MW00388358

Buried Scars

JANE BLYTHE

Copyright © 2024 by Jane Blythe

All rights reserved.

No part of this book may be reproduced in any form or by any electronic or mechanical means, including information storage and retrieval systems, without written permission from the author, except for the use of brief quotations in a book review.

Cover designed by RBA Designs

❀ Created with Vellum

Acknowledgments

I'd like to thank everyone who played a part in bringing this story to life. Particularly my mom who is always there to share her thoughts and opinions with me. My wonderful cover designer Letitia who did an amazing job with this stunning cover. My fabulous editor Lisa for all the hard work she puts into polishing my work. My awesome team, Sophie, Robyn, and Clayr, without your help I'd never be able to run my street team. And my fantastic street team members who help share my books with every share, comment, and like!

And of course a big thank you to all of you, my readers! Without you I wouldn't be living my dreams of sharing the stories in my head with the world!

CHAPTER

One

He was getting too old for this.

That was what Rafe "Panther" Neal was thinking as he and the rest of his team swam through the cold ocean. The same ocean that, just three months ago, they had swum through on their way to find a yacht that supposedly had the second in command of a notorious human trafficker on board.

Leonid Baranov was wanted by almost every agency in every country worldwide. The Russian oligarch was richer than any person needed to be, and instead of contributing anything good to the world with his money, the man used it to buy and sell people. While he wasn't a major player in any specific human trafficking ring, he was a sick and sadistic monster who got a rush out of buying high-value victims.

Sons and daughters of politicians, royalty, and businessmen had joined his collection over the years. Of all the victims unlucky enough to pass through what had been dubbed the House of Horrors, only four of them had ever survived.

One had committed suicide shortly after being rescued. Another had been tortured and killed not long before Panther and his team— Prey Security's Bravo Team—had been set to meet with him. One had been snatched from the home she had been living in under a new identity, her young daughter murdered before her eyes.

The last was the wife of Bravo Team's leader, Axel "Axe" Lindon.

They were the team who had come so close to catching Leonid Baranov once and for all. The billionaire had bounties out on all of their heads, which had forced him and his team to leave Delta Force and move to the private sector, now working for the world-renowned Prey Security.

Beth was one of the three victims they had rescued the day they came so close to destroying Baranov. Something about her drew all of them in, and they had quickly adopted her as a little sister of sorts since she had no family to care for her. Or at least the rest of them had. Axe had known Beth was his from the moment he laid eyes on her. He had helped her heal, and the two had grown close. Once she was ready for more, he'd asked her out.

The two had married two years after they rescued Beth, and he'd never seen either of them happier.

Until nineteen months ago when Beth had simply vanished.

Like a puff of smoke, she was gone.

No matter how hard they searched for her, using every one of Prey's vast resources, they hadn't been able to find her.

Then ten months ago, she reappeared with no memory of who she was or what had happened to her in the eight months she was missing.

Since then, they'd all had to stand by and watch Axe and Beth drift further and further apart. They needed answers, needed to know what had happened to Beth while she was gone, and to know that Leonid Baranov was no longer a threat.

Which brought him right back to why he felt like he was getting too old for this. He might be only thirty, but the things he had seen and done made him feel so much older.

Thirty, divorced, and a single father to an eight-year-old son he adored more than life itself, watching the guys on his team fall in love this past year had gotten him thinking. He'd always believed he was happy enough with just him and his kid, but Andy was growing up fast, and he couldn't help but feel that his son was missing out on something by not having a mother figure in his life.

Sure, the boy had his teammates' women who spoiled him rotten, and Mrs. Pfeffer, the babysitter who looked after him while Panther and his team were away was a great influence on Andy. But it wasn't the same.

Shoving away thoughts of his son and his future, Panther caught sight of what they'd been looking for.

"Found it," he said into his comms as he dove deeper toward the wreckage of the yacht.

Three months ago, when they'd been tracking Tomas Butcher, Baranov's right-hand man, the yacht had been blown up moments after they were able to bail off it so they weren't taken out along with the vessel. That same night they'd gotten a glimpse of a woman with Butcher as the man boarded a helicopter and took off, seemingly disappearing as there was no record of where the helo landed or where the man had gone afterward.

Bravo Team was desperate for answers.

Desperate enough that they had come back to attempt to find the wreckage and see if any clues could be gleaned from it. Sarah Sanders had had a child. They might not know why the girl had been murdered instead of being taken along with her mother, but there was a chance that Sarah was the woman who had been on the yacht with Butcher that night.

It didn't make sense, the timeline didn't add up, but then nothing about this entire mess made sense.

So there they were, scouring the depths of the ocean in search of a wrecked yacht that probably wouldn't tell them anything they didn't already know.

A shape appeared beside him in the dark, murky ocean water, the beam of a flashlight joining his own. "That's it. At least what's left of it," Axe said.

Even though he couldn't see his friend's face, it wasn't necessary for Panther to know that Axe's expression would be a mixture of pain and impotent fury. Nothing was worse than knowing the person you loved most in the world was hurting, and you couldn't make it better. Axe was a mere shell of the man Panther had always known since Beth had been snatched and then returned to him with no idea who he was.

Another flashlight danced about. "Doesn't look like there's much of it left," Sebastian "Rock" Rockman said.

"All we need is one clue to give us a direction to move in," Mason "Scorpion" Markson reminded him.

Reminded all of them.

They all felt lost and disillusioned when it came to Beth and her disappearance. All of them were feeling like they had failed her, and felt like they were running around like a dog chasing its tail. They were trying but they weren't getting anywhere, and Panther could attest to the fact that it was beginning to feel like they never would.

"We do a quick search now, grab anything we can find, then tag everything so Eagle can send back a team to collect and bring it all up," Gabriel "Tank" Dawson told them. When Beth had first gone missing, Axe had stepped down as leader of Bravo Team and Tank had stepped up. Although Axe was back now, the two seemed to share the role of leader, Tank stepping in whenever it seemed like Axe was unable to.

"What exactly are we hoping to find?" Patrick "Trick" Kramer asked. "We know Baranov, the man is meticulous, there's no way he would have allowed Butcher to leave anything behind on the yacht. And even if he wasn't thorough because he was planning on blowing up the yacht, it's been three months, whatever wasn't destroyed in the blast has likely been destroyed sitting underwater for so long."

They all knew that. It was why they'd never searched for the wreckage right away. Baranov meticulously cleaned away any DNA, prints, fibers, or anything else that could possibly link him to a crime and be used against him. Whatever was on that yacht wouldn't be anything they could use to find out where Baranov was hiding.

But things had changed.

The information they'd gotten a couple of days ago had opened up a whole new world of possibilities, and so they had returned to see if they could find anything that might help, no matter how slim the chances.

DNA tests had been run on the blood they'd found at the farmhouse, blood that they initially assumed belonged to Sarah. Only the tests had proved that while it wasn't Sarah's blood there was a close DNA match. That was how they knew the blood had belonged to Sarah's daughter.

But they were able to get more from the DNA.

They were able to determine paternity.

The father of Sarah's child wasn't someone from the small farming community she had moved to, and it wasn't Leonid Baranov.

It was Tomas Butcher.

They had no idea what that meant, how old the child was, and whether he knew about his daughter. But a woman who fit Sarah's description had gotten onto that helicopter with Butcher the night the yacht exploded, and they were all desperate enough to clutch at straws and come back to search for the yacht in the likely vain hope that it could somehow lead them to Butcher, Baranov, Sarah, and the answers Beth needed—that they all needed—to move forward.

~

February 14th
   6:38 P.M.

What was she going to do if this didn't work?

Elle Cavey couldn't even allow herself to go down that path, because if she did, she was going to lose whatever sanity she had managed to cling to these last few weeks.

She already knew the answer to that question anyway.

If this didn't work then it was over. She'd have no choice but to give up. This was quite literally her last chance, her only hope, the only possibility that she might get what she needed.

Elle had never experienced pain like this before.

Ever.

It wasn't physical pain. That she could handle with relative ease. This was so very different. It ran deeper than just emotional or psychological pain. It was the kind of pain caused by having the thing most precious in your entire world ripped away from you.

Her sweet little girl was gone.

Abducted.

And it was all her fault.

Elle's seven-year-old daughter Ruthie was her whole world, her whole heart, and soul. It had been just the two of them since Ruthie was a baby, and Elle's now ex-husband had decided that fatherhood wasn't for him and walked away. He'd signed over his parental rights, not contested anything in the divorce, just walked away like the two of them meant nothing to him.

Other than school and Ruthie's gymnastics class they were always together.

Just the two of them.

Two halves of a whole.

Now one of those halves was gone, and Elle was left all alone.

The pain in her chest was too great, and she swerved over to the side of the quiet country road, lowered her forehead to the steering wheel, and let her tears flow. How many tears had she shed since she walked into her backyard that bright winter's day to find it empty?

Millions.

Billions.

And yet, whenever she thought she must have cried herself out there were more.

Each tear that fell felt like a drop of blood leaving her body. It felt like sooner or later she wouldn't just cry herself out, she would cry herself dead. Because no tears meant no more hope, that she had accepted she was never going to get her daughter back.

Without her child, she had nothing to live for.

Each day she battled the desire born of desperation to just let go of all the pain and fear and end it all. It was only because she knew that her daughter was still alive, and without her fighting for Ruthie, her child would become just another statistic.

"You have to live, you have to fight, you owe it to your baby girl," Elle said aloud. These were the same words she'd uttered in her darkest moments when suicide seemed like the best option because living without her daughter was just too much. The same words she uttered every morning when she dragged herself out of bed after a fitful night of tossing and turning. The same words she uttered every night when she had to force herself not to climb into Ruthie's bed because when she touched her nose to her child's pillow she could still get a gentle whiff of Ruthie's lavender shampoo, and she didn't want to lose that tiny connection she still had to her daughter.

The words had saved her more than once, and like they always did, they saved her again now.

Somehow, she was able to get herself back under control. Take her pain and fear and shove it down just below the surface so she could function.

Functioning was about the best she could hope for these days. What she was doing certainly couldn't be described as living. It was surviving at best. There was no joy, no laughter, and no smiles. Most days she barely ate, which was now obvious when you looked at her, she'd lost a lot of weight in this last month. She was surviving on a couple of hours of sleep a night at best, and that was usually restless and filled with nightmares that were even worse than the waking nightmare she was living.

Elle was driven by only one thing.

Find her daughter.

Bring her home.

Worse even than knowing Ruthie was out there somewhere, scared and alone, begging for her mommy to come, was knowing that she had no one to blame but herself for her daughter's abduction.

It was her fault.

All hers.

No amount of empty words from the cops, or the shrink they insisted speak with her was going to change that. It was simply a fact. Ruthie hadn't been taken out of opportunity, she wasn't in the wrong place at the wrong time.

No.

Her daughter had been targeted.

Taken specifically because she was Elle's daughter.

How was she supposed to live with that guilt?

Did Ruthie know it was her mommy's fault that she had been taken from her home, her friends, her school, her life? Did her sweet, little, baby girl hate her?

Another sob burst out, and although she did her best to get it under control, she couldn't. Elle wept until she could barely breathe, the pressure in her chest so severe it was slowly smothering the life right out of her.

"You have to get it together. If you don't, they won't help you."

The words were enough for her to wipe away the worst of the tears flooding down her cheeks, and pull the car back onto the road.

If she got there and they wrote her off as just a hysterical mother whose daughter had been taken, then they wouldn't help her. If that happened, she knew it was the end of the road for both her and Ruthie. This was her only hope at getting her daughter back and she couldn't waste it.

Desperation had her coming to the only people she believed might be able to help her. The cops had done nothing, neither had the FBI. Oh, they had at first. A whole team of them had come out to her house, they'd questioned her, and treated her like a suspect. Elle hadn't cared because as soon as they cleared her they could look for her daughter. So she'd given them access to everything, answered all their questions, and done everything they asked of her.

But in the end it hadn't changed anything.

Just because she had been cleared as a suspect early on didn't mean there had been any other viable ones. Everything they did wound up leading nowhere, and then two days ago they had sat her down and explained that they had exhausted their leads and there was nothing else they could do.

They'd told her they weren't giving up. They would continue looking for new leads, but no one would be staying in her house waiting for a ransom call that had never come. No one would be calling with regular updates.

Ruthie would just fade into the background until she was just another cold case.

Not that they'd used those words, of course, but she wasn't stupid, she could read between the lines. They had already given up on Ruthie and didn't believe that she was still alive or that they would ever find her.

Being told that killed her.

How could they give up on her daughter after only a month?

One month wasn't long enough to just give up on a child in need. It had been one hellishly long month that felt more like an eternity, but she hadn't expected them to give up so soon.

Elle would *never* give up on her baby girl. Not for anything.

So she was there, ready to meet a group of men who, if she was honest, sounded incredibly intimidating and maybe even a little scary. But they were possibly the only ones who could save her daughter.

"I'll find you, my little unicorn girl, I promise. I won't ever give up on you. Even if you hate me forever, I'll bring you home."

With that vow on her lips, Elle pulled up to a large gate. If you didn't know it was there you'd never even find it. Thanks to the directions she'd been given she had located it and now, sitting there looking at it, she prayed it was like the wardrobe in *The Lion the Witch and the Wardrobe* and was about to lead her to a magical land filled with people who could do what felt like the impossible and bring her baby back to her.

"Please do the impossible," she murmured as she climbed out of her car.

Drawing a deep breath, she shivered in the cold, realizing she'd forgotten to put on her coat when she'd left, and hurried over to the gate. She punched in the code she'd been given, praying it worked even though she had no reason to doubt that it would.

Still, when it beeped green, and she heard the lock disengage, she sent up a silent thanks, then pushed the gate open and walked back toward her car.

She never made it back inside.

A hand clamped around her mouth, silencing her scream before it could escape, and she was yanked up against a chest that felt carved from stone.

CHAPTER

Two

February 14th
7:09 P.M.

This had to be her.

She had the code to the gate and fit the description he'd been given. Long chocolate brown hair that hung halfway down her back and light brown eyes that were full of intelligence and strength, but also heart-breaking pain.

Pain Panther could much too easily identify with. She was a mother, he was a father. They both knew what it was like to have your heart walk around outside of your body, and to have that heart snatched away …

That was something he didn't even want to consider.

But whether he wanted to consider it or not, he could empathize with it, and that was the only reason he had agreed to help in any way he could.

The strength he'd seen in the woman's eyes was echoed in the way she struggled against his hold. She couldn't break out of it, he was a former Delta Force operator who could keep a grown man from breaking out of this hold, and even though he'd kept it gentle, not wanting to harm her, there was no way this small woman could get free.

Didn't stop her from trying though and he respected that.

Even though he didn't want to add to what this woman was already going through, and he was ninety-nine percent sure she was who he believed her to be, he had to be sure. This was where his son lived, where the women his friends loved lived, he wouldn't—couldn't—do anything to jeopardize their safety.

"It's her, fingerprints confirm it," Rock's voice in his ear told him.

Good.

Now that he knew this was indeed Elle Cavey, he could stop scaring the life out of her.

"Shh, I'm here to help you," he said softly, holding his lips just above her ear.

It took a moment for his words to penetrate her panic, but he knew the second they did because she went completely still. Still, he waited a moment longer before removing his hand, not wanting her to scream and disturb the other person inside his cabin.

"Panther?" she asked when he finally released his hold on her and stepped back.

He expected her to scurry away from him in fright like a timid little rabbit. With his height, his muscle mass, his thick dark hair, and golden-brown eyes, he knew that he could be an intimidating sight, especially to a woman who had already gone through so much and was teetering on the edge.

But that's not what she did at all.

Instead, she did the opposite. Elle moved closer as though seeking his protection, his reassurance, the help only a man like him could give her.

"Yes," he replied, somehow managing to tear his gaze away from her expressive face long enough to remember that he was supposed to be helping this woman, not ogling her.

Again, the woman did the absolute last thing he expected. Bursting into noisy tears, she launched herself at him, throwing herself into his arms. "Thank you. Thank you. Thank you. You're the last hope I have left of getting Ruthie back. Thank you so much for agreeing to help me."

Her garbled words did something to him. They stirred up something in his heart, twisting it inside his chest. Something he hadn't felt in a long time, not since he was young and naïve. Something he remembered from the first time his son had been placed in his arms. He hadn't wanted to be a father then, hadn't been ready, the timing had been all wrong, and yet the moment he had been given his son, his heart had swelled with this deep, dark protectiveness. A knowledge that there wasn't anything he wouldn't do to protect the tiny bundle in his arms.

Now, as he held this fragile woman in his arms, a woman he knew was a whole lot stronger than she felt—had to be to have gone a whole month knowing her child had been taken from her—he felt a glimmer of that same protectiveness.

Panther didn't date, didn't have the time nor the inclination. Even though he had been thinking about it lately as he'd watched his teammates getting bitten by the love bug one by one, he hadn't intended to just jump on in with the first woman he met. But this woman was provoking all sorts of completely inappropriate protective urges.

She was a client.

Nothing more.

A stunningly beautiful client but still just a client.

Clearing his throat, suddenly feeling every bit the geeky kid he'd been in school, Panther released his hold on the woman and took a step back, putting a little space between them as though that would help with these possessive feelings he was having.

"Uh, why don't we walk to my cabin? It's only half a mile down the driveway, and it looks like you could use the fresh air." His voice came out a little harsher than he'd intended, but this woman and her beautiful, pained strength were messing with his head. He could not look at her and not see himself in her position. If someone took Andy from him he didn't know how he would survive, yet this woman was still standing, still fighting, and he respected the hell out of that.

"Okay, sure." She nodded so fast he actually worried she might snap her neck. It was clear that she would do whatever he asked her to, probably out of fear that his help would be withdrawn if she refused.

Panther found he didn't like the idea that she didn't trust him to help her just because he could. There were no strings attached. She could tell him no, or disagree with him, and he would still do everything within his power to find her daughter. His help wasn't—and never had been—conditional.

Following his lead, she started walking down the driveway, not even bothering to check on her car, which he stupidly realized they'd left running on the other side of the gate.

"Hold up," he said.

Elle stayed exactly where he'd left her as he returned to her car, drove it through the gate, turned the engine off, snagged her purse, and then locked both the vehicle and the gate before returning to the desperate mother.

"Fresh air will do you good," he mumbled as he started walking again, Elle trailing along behind him like a lost little puppy. Actually, she looked like she needed a whole lot more than some fresh air. Beneath the dark circles under her eyes and the blotchy red skin that told him the tears she'd shed in his driveway weren't the only ones tonight, she was pale as the snow. It was obvious in the way her clothes hung off her that she'd lost weight since her daughter's abduction. Elle looked like she was hanging on by a thread, and surprisingly, Panther found he didn't just want to return her child to her, but take care of her as well.

What was going on with him?

Despite believing he wasn't ready for kids, when his girlfriend wound up pregnant, she'd talked up how great it would be with the three of them as a little family of their own, and he'd fallen for the whole idea. And it had been great for the first year at least. Then his wife had announced she wasn't ready for motherhood after all and dumped both of them.

That was seven years ago, and in all that time there had never been another woman who had caught his attention. There had been a couple of brief affairs that were more to do with satisfying his needs than anything else. But with a son at home, he hadn't wanted Andy to get the impression it was okay to use women for your own needs, so as his son got older, Panther had taken to attending to his needs himself.

Now, in just a couple of minutes, this woman had him all tied up in confused knots. It wasn't appropriate to want her sexually, it wasn't what she'd come there for. Her child was missing, and he might be able to help. It also wasn't appropriate to want to take care of her, again she was there for his help finding her child, not for him to worry over her getting sleep and a decent meal.

So why couldn't he shake the need to wrap her up in his arms, carry her inside, and make sure she was taken care of while he did what he could for her little girl?

Panther liked order and structure. He'd never liked anything he couldn't explain or understand. Even as a small child, he had been compelled to figure out all the things he didn't know, eventually leading him to his love of computers. This woman and the protectiveness she stoked wasn't something he could explain, and that made him feel compelled to figure it out.

Just as they reached his place, the door to his cabin creaked open, light spilling out onto the porch as a small figure stood shadowed in the open doorway. "Is everything okay?"

~

February 14th
   7:27 P.M.

"Who's out there?" a sweet little voice called out.

The voice clearly belonged to a child. A little boy.

Panther's child.

Elle didn't need to see the boy to know she was looking at his father. It was written into every nuance of the man standing beside her. The way his body had gone stiff, and his hands flexed and then curled into fists at his side. It was the way his face went impassive but his eyes remained a swirling pit of emotions.

Panther was a father.

No wonder she had been sent specifically to him. If he had a child, then he would be able to imagine what it felt like to have them ripped away from you.

It was like losing a piece of yourself.

Not just *a* piece, but the biggest piece. The only piece that mattered. Your reason for existing.

"Y-you have a s-son?" she stammered.

He hesitated as though deciding how to respond. Since he knew she was no threat to him or his little boy, it was probably because he didn't want to upset her given that her daughter had been abducted.

She was sure he didn't want to hurt her more by reminding her that his son was safely at home while her daughter was out there someone, terrified and alone.

But his little boy couldn't hurt her any more than she could hurt him. Knowing how much having her baby ripped away from her hurt, she would never wish that kind of feeling on another parent. Not even someone she hated, let alone a man who seemed good, kind, and honest, if a little gruff, although she could hardly blame him for not being thrilled that she'd thrown herself at him.

It was just that he was the first real solid thing she'd had this last month. The first thing that gave her real hope after those first few days when she was so sure the police would find her daughter and bring her home. Even though it had been the same team of cops working Ruthie's case, none of them had done anything to try to connect with her on a friendly level. To them, she was just the woman with the missing kid.

In the few minutes she'd known him, Panther had shown her more compassion. It wasn't anything he'd said, or even anything he had specifically done, it was just his eyes. So pretty, and golden, they had practically glowed with empathy and a determination that stopped her from losing all hope.

Elle couldn't be more thrilled that his little boy was safe and sound, she hoped he never felt the pain of losing his son.

"Please," she whispered. For some reason she couldn't explain, it felt important to her to know this was Panther's son, to know that this man would truly do everything he could to find her daughter.

"Yes."

"How old is he?"

"Elle, we don't ..."

"How old?" she repeated.

"Eight."

"Just a year older than Ruthie," she murmured. "What's his name?"

"Elle ..."

"Please." Begging wasn't above her right now. Heck, nothing was above her. Anything she was asked to do to bring Ruthie home she'd do without hesitation. Panther probably felt like he was torturing her, imagining it must be awful for her to be around children given her own had been taken. Elle might have thought that would be the case, but for some reason, this man and his son provided comfort with their presence not torment.

"Andy. His name is Andy."

The boy chose that moment to jump down the cabin steps as only a small boy could do, completely free and with abandon. Walking cautiously toward them, the little boy stopped beside his dad. While the child had lighter hair than his father's, and his eyes held more of a hazel gleam than the golden-brown of Panther's, there was no mistaking that the pair were father and son. It was in the confident way they stood, the protective vibe they both gave out.

For a book she'd been writing last year, she'd actually wound up calling Prey and asking if she could speak with someone to get some thoughts and ideas to make sure her story was as accurate as possible. Meeting one of the infamous billionaire Oswald siblings, Sparrow and her husband Ethan, along with their two children, then thirteen-month-old Connor and two-month-old Charlotte, had been a whole lot of fun. The family were so sweet and held nothing back, both Sparrow and Ethan sharing their experiences in the military without reservation.

Given that she had met Sparrow and Ethan she knew what these types of people were like, the kind who joined the military, who wanted to protect and save, and she could already see that one day little Andy was going to be a hero like his daddy.

"Who's this?" Andy asked, looking up at her with curiosity.

"This is Elle," Panther made the introductions. "And this is Andy."

Andy studied her with serious hazel eyes, and when he spoke his voice was gentle and seemed so much older than his eight years. "Is my daddy going to save you?"

Fresh tears streamed down her cheeks at the child's innocent words.

So sweet, so confidently spoken, like he couldn't imagine that his daddy wouldn't save someone.

Elle hadn't shed this many tears since the first few days after Ruthie had been kidnapped. "I hope he is. He's the only chance I have of ever seeing my little girl again. It's my fault he took her," she said, turning her attention to Panther. He'd agreed to help her, but he had to know everything, including that this was all her fault. If he decided that he didn't want to help her after that, she would have no choice but to leave. "The man who took her, he is ... was ... is ... I don't know anymore ... but he is or was a fan of mine. He thinks we're in love, he took my daughter because I rejected him and I'm terrified of what he's going to do to her." She swallowed hard and made herself say it even though she didn't want to. "What he's *already* done to her."

Admitting that her daughter had already been harmed beyond repair tore at her skin as effectively as if she'd walked through a rose bush. Trying to figure out exactly what the man had done to her sweet little girl was like picking off one of those thorns and using it to gouge away at her own skin.

If nothing else, Ruthie had been terrified, but what else? Had he starved her? Deprived her of water or sleep? Was he keeping her warm? Ruthie had always been a cold body. As much as she loved winter and playing in the snow, it always took her ages to warm up again afterward. The two of them would snuggle on the couch in front of the fireplace and watch movies, curled up under blankets, drinking hot chocolate, and eating cookies fresh from the oven.

Now her little girl was gone, and there was no way she could make sure that Ruthie was okay.

Even if the kidnapper was taking care of the basics like food, and water, and a bed, what else had he done to Ruthie? Had he hit her? Cut her? Whipped her?

Had he ... raped her?

The thought of that happening to her innocent seven-year-old daughter was too much, and a new wave of tears streamed down her cheeks. Panther hadn't asked her any questions or made any comments, but he had to be thinking she was a terrible mother to have allowed someone to hurt her child.

A glance at him told her nothing of what was going on inside his head. All she saw was a huge man standing ramrod straight beside his son, with his fingers curled into fists so tight that even out there in the dim light from the cabin, she could see his knuckles had blanched.

He had to hate her.

Had to blame her because she blamed herself.

Maybe he didn't want her anywhere near his son.

Elle worried that she had ruined this before it even started, but when she forced herself to meet his gaze it wasn't anger, blame, or even empathy that she saw there. Instead, it was impotent fury. Panther wanted to help her, but he didn't know how. He couldn't magically produce her daughter for her, and that was really the only thing that was going to provide her with any meaningful help.

It was all she wanted and she would make a deal with the devil if that was what it took to get her baby girl home.

In the end, it wasn't Panther who found a way to comfort her, it was his son. Taking a step toward her, little Andy reached out, touched her hand with his own small one that reminded her so much of Ruthie's.

"My daddy will find her, don't be sad," he said with such confidence and compassion that a part of her believed him.

With tears still streaming down her cheeks, Elle reached out and ruffled Andy's hair. "You know what, Andy? I think you're right. I think your daddy is going to find my daughter."

CHAPTER

Three

February 14th
7:41 P.M.

Normally, Panther didn't allow his son to have anything to do with the darkness that shrouded his life.

Work was work, but home was home.

Home was a safe place he had to create for his son. Andy was everything to him, and while he wasn't pleased to have his little boy out there with a client, he couldn't seem to summon the words to tell Andy to go back inside.

It was the way his son hadn't hesitated to approach a woman he didn't even know. The empathy in his little boy's words and actions. In this moment, Andy seemed so grown-up, so much older than his eight years, and Panther couldn't be prouder of him.

That wasn't the only reason he couldn't bring himself to separate Elle and Andy.

The way Elle looked at his son, even in the midst of the horrific ordeal she was living, with such respect and admiration, did something to his heart.

Had his ex ever looked at their son with even half as much emotion as Elle was currently showing the boy?

It hurt to say Marcia hadn't.

Not once.

Despite all her talk about how amazing it would be to get married and raise their unplanned baby together, she hadn't taken to motherhood at all. They'd been young, and Panther had been working hard to make it through his training and hopefully get a place on Delta Force at the end. He'd wanted to support his family even if he'd been unsure if he was ready for the responsibility. Marcia hadn't wanted to give up her lifestyle of hanging out with friends and going to clubs and bars to look after an infant.

But the way Elle smiled at his son ... that was everything. Not that he'd had any doubts about what kind of mother the woman was, but if he had, this moment would have wiped them all away.

Elle Cavey was exactly the kind of mother he wished his son had had.

When she shifted her gaze to meet his, those tear-drenched brown eyes were filled with such trust that they speared an arrow straight through his heart.

It wasn't that he wasn't used to people trusting him. His son trusted him to provide everything he needed, his team trusted him to have their backs, and victims trusted him to save them, but something about this trust Elle was handing him felt different.

Unsettled and wanting to move on, focus on the reason the woman was there, so he could get her daughter back where she belonged, Panther cleared his throat.

"Okay, let's go inside and you can tell me everything," he said, reaching for Andy's hand. His other hand, somehow, with no conscious thought on his part, found its way to the small of Elle's back as if it was the most natural thing in the world, and he guided her up the porch steps. He felt her reaction to his touch, the way her body straightened, the slight inhalation of breath at the arc of attraction that seemed to spark between them.

Panther felt it, too, and he didn't like it.

He wasn't looking for a woman to date. He'd tried marriage, and it hadn't worked out well for him. Not that he regretted his relationship with Marcia and their short-lived marriage because it had given him his son.

Andy was at the center of everything Panther did. It wasn't easy to leave his little boy at home to go off on missions, but he wanted to do whatever he could to make the world a slightly safer place for his child to grow up in. A child of a broken home himself, the last thing Panther wanted to do was bring into his son's life another woman who sooner or later would wind up leaving him.

Being constantly shuttled between his parents, feeling like he didn't belong anywhere, then watching as both his mom and dad remarried and had new families, leaving him out in the cold, had made Panther wary of marriage. Then having his wife leave him a single dad of a one-year-old had sealed the deal.

He wasn't looking for anything with a woman.

Ever.

His priority was his son, job, and Bravo Team family.

Nothing else.

Given that her seven-year-old daughter was missing, Panther highly doubted that Elle was looking for anything, serious or otherwise, with a man.

She was there for help finding her child. That he was picturing her naked and in his bed—and worse, sitting around his kitchen table laughing and joking with his son—was completely and utterly inappropriate.

Disgusted with himself, Panther was about to order Andy off to bed so he could get to work looking for Ruthie Cavey, but apparently, his son had other ideas.

"You need tea," Andy announced to Elle as they entered the cabin, immediately reaching for her hand and tugging her through and into the kitchen. Of all the cabins belonging to his teammates on the compound his was the biggest. The front door opened onto a large living room, with a staircase in the corner leading up to three bedrooms and two bathrooms. To the right of the living room was Andy's play-room, to the back of the living room was a huge kitchen diner, and leading off that was Panther's office.

"Umm, tea?" Elle asked, confused, allowing Andy to guide her over to the table.

"Mrs. Pfeffer says tea makes everything better," Andy explained. It seemed like his son had taken an immediate liking to Elle. Home-schooled and having spent almost his entire life on the remote compound, it usually took the little boy a while to warm up to new people, but not Elle. Andy had jumped in on sight.

"Uh, who's Mrs. Pfeffer?" Elle asked, turning her gaze to him.

"She's a retired school teacher who tutors Andy and looks after him if I'm away," Panther explained. His son wasn't the only one who usually kept his distance, Panther never usually talked about his private life, let alone his son, with a client.

Yet for some reason Elle felt different.

Crazy.

Totally crazy.

The woman was there for one reason and one reason alone.

Yet his mouth seemed to disagree and kept right on talking as he went to fill Mrs. Pfeffer's kettle and grabbed some teabags from the pantry. "She's English, and you know how they are about their tea. She lives in town, I've offered to build her a cabin of her own out here, but she says she'd miss the hustle and bustle." No idea why he was telling her all of this, Elle didn't care, and it wasn't relevant, but for some reason he was rambling like he was nervous on a first date or something.

"It's nice you have her. I take it you're a single dad?"

"My mom didn't want me," Andy announced like it was no big deal at all as he chose his favorite mug and set it on the counter next to the stove where the kettle was boiling.

"Oh, I'm so sorry, sweetheart. Ruthie's daddy didn't want her either. But it looks like you have the best daddy in the world," Elle said.

Andy beamed up at him. "My daddy is a superhero like Spiderman and The Hulk."

"Your daddy is a superhero," Elle murmured her agreement, and the hope in her eyes as she looked at him almost stole his breath. Her daughter had been missing for a month, there was every chance that the child was gone for good and he wouldn't be able to find her. Panther knew Elle had come as a last resort and if he failed her ...

If he failed her then she would never get her daughter back.

If that happened, he wasn't sure how he'd be able to deal with the guilt of letting her down.

When the kettle boiled, he made the tea, and allowed Andy to carry the mug over to the table to Elle, before deciding he'd wasted enough time and now he had to get down to business.

"Off to bed, buddy," he told Andy. "Go up and get your pajamas on, brush your teeth, and I'll be up to tuck you in in a few minutes."

Looking from Elle to him and then back to Elle again, when Andy finally turned serious hazel eyes on him, Panther wasn't surprised by what his son said. "You don't have to tuck me in, Daddy, I can do it myself. You need to help Elle find Ruthie."

In that moment, all his fears of not being a good enough father, all the guilt about being gone so often, his worries that he wasn't giving his boy what he needed evaporated like a puff of smoke. Andy was only eight, and he was already someone Panther could be proud of. Intelligent, sensitive, compassionate, and with a heart so big there wasn't anyone he couldn't care about. Andy was everything Panther had hoped his son would grow up to be.

"Goodnight, Dad." Andy wrapped his skinny arms around Panther's waist, and he leaned down to kiss the top of his son's head. "Night, Elle." There was no hesitation on Andy's part, he just walked over, hugged Elle hard, and then ran out of the kitchen and up the stairs.

"You have an amazing little boy," Elle whispered, tears glimmering in her eyes.

"The best," he agreed.

"H-he sent me this," she said, fishing something from her purse and holding it out to him with a shaking hand. "I'm so terrified about what he's going to do to my baby."

While he wouldn't say the words aloud, and only knowing the bare bones about the case, Panther also feared for the little girl's safety, and the sanity of the desperate mother sitting before him.

～

February 14th
   7:54 P.M.

Elle's hand shook badly as she held out the photos that had been hand delivered to her home. She had no idea how he managed to get in and out with her expensive security system, but somehow he did. He'd done it when he abducted her daughter and many times both before and after he'd taken Ruthie.

At first it was letters.

Love letters.

Creepy love letters.

Little notes telling her how much he loved her and how much he wanted the two of them to be together. Of course, she had reported them immediately, but the guy never left any forensics behind, and after a short investigation the cops seemed to just brush it off as harmless fan mail. Implying that if she wanted to put herself in the public eye as a well-known romance author, she should accept that it was going to come with fans.

But it wasn't harmless.

This guy left the notes *inside* her house. He never entered while she was home, so he was watching her and knew when her house would be empty. No matter how many times she changed the code to her security system, he always seemed to crack it, so he had the skills to bypass the system. Just because he never threatened her with violence didn't make the notes okay. There was a clear undertone of possession in them, like he already viewed her as his, there was absolutely nothing harmless fan mail about them.

Maybe if someone had paid attention to her, he wouldn't have taken her daughter.

After Ruthie was kidnapped, the love letters started including photos. They were always of the same thing. Her daughter sitting in a room, fancy and ornate enough to belong to a princess, dressed in a ball gown, crying.

Sobbing.

Her baby was crying, and she wasn't there to make everything better.

That was every mother's worst nightmare, only there was no waking from this because it wasn't a dream, it was real life.

Taking the photos from her, the grim look on Panther's face was enough to confirm her suspicions that he saw this the same way she did. Her baby was never coming home. Elle hadn't wanted to admit it, not even in her darkest moments, but right then, seeing the expression on Panther's face forced her to confront reality.

The world felt like it was disappearing around her, leaving her trapped in a dark, empty place where there was nothing but pain, fear, sadness, regret, guilt, and grief.

Soul-destroying grief.

"Hey."

Large hands clasped her shoulders, giving her a firm shake, and Elle blinked away the darkness and looked up to find Panther before her, knees bent so they were at eye level. This man exuded strength and confidence, and she wanted to absorb both because she was tapped out.

He had been her last hope, but he didn't think finding Ruthie was possible. She'd seen the truth in his eyes, and it had broken her, drained her of the remaining strength she had somehow been managing to cling to.

"Listen to me, Elle." Those large hands shifted until they cradled her face, his thumbs stroking along her cheekbones, catching tears she hadn't even realized were falling. "I promise I will do everything I can to find your daughter and bring her home to you, but I need you to do something for me."

"Anything," Elle hurriedly agreed. Whatever it took, walk through hell, deal with the devil, it didn't matter so long as Ruthie was home and safe.

"I need you to hold it together." Panther glanced over his shoulder to the door where his son had disappeared just moments ago. "I can't imagine what you're going through, if I'm honest I don't even want to. But I will work this as hard as I would if it was Andy who had been taken."

That promise meant everything to her. "Thank you."

Panther gave a single nod. "You good?"

No. But for now, she could find a little more strength to keep moving forward. When she nodded, he released her and she immediately felt the loss. Begging him to hold her was completely inappropriate no matter how much her body seemed to crave his touch. So she clamped her mouth closed, and instead, focused on the pictures he was now flipping through.

The fact that her daughter always looked clean was the worst thing about them. It was obvious she was being bathed regularly, but by herself or did the man do it? Did he touch her little girl's naked body? Had he hurt her?

Not having answers was driving her to the point of insanity.

"H-he took her because of m-me. Because he's obsessed with me, but I don't know who he is. I don't know who he is," she repeated on a sob. How much easier this would be if she could just give the cops a name, and they could go to his house, arrest him, and bring her daughter home.

But she didn't know his name.

She had no idea who he was or why he had decided to fixate on her.

Over the last month, the cops hadn't had a single viable lead to her stalker and her daughter's abductor's identity.

Was it stupid to think that Panther could achieve what the police and the FBI had been unable to? Was she just deluding herself into thinking the outcome would be any different?

"No," Panther said with such authority that Elle startled. "Whoever he is, he took your daughter because he chose to. Because he wanted to carry out his own sick, twisted plans. It is *not* your fault. You are not responsible for the actions of other people."

All she could do following his outburst was stand there and stare at him in shock. Not even the cops had been so adamant in telling her that it wasn't her fault. Their responses had been lukewarm at best, and she couldn't help but feel that they were judging her, blaming her, even as they pretended not to be.

Or that was her own guilty conscience talking.

If she'd just done more, pushed harder, hired private security, something, anything, then maybe this wouldn't have happened.

A thumb and forefinger pinched her chin just hard enough to sting, and her face was tilted up so she could meet Panther's glowing golden eyes. "Not. Your. Fault," he repeated.

Before she could say anything, her cell phone began to ring, an unknown number showing on the screen.

"Answer it," Panther said.

Elle nodded. It was probably another newspaper or blogger wanting to interview her. She turned them all down, it sickened her to think that they thought she would use her daughter's kidnapping for publicity she didn't even need. Book sales were going better than she ever could have hoped for, and she had a few offers to turn them into movies. Her career was doing great, she didn't need to use her personal tragedy to prop it up, and even if sales weren't doing well she would never use her daughter's ordeal like that.

Ever.

And it made her feel shallow and pathetic to have anyone think that she would.

"Hello?" she said as she accepted the call.

"Mommy!" Ruthie's hysterical voice would have made her fall to her knees, but Panther was there, wrapping an arm around her waist and holding her up.

"Baby! Ruthie, my sweet little unicorn girl, I've missed you so much. I love you so much, baby. I love you more than anything in the whole entire world. You are my world. Where are you, baby? Tell Mommy where you are so I can come and get you. Are you okay, little unicorn girl? Are you hurt?"

"I don't know where I am, Mommy. I don't know," Ruthie sobbed. "The man, he said you have to come to him, that we all have to be together. Like a family. He says we're a family, Mommy. He says if you don't come he's going to hurt me. Mommy, come here, please! I'm scared, Mommy. Come, I want you to come. I want to go home. I miss you, Mommy. I want you. I want to go home. Please, Mommy, come to the man's house. Please, Mom—"

The call ended abruptly, and Elle screamed.

For a few precious seconds, she'd had contact with her baby girl and now it was gone, and it felt like Ruthie was being ripped away from her all over again.

"No!" she screeched, vaguely aware of the fact that she shouldn't be yelling, that she didn't want to scare or upset little Andy. But she wasn't in control of herself or her actions right now. She was consumed with terror for her daughter. "Ruthie? Baby? Come back! Don't leave me again, baby, don't leave me. Mommy needs you, Ruthie. Come back to me!" Her own sobs became hysterical as she collapsed against Panther, convinced that was the last time she would ever hear her sweet little girl's voice.

CHAPTER Four

February 14th
8:09 P.M.

Her desolate sobs filled with a pain so deep there were no words to adequately describe it, tore at Panther's heart.

Shredded it.

Left it in tatters on his kitchen floor.

All he could see inside his head was himself in Elle's position, his sweet little boy snatched away from him, helpless, unable to get his child back, the fear and terror that would be coursing through his body.

Honestly, he was surprised that Elle had held it together as well as she had.

Wrapping his arms around her and holding her didn't seem like he was doing nearly enough to help. His desire to find Ruthie had grown into a need. He had to find this child, there was no other option. There was no way he could send this woman away empty-handed and still be able to function as a member of Bravo Team.

Panther had no idea why he cared so much, nor did he intend to worry about it. His whole focus was on the woman sobbing her heart out in his arms.

"Daddy?" Andy appeared in the doorway, his worried eyes on Elle. "What's wrong?"

In his hold, Elle went completely still, somehow managing to stifle her sobs from one heartbeat to the next. "I'm sorry," she whispered quietly enough for only him to hear. "I never meant to upset your son."

Tightening his hold on her for a moment, Panther then took a step back, letting his arms fall to his side, suddenly missing the feel of Elle's slim body pressed against him. "Sorry we disturbed you, bud, but everything's okay."

"Are you sure?" Andy's gaze was on Elle, not him, as though he needed to hear her reassurance before he could believe it.

"I'm sure," Elle told him. "I just got upset about Ruthie but didn't mean to disturb you. Do you want your daddy to go and tuck you in?" There she went again, worrying more about his son being taken care of than she did herself. She had to be desperate to give him every piece of information she could so he could start looking for her child, but she was still taking the time to make sure his child was okay.

Looking between the two of them with an expression so much older than his years, Andy shook his head. "No. You need Daddy more than I do right now."

With one more sombre look, Andy disappeared back upstairs. Panther couldn't be more proud of his boy. Growing up without the benefit of being surrounded by other kids made Panther worry that his son was missing out on learning the skills he needed to grow up into a well-adjusted young man. But that obviously wasn't the case. Andy was intelligent, empathetic, creative, and already had a well-developed intuition.

"He's a great kid," Elle said softly as she sank into a chair at the table with a weariness that told him she was getting dangerously close to reaching the end of her rope.

"The best," he agreed. Heading to the fridge, he began pulling out ingredients and setting them on the counter.

"What are you doing?" Elle asked warily.

"Cooking you some dinner."

"I'm not hungry, and I didn't come here looking for the services of a chef, I came looking for someone who can find my daughter."

"You're getting both," he said simply as he filled a pot with water, turned it on to boil, and then began chopping vegetables.

"I'm really not hungry." Out of the corner of his eye, he could see Elle rubbing at her stomach as though the thought of food made her sick. Panther was sure that it did. She had been living on adrenalin and not much else this past month, but one thing you learned fast if you wanted to survive Delta Force, and that was you took care of your body whether you felt like it or not. It could be your greatest asset or your greatest enemy, it was up to you to decide.

Only this time, he was going to make the decision for Elle.

"When was the last time you took care of yourself? Ate a proper meal? Took a long hot shower? Got a full night's sleep?" They were all rhetorical questions, but he posed them all to her anyway because Elle had to understand that even though she was scared out of her mind, taking care of herself was non-negotiable. Her daughter was counting on her, so Elle couldn't afford to run herself into the ground and collapse.

"Ruthie is missing," she said as an explanation.

The water in the pot was boiling, so Panther poured in some pasta and then turned to face her. "Exactly. And your daughter is counting on you. That means you take care of yourself whether you feel like it or not. That starts with a nutritionally balanced meal and then a shower."

Her brow furrowed into the most adorable frown. "I can't take a shower here. I don't have my shampoo, or conditioner, or body wash, and ..." Her cheeks turned the sweetest shade of pink. "I don't have any clean clothes."

"I'll lend you something to wear." If she was going to keep throwing up roadblocks, he would keep plowing through them. It was obvious no one in Elle's life had stepped up to make sure she was okay while she was living through a hell none of them could understand. If she didn't have anyone else to take care of her, he'd do it himself.

"But don't we ... have to talk about Ruthie? I don't know how much you know, and I've been keeping notes. I couldn't help myself. I started when I got the first letter. The cops have the originals, but I have pictures, and detailed notes on everything I know about—"

"Elle," he said, cutting her off. "We'll talk about everything. I promise. I know enough about the case to get started. Sparrow made sure I was given access to the file the police have. I want to hear everything you have to tell me as well, but for now, I need you to take the next hour to focus only on yourself. Can you do that for me?" Panther was aware it was like asking her to cut off her own arm. A parent couldn't just turn off their fears for their child, especially when that child was in danger, but right now, Elle was letting herself get too close to hitting a brick wall, she needed this, he knew she did.

"Well ..." she hedged, obviously still undecided.

"While you shower it will give me time to read through the files, make a list of questions to ask you," he added. This was all happening at the last minute. Sparrow had called only a few hours ago to ask for this favor. Normally, she would have asked her older sister, but Raven's three-year-old son had decided that trying to use the trampoline to catch a balloon stuck in a tree was a good idea and wound up breaking his leg, and now Raven and her husband Max were preoccupied trying to keep an active toddler still and quiet. While he had read through the file, he really did need to take a closer read, and it would be easier without Elle hovering.

"Okay," she finally agreed.

"Perfect. Take as long as you want in the shower, then make yourself comfortable in the living room and I'll be through with dinner and we can talk. Use my bathroom upstairs, the other one is filled with all of Andy's stuff." The thought of her in his bathroom, naked and soapy in the shower, made him have to turn his back quickly, pretend he was busy with the stove, so she didn't see the bulge in his pants and leave immediately thinking he was completely unprofessional and sleazy on top of that. "Door at the end of the hall is my bedroom. Grab a pair of sweatpants and a sweatshirt and stick your clothes in the machine when you come back down."

With a look that said she still wasn't completely certain about this, Elle gave a slow nod, lifted herself out of the chair like her limbs weighed too much, and disappeared through the door.

Alone, Panther finished up the vegetables, drained the pasta, and added it along with some sliced chicken breasts and plenty of cheese, into a casserole dish. This was Andy's favorite meal, and since it contained carbs, vegetables, meat, and dairy he considered it a parenting win.

Dinner attended to, Panther grabbed his laptop and sat down at the kitchen table, bringing up the file Sparrow had sent him. Time faded away as he read through everything the cops had on Ruthie's case. As he did, he made a list of questions to ask Elle, just like he'd told her he would.

When the timer went off to tell him that dinner was ready, he took it out of the oven and served two plates even though he'd eaten earlier with Andy since he suspected he would get Elle to eat more if they both ate together. Tucking the laptop and notepad under his arm, he balanced both plates and carried them through to the living room, stopping abruptly at the sight that met his eyes.

Curled up on his couch was Elle, the tortured lined in her face finally smoothed away by sleep. Dressed in a pair of his sweatpants and one of his hoodies, she looked tiny and delicate in the too-big clothes. Seeing her dressed in his clothes filled him with a surge of possessiveness.

Carrying everything back into the kitchen, he covered the plates and set them on the counter to cool before going in the fridge. Guess feeding Elle would have to wait till morning because no way was he waking her when she was actually getting some sleep. He had intended for her to go home after they'd talked through her daughter's case, but now he returned to the living room and very carefully scooped her into his arms. She'd be spending the night there.

Upstairs, he headed straight for his room. While he couldn't put her in Andy's room, he was sure Mrs. Pfeffer would be fine with Elle sleeping in her bed. Not that he did that. He bypassed both bedrooms and headed straight for his own. Lying her in the middle of his king-size bed again emphasized how small and vulnerable she was, and Panther couldn't help but smooth a hand over her silky brown locks as he tucked her in.

This woman might be a job, but he liked seeing her in his bed as much as he liked seeing her dressed in his clothes.

Yep, he was in big trouble.

~

February 15th
2:32 A.M.

"Mama."

The sweet little voice called out to her from the darkness.

"Ruthie?"

"Mama."

Spinning in a circle, Elle couldn't see her daughter.

Darkness was everywhere.

It was like a fog, only instead of being floaty and white, it was thicker, blacker, and it covered everything.

"Ruthie? Baby? Where are you?" she called out, the circles she was turning in became faster and more frantic. Where had Ruthie gone? She was right there, right beside her, holding her hand.

She hadn't looked away. Had she?

The small fingers curled around her own had been enough to reassure her that her daughter was okay, safe, close ... maybe she had looked away, just for a second.

A second was all it took.

One moment in time and you lost everything that mattered.

But she didn't look away, she wouldn't. Turning her back on her precious daughter wasn't something she would do.

Not ever.

Not even in the safety of their own backyard.

She was careful.

She was always careful.

No.

Elle wouldn't leave Ruthie alone, not for anything, so where was her little girl? How had she been swallowed up by the black fog? Where was her daughter? Where was her little unicorn girl? The one who brought magic and whimsy into her life?

"Where are you, baby girl? Answer, Mommy, please, sweetie. Tell Mommy where you are!"

Her cries went unanswered.

Silence swirled around her. Taunting her.

"Mama."

The voice was everywhere and yet nowhere. It sounded close and yet far away. It was the faintest hint of a sound, yet it was also deafening.

"Where are you, Ruthie?" Elle demanded, fear made her voice come out sharper than she intended, and she could hear her baby crying. *"I'm sorry, Ruthie. I'm sorry, baby. Mommy is so sorry. Where are you, baby? Where are you, little unicorn girl?"*

Nothing.

No answer.

Just the sound of her daughter sobbing.

"No," she screamed in pained frustration. *Ruthie was gone, and it was all her fault. Now she would be forced to live her life to the sound of her daughter's cries.*

It was too much.

She couldn't go on like this.

Didn't want to go on like this.

All she wanted was to hold her baby in her arms again.

"I'm sorry, Ruthie. I'm sorry. I'm so sorry," she wept over and over again.

"Elle."

"I'm sorry, my sweet unicorn girl. I failed you. It was my job to protect you, to keep you safe, to never let anything hurt you, and I failed. I failed."

"Wake up, Elle. Now. Damn it, wake up."

"I love you, baby girl. Do you know that Mommy loves you? Do you know that Mommy would do anything for you?"

A sharp, stinging pain in her cheek had her bolting upright.

Elle's eyes snapped open, and instead of the black, swirling fog she expected to see the room was bathed in light.

Disoriented at the sight of the unfamiliar room, the walls were a light gray instead of the soft pink of her bedroom, and the quilt beneath her shaking hands was dark grey instead of frilly and white. The bed felt wrong, and there was no soft breeze floating over her now icy cold skin from the window behind her bed that she always kept open.

Where was she?

Panic flooded her system, and she began to scramble backward when her gaze fell on the man leaning on the side of the mattress. One knee was by her hip, his other foot planted on the floor. He was wearing only a pair of pajama pants that hung low on his hips, and his torso may as well have been chiseled from marble by Michelangelo himself.

Her mouth dropped open as fear and confusion turned to embarrassment. There she was ogling him, and she didn't even know where she was or why Panther was standing beside her ... no not her ... *the* bed.

"I umm ... what ... I'm sorry ... I don't ... where am I?" Elle stammered, averting her gaze before she did something completely stupid and inappropriate like reach out and trace the lines of his six-pack.

"You fell asleep on my couch," Panther told her.

The last thing she remembered was feeling rejuvenated by the long, steamy, hot shower. It had been weird being naked in a stranger's bathroom, but Panther was right, the shower had helped, it washed away the fog and relaxed her tense muscles. By the time she'd gone searching through his dresser her eyes had felt heavy, but she'd ignored it, dressing and heading down, marveling at the fact that the smells coming from the kitchen had her stomach rumbling.

It had been a long time since she'd felt hungry. Elle ate because it was necessary, snatching a slice of bread here or a piece of fruit there, but mostly living off coffee. Same with showering. When she realized she was smelly, she hopped in the shower, rushing through it in case there was a call saying her daughter had been found.

But last night, she'd made herself stay under the spray, letting the water work its magic and allowing herself a moment to just ... be.

Obviously, it had helped more than she realized because she must have fallen asleep the second she curled up on the soft leather couch. She didn't remember a single thing after that. Panther must have found her and carried her to one of the bedrooms.

As she looked around, noted the pictures of Andy, and recalled rifling through the dresser opposite the end of the bed earlier, she realized that Panther had brought her to *his* room. She'd been sleeping in *his* bed.

And from the sight of his messy, dark locks, she'd woken him in the middle of the night.

Andy.

Had she woken the boy as well?

"I'm sorry, did I wake you? I didn't mean to fall asleep, I didn't intend to spend the night here, I was going to go home after we talked, the shower, it must have relaxed me too much, and I was dreaming, and I must have been calling out, apparently I do that, and—"

"And do you intend to put any full stops in that sentence or just keep babbling indefinitely?" Panther asked, amusement dancing in his golden-brown eyes, and Elle couldn't look away, mesmerized by them.

He was so handsome, and even though she was supposed to be there for him to help her find her daughter, he'd gone above and beyond. Taken care of her. When was the last time anyone had bothered to take care of her? Her parents had been too busy with all their strict rules and expectations to actually spend a second of their time coddling her in any way. Her ex-husband wasn't a bad man per se, but he was more interested in relaxing after work—if he even had a job—and playing his video games than to help around the house or take care of her or her needs.

But Panther ...

A man who didn't even know her had gone out of his way to look after her even though it was absolutely going above and beyond.

"I babble when I'm nervous," she admitted, offering him a shy smile. "Was I screaming in my sleep?"

"Crying more than screaming."

Elle winced. "Did I wake Andy, too?"

"Nah, the kid could sleep through an air raid, I don't know where he gets it from."

"I woke you, though. I'm sorry. I was always a vivid dreamer, but since Ruthie ... disappeared ... I seem to talk in my sleep. Scream usually, although I've been told I cried a few times as well."

"It's okay, Elle," Panther said gently.

For some reason, she didn't like the idea of him being just Panther. They weren't friends, but he was searching for her daughter, and she prayed he was going to do what no one else had been able to do. She should know his real name, after all, if he brought her baby home, if she ever had other children, she was going to name them after him, and she could hardly call them Panther.

"What's your name?" she asked before she could stop herself. Sparrow had only ever called him Panther and hadn't told her anything else about him other than that if anyone could help her find Ruthie, it was him.

A strange look came over his face, almost making her regret asking, but she didn't back down. If he didn't want to tell her he didn't have to, but she honestly didn't see what the big deal was. It was just a name.

Just when she thought he wasn't going to answer, his voice spoke softly. "Rafe. It's Rafe."

"Rafe," she echoed, it suited him. "I'm sorry for falling asleep last night. You made dinner and everything, and I'm sorry for waking you in the middle of the night."

"It's okay, Elle. I don't mind. I'm glad you rested, and nightmares under these circumstances are perfectly normal. Do you think you can go back to sleep?"

There was no way she would sleep again right now, not while her body, her mind, and her heart were still buzzing from her dreams. "I don't think so."

"Then how about we get up and I get you something to eat."

When he went to move away from the bed, she reached out and touched a hand to the top of his. "You don't have to. You can go back to bed, I can look after myself."

Something dark passed through his eyes, but it was gone so quickly she wondered if she imagined it. "I don't have to, Elle, but I want to."

With that, he was gone, leaving her staring after him, trying to figure out a man who was only supposed to search for her daughter but seemed to be doing so much more.

CHAPTER

Five

Giggling.

The sound drew Panther's attention away from his laptop.

Usually, when he worked from home, which wasn't all that often, the house was quiet. If it was a school day then Mrs. Pfeffer would be in the playroom with Andy running through his classes for the day. There might be a bit of sound as Andy asked questions or Mrs. Pfeffer talked, but all in all, things were quiet and there definitely wasn't the kind of giggles he could now hear coming from his living room.

Working in the cabin wasn't what he normally did. The large compound he and his team had purchased when their Delta Force careers had gone up in smoke was seventy acres. Each of them had an acre of their own with their cabins, and the remaining ten acres was a communal area with a large building and a training range they used to run scenarios. In the building they had several conference rooms for planning ops, a hang out space, and Panther had a huge office filled with all the equipment and electronics his heart could desire.

But today, he hadn't wanted to go and work there. Today, he'd needed to stay home, close to his son. There was no way he could work this case and search for Elle's kidnapped daughter and not feel a burning need to keep his own child close.

So he'd called Mrs. Pfeffer and told her she didn't need to come in today. Even though it was the weekend when he'd gotten a call from Sparrow asking him to look at Ruthie Cavey's case, he'd asked the nanny if she was available if he needed her. Of course, Mrs. Pfeffer was, he'd lucked out finding her to help with Andy, but he also knew she could easily find something else to do, the woman was the epitome of the social butterfly.

Since Elle had woken him before three, they'd had time to go through her daughter's case in great detail before Andy got up. His son had been delighted to see that Elle was still there, and even though the woman had offered to leave after breakfast, Andy had begged her to stay. Panther could have put his foot down, told his son to let Elle leave, but he'd sensed she didn't really want to go home alone to her empty house where all she would do was worry about her daughter, so he'd told her it was fine if she wanted to stay. This way at least he could help her by giving her something else to do to split her attention between her fears for her daughter and playing with his son.

It had been almost four hours since he left Andy and Elle in the kitchen cleaning up after breakfast. Once he got his head buried in his computer, he could go for hours without coming up for air. If he didn't have a child who needed feeding, bathing, and attention, he would likely forget to eat. In fact, when he was digging for some obscure piece of information he and his team needed, he had been known to forget to eat and sleep, and forget about taking a shower, that was at the bottom of his list.

Now, though, the sounds of carefree giggles couldn't be ignored.

The kitchen was empty, everything packed away. How many times had Mrs. Pfeffer scolded him and Andy for leaving the kitchen in a mess for her to clean up? Hundreds over the years she'd been taking care of his son. It wasn't that he tried to be lazy or thought cleaning up was a woman's job, it was just that time with his son was precious, and he didn't get as much of it as he would like. So, when he did get that one-on-one time with Andy, he didn't want to waste it cleaning up the kitchen.

His son was his whole world, and Panther vowed he was going to start making more time for the two of them to hang out together. Already Andy was growing so quickly, it wouldn't be long until he was a teenager and didn't want to spend time with his dad.

These years were so precious, and he had let more time than he should slip through his fingers already.

No more.

Andy was and should be his priority. As important as his work was, his child was still number one. Now closely followed by a little girl with long brown locks and big gray blue eyes. A child who had haunted his dreams even before her mother's screams woke him up.

I'm going to find you, princess, you just hold on for me.

That promise was renewed as he stepped through the kitchen door and found his son and Elle engaged in what looked like a pretty epic Nerf gun battle. They'd pulled all the cushions off the couch, and looked like they'd collected the pillows from the beds, too. Furniture had been moved, the pillows and some blankets added to make forts, and they were firing away at each other, lost in their game.

"Hey, Andy, intruder!" Elle suddenly called out, and as though the two had practiced it, they both turned and fired, raining down a bevy of foam bullets on him.

Their squeals of delight warmed his heart, and he was glad he'd fibbed and asked Elle if she could watch Andy so he could work since his nanny was sick and couldn't come in. Seeing his son having so much fun with Elle gave him this weird feeling in the pit of his stomach. Panther couldn't deny he was attracted to Elle. What wasn't there to like? With her long brown locks, soft curves, and big brown eyes, she was beautiful. Add in the fact she was strong and brave, fighting for her daughter with everything she had, and any man would be lucky to have her.

Most importantly to him, though, was that Elle was a good mother.

Was he really standing here watching her play with his son and making a pro list in his head of asking her out?

The thought shocked him, leaving him completely immobile.

"Daddy, you're dead," Andy called out, firing another few bullets at him. "See? Dead."

Elle had grown quiet, her easy smile falling from her lips, replaced by anxiety he itched to soothe away with soft kisses. "I'm sorry. I should have asked before we made all this mess. I'll clean it all up before I go."

"You can't go now, Elle," Andy protested. "We were going to make lunch, and then we were going to play Mario Kart. My dad is going to build me a go-kart in the spring."

"Umm, a go-kart sounds super cool, but maybe we can play Mario Kart some other time," Elle said, clearly uncertain now since he still hadn't said anything. It wasn't that he didn't want to, it was that he couldn't. All he could see as he watched her in his living room, playing with his son, was more mornings like this, only with a little pigtailed girl joining in the fun.

It hadn't even been twenty-four hours since he'd met this woman, how could he already be picturing her as any sort of permanent fixture in his life?

Shaking away his own stupidity, he brushed his feelings off as a mixture of loneliness on his part—he was the only member of his team now without a woman—and his driving need to bring her daughter home to her.

Realizing he still hadn't said anything, Panther shot out a hand to stop her when Elle tried to sidle by him to get into the kitchen, probably to grab her purse so she could leave. "Stay. Please."

"Yeah, Elle, stay," Andy added, bouncing about like he did when he was excited. And no wonder his son didn't want Elle to leave. When was the last time somebody had played with him like this? Mrs. Pfeffer was in her seventies. When she played with Andy it tended to be board games, and he was so busy that the time he did get with his kid they usually kicked a ball around, or played video games.

"I don't have to stay," Elle said cautiously, even though it was obvious she wanted to.

"We want you to. Andy wants you to, and so do I," Panther added honestly, surprised that it was actually true.

"Then I'd love to stay for lunch, if you're sure I'm not in the way and intruding."

The fact that her concern was interrupting his time with his son and not that she wanted him to stay glued to his laptop, searching for her missing daughter, made him like her that much more. Elle was something else, and one way or another, he would bring her daughter home to her, even if that was only the closure of a body to bury.

Although he prayed it didn't come to that.

"Elle said we could have pizza for lunch," Andy said, shoving past them into the kitchen.

"I did not, you sneaky little munchkin," Elle said with a laugh. "I said you could ask your dad if we could make Ruthie's favorite mini pizzas for lunch." Pain chased away her smile as she realized she'd just mentioned her daughter. How many times a day did the gut-wrenching, soul-destroying pain of remembering her daughter was gone hit her?

Panther didn't even want to think about it.

"Hey." He caught Elle's hand as she went to walk past him into the kitchen. "I'll find her. I'll bring her home to you."

The smile she gave him was both grateful and reserved. She knew he couldn't make her that promise, but she appreciated that he would give it everything he had. "At first, I wasn't sure why Sparrow sent me to you, especially given Raven's history with Cleo. But now I get it. You're a great father, and there is no one I would trust more to look for my daughter than you."

When she stood on tiptoes and touched a kiss to his cheek, Panther felt it right down to his heart.

～

February 15th
12:38 P.M.

Tears stung the backs of Elle's eyes as she cleaned up the kitchen.

It wasn't just the sounds of muted laughs coming from the living room that were so bittersweet it hurt, it was everything. Sparrow making Ruthie's case important enough for Prey to look at even though this wasn't their usual kind of work. Rafe being nice enough not just to try to find Ruthie, but to allow her to spend time with his son while he worked, seeming to sense she needed to be around a child right now even if it hurt. Andy being so sweet and funny, playing with him had reminded her of her daughter, but it had also been about him, making him smile, making sure he was having fun.

Then there was lunch.

Mini pizzas weren't just Ruthie's favorite, they were a special meal that just the two of them shared. They weren't really pizzas, but for Elle's birthday the year Ruthie was four, her daughter wanted to make her mommy a special birthday lunch. Being only four, it wasn't like her daughter knew how to cook, but that wasn't the kind of thing that stopped a child like Ruthie.

Nope, her daughter just raided the pantry and came up with her own thing.

Ruthie was a free-spirited little girl. She was smart, polite, funny, sweet, and so friendly she had never met a person who didn't come to love her within minutes of meeting her. But Ruthie never followed the crowd, she made her own way, and that was evident in the mini pizzas she shared with such pride.

Nothing more than a rice cracker with ketchup and a slice of cheese. They didn't actually taste all that good, but Ruthie had been so proud of herself and so excited that the meal had quickly become their favorite.

Now she'd shared that special tradition that had been for just the two of them with Rafe and Andy, and she felt ... odd. Not unhappy, Andy had been so excited to ask his dad for pizza for lunch, and it had seemed like the most natural thing in the world to tell him about Ruthie's mini pizzas. Andy had been just as proud of himself as Ruthie had been to make them all on his own, and he'd loved them. Rafe had said he liked them, too, but she wasn't sure if that was just him being nice and not wanting to hurt her feelings.

Father and son were busy with Legos in the living room while she cleaned up. They'd wanted to help, but she needed this moment alone before joining the boys to play Mario Kart. Elle knew spending time with Andy might be what she needed to feel closer to her daughter, but she couldn't help but feel like she was setting herself up for heartbreak.

It wasn't like the boy could be in her life forever.

If—*when*—Rafe brought her daughter home, she and Ruthie would return to their lives as Elle focused on doing whatever her child needed to heal. And if the worst happened and Rafe couldn't help her, then she could hardly move into his house and play with his son every day for the rest of their lives.

The little boy reminded her so much of Ruthie. Andy was a free spirit, too, only in a different, more serious way. There was no doubt he had inherited the protective gene from his father and she was positive he was going to excel at whatever he wound up doing in life.

Ruthie would love him, too. Her daughter had been desperate for a sibling for as long as Elle could remember. It didn't matter how many times she explained that you needed a mommy and a daddy to make a baby, Ruthie kept insisting that she didn't care that there was no daddy, she still wanted a baby brother or sister.

"Hey."

The hand touching her shoulder made her shriek as she spun around, her hand flying to her chest where her heart hammered like it was attempting to singlehandedly build an entire village.

"You scared me," she told Rafe, a teeny hint of accusation in her tone.

"I called your name, you didn't hear me. Are you okay?"

There was genuine concern in his voice and it chipped away at her resolve. She didn't want to cry anymore and certainly didn't want this man to think she wasn't so very grateful for everything he was doing for her, but she couldn't seem to stop.

Too many emotions, too much pain, too much grief, no one to share the burden, not even a little bit.

Only when a strong set of arms closed around her, and she was urged to lean against a chest that was so sturdy it may as well be an oak tree, Elle realized that wasn't quite true.

Rafe was here.

Holding her, soothing her. He'd been there last night, too, when she woke from a nightmare.

In less than twenty-four hours, he'd been more supportive than all the people who were supposed to love and care about Ruthie put together. Her parents had literally told her that if she followed the path they set for her, dedicating her life to medical research instead of wasting it as a romance author, then she wouldn't be in this predicament. Even though he'd signed away his parental rights, Elle had called her ex to tell him about Ruthie, he was, after all, her father, and he had to love her in his own way. His response was 'call me if you find her'. Like their daughter was a missing sock or Tupperware lid.

But Rafe had shown true empathy and concern, not just for Ruthie but for her as well.

"I'm sorry," she cried into his shirt, fisting her hands in the soft material that smelled just like Rafe.

"For what?"

"For intruding on your time with Andy. For falling asleep here last night instead of going home. For taking your bed. For waking you in the middle of the night. For making such a mess when I was playing with Andy."

Large hands covered her shoulders and she was eased back. "I don't care that you and Andy made a mess. Kids are messy, we both know that. I ... liked seeing you playing with my son."

His admission started a fresh wave of tears. "I can't seem to stop crying. No matter how many times I think I must have used up all my tears for a lifetime more still manage to come."

"Course they do, Elle. Your baby was taken from you."

"I would go to him if I knew who he was or where he was," she whispered brokenly. It wasn't wanting to protect her own safety that stopped her from going to the kidnapper, it was that she had no idea who he was, and therefore, no idea where he was. Whatever relationship he believed the two of them—three of them if you included Ruthie—had wasn't reality. He might know her, but it didn't go both ways. There wasn't anything she wouldn't do for her child, including sacrificing her own life.

"They're everything, aren't they?" Rafe said.

"My parents ... they weren't the most loving ... and my ex was selfish ... until Ruthie, I didn't even know you could love someone the way I love her." During her pregnancy, Elle had been afraid that she wasn't capable of loving her child the way they deserved. Turned out she shouldn't have worried. From the moment that red, squawking little infant had been placed in her arms, Elle had loved her with a ferocity she didn't know existed.

"Raising them alone is the hardest job in the world."

"The hardest," she agreed. Not how she had planned it. She and her ex had been married for two years and discussed having kids. The pregnancy was planned. There was no way she could have guessed her husband would bail while she was sleep-deprived and trying to build a career and take care of a newborn at the same time.

"I wouldn't change it for the world."

A soft laugh came out through her tears. "Me either."

"Elle?" Those hands on her shoulders tightened to a point just shy of pain. "Even if I knew where he was, I wouldn't let you trade yourself for Ruthie. I'll get your daughter home where she belongs, but I won't allow you to die in the process."

It wasn't his choice.

Her daughter, her life, her choice.

Yet from his expression, she could see Rafe wasn't trying to be controlling, or demanding, or anything.

He was worried.

About her.

There was something between them, she couldn't deny it. Attraction at the very least. Elle wasn't opposed to dating again, she wasn't single because she'd sworn off men or relationships, she was just too busy.

But this thing brewing between her and Rafe was more than attraction. They got what it was like to be a single parent, they would both always put their kids first. They'd both had partners walk out of them so they would never do that to another person.

If there was one person in the world she believed could bring her baby home to her, it was this man staring at her so silently, with such a confused expression, like he didn't know what to make of her, but that some part of him had already claimed her.

CHAPTER Six

February 15th
5:22 P.M.

"Why do I keep landing on the chutes?" Elle asked with what could only be described as a frustrated huff.

Damn, she was adorable when she huffed like that.

Panther almost couldn't take his eyes off her.

It had been like that all day. The more time they spent together, the deeper his attachment to her grew.

She was so vulnerable yet so strong.

Even though her entire world had been ripped out from under her, she was still going, still fighting for her daughter, still loving and caring for others. The way she was with his son was everything he had always wished for in a mother for Andy. Everything he had been too scared didn't exist.

Now that he was staring in the face a future that he could actually have—provided he could find this woman's daughter and bring her home—he realized why he'd avoided relationships these last seven years.

When Marcia had left, skipped out on her life leaving him quite literally holding the baby, it had hurt.

Hurt him. Because Andy didn't remember his mother.

But if Panther let someone else into their lives. Allowed his son to become attached, and she wound up leaving them, it would be his son who got hurt.

His child's pain was the one thing he couldn't bear.

Elle would never walk away. It might have been only forty-eight hours since he met her, but he already knew that with absolute certainty.

"You landed on one ladder," Andy said with an encouraging smile. Panther wasn't the only one smitten with their guest, Andy already adored Elle. Earlier after he'd comforted Elle in the kitchen, he'd gone back to play Ninjago with Andy. Aware of the clock ticking on Ruthie's life, after thirty minutes or so he'd told his son he had to go back to work. While he'd been expecting disappointment from Andy, the usual reaction when he had to stop playtime for worktime, Andy merely nodded and bounced off to Elle asking her to race him in Mario Kart.

"Yeah, about fifty rolls of the dice ago." Panther snorted in amusement.

Turning narrowed eyes on him, Elle planted her hands on her hips. "It was only ten rolls ago, but that's the only ladder I got, I keep getting those chutes."

"I think someone is a bad loser," he teased. While he definitely enjoyed winning, neither he nor his son were ultra-competitive. Maybe it was because so much of his life revolved around working as part of a team where every person played an important role that he never worried himself with winning and losing.

"I am not." She huffed again, making him laugh. "Chutes and Ladders is a terrible game anyway. It's all chance, no skill."

This time both he and Andy laughed at her irritated frown.

"Does Ruthie like Chutes and Ladders?" Andy asked. His son had been peppering Elle with questions about the little girl all day. At first, Panther had hurried to shush his son, not wanting to upset Elle by making her talk about her daughter, but she had assured him it was okay, that she thought of Ruthie every second of every day and that it helped a little to talk about her.

"She does, but her favorite game is Jenga. She's really good at it, too. She has these nimble, little fingers that seem to slide blocks out without causing a single ripple even with the most precarious of towers." Elle laughed, the sound simultaneously both warm and sad. "She always giggles when we play, she's happy whether she wins or loses. I guess I'm the only bad loser in the bunch." She gave another laugh, this one self-deprecating.

"Dad, I'm hungry," Andy said as he rolled the dice for his turn and landed on another ladder, moving up two spaces away from the end.

"Oh, look at the time," Elle exclaimed, glancing at the clock hanging on the wall. "I'm sorry, I didn't realize it was dinner time. I've taken up your whole day." She stood so quickly her chair wobbled. "I didn't mean to stay all day. I'll get out of your hair. Let you two hang out together for a while. You have my number. You'll call if you find anything, right? Even if it's small I want to know. I don't care about getting my hopes up if it turns out to be nothing. If you find something I want to know. I *need* to know."

The woman who had spent the day playing with his son evaporated, and he could sense Elle's growing panic. The last thing she wanted was to go home alone where all she would do was obsess over Ruthie. Despite them knowing one another only a couple of days, she was drawing strength from him and his son, security, and comfort, and Panther found he liked knowing that.

All these years of being adamant he and his son didn't need anyone else, and then one woman whose love for her child equaled his own had changed everything he thought he knew.

It would be so easy to slip into a life with this woman.

Scarily easy.

And what was even scarier was that he *wanted* it.

Wanted to take this woman out on dates and learn everything about her. Wanted to get to know her daughter and be the father figure the little girl's father wouldn't be. Wanted the four of them to hang out and do family stuff together.

Crazy, but Elle and Ruthie had kicked his protective instincts into overdrive, and he couldn't stomach the idea of her going home alone where no one would be watching out for her.

"Stay, please." He'd said those words to her before and they were easier to say this time. He was worried about her being alone, and he wanted to be the one to take care of her, make sure she was eating, and be there if she had more nightmares.

There was a brief hesitation as her gaze flew to meet his. "Are you sure? I don't want to intrude. I know how precious time is with them."

"You're not intruding." Absolutely the truth.

"Then I would love to have dinner with you two handsome men," she said with a shy smile.

That smile gave him an idea, and he snapped his laptop closed and stood. "You two go play for a bit, I'm cooking dinner." Something special, and he was going to get out the good china. It was something Marcia had insisted on buying even though, at the time, they'd been struggling just to pay the bills let alone buy an expensive dinner set. After she'd left, he'd kept it, and for some reason, it had gotten packed up along with everything else and brought there. He hadn't used it, not even once, but tonight he wanted to do something nice for Elle. Not that he could take her mind completely off her kidnapped daughter, but he could do something that would distract her at least a little.

"I can help cook," Elle offered immediately.

"Nope. I got it handled. You two go relax, I'll call you when dinner's ready." He shooed them both out of their chairs and began to pack away the board game.

"We can watch the Mario Bros movie," Andy said as the two disappeared into the living room. "I've seen it almost twenty times already," his son boasted.

"Twenty times?" Elle sounded shocked. "Then you don't need to see it again. How about we read? Ruthie and I love to curl up and read to one another in the evenings, especially on winter nights like this when it's cold and snowy outdoors. If you want I could read to you, or you could read to me, or we could take turns."

"Let's take turns," Andy exclaimed in delight, making Panther smile. His son loved being read to, but with such a busy schedule he rarely had the time. Mrs. Pfeffer would read to him sometimes, and he always raved about the voices she put on for him.

That smile remained on his face as he got the oven on and began preparing vegetables. He'd do roast potatoes, carrots, and pumpkin. There were some chicken breasts in the fridge, he could season them and throw those in the oven, too. Then he'd set the table, pick some flowers from the yard, and go and put something nice on. Panther was sure there had to be some candles around here somewhere, too.

How long had it been since he had this energy buzzing through him?

Between his job and being a single dad, there was barely a spare second to think about the future, but even when he did, he hadn't been willing to risk his son's happiness on a woman who could so very easily break Andy's tender little heart. His heart, too.

It wasn't like he was ready to offer Elle forever, even if she didn't have too much going on to think more than a couple of seconds into the future, but he wanted to see if there could be something amazing between them.

For the first time since his wife announced she wanted a divorce and no part in raising their son, Panther felt hopeful about the future.

A future that could far too easily slip through his fingers.

Because it all rested on one thing.

His ability to find Ruthie and bring her home. If he couldn't, he was afraid the brave, strong, vibrant woman who could fill the hole in his and Andy's lives would fall apart and become but a shell of who she was.

~

February 16th
  3:02 A.M.

Yesterday, the couch had been comfortable enough that Elle had slipped right off to sleep without even realizing it.

Tonight—this morning really—it felt like the most uncomfortable surface on the planet.

What had changed?

Maybe it was knowing she was a coward.

While Rafe tucked his son into bed last night, she had pretended to fall asleep on the couch. Why, she wasn't altogether sure.

A myriad of reasons probably. Partly, she was afraid that if he saw her awake, he'd tell her she'd finally outstayed her welcome and it was time for her to go home to her own house, and that he'd call when he had news.

There was no way to adequately explain it but *here* was where Elle felt the safest. She didn't want to leave. It was stupid because she was only there because Rafe was looking for Ruthie and he felt sorry for her, and sympathized with her as a fellow single parent. And while she didn't want his pity, she couldn't deny that even if it looked like pity to her eyes, it felt different to her heart.

That dinner ... Rafe had gone all out. No other way to describe it. If his son hadn't been sitting at the table along with them, and she wasn't wearing jeans and a sweater, it would have felt like a date.

Only it wasn't a date.

The more time she spent with Rafe and Andy, the more the lines felt like they were getting blurred. She wasn't there to meet a prospective boyfriend, she was there for help finding her kidnapped child. Yet, she couldn't deny that if she was going to start looking for a partner, Rafe pretty much ticked every box she could have. Most importantly, he was also a father so he understood that her priority was her child and not herself and her own needs, wants, and desires.

If she was honest with herself, Elle knew why she couldn't sleep, and while some of it was the same as always—fear for her daughter—some of it was that tonight she wasn't wrapped up in Rafe's comforting scent. After putting her own clothes back on after they finished in the drier yesterday morning, she realized she missed being wrapped in Rafe's clothes. Missed his big bed and its woodsy male scent. Part of her pretending to be asleep was hoping he might pick her up and take her up to his bed again, where she could find some molecule of security that had been missing from her life since this whole mess started.

He hadn't taken her up to his bed, though. When he'd come into the room and seen her "sleeping", he'd switched off the lights and the TV, gathered his laptop up, and disappeared. She assumed into his office since it was too early for bed.

Leaving her alone.

Always alone.

If she didn't have Ruthie she didn't have anyone.

No siblings, her parents hadn't wanted her, her husband left, and now her daughter was gone. If Rafe couldn't find Ruthie, then honestly, Elle couldn't find another reason to keep going. As much as she adored writing, it was her passion, the language of her soul, above all else, she wrote for herself to tell the stories that cried out to her to be told. But was writing enough to sustain her without her child?

Elle feared it wasn't.

She feared that without her daughter, she might do something she didn't really want to do because it seemed like the only option left.

So long as she had proof Ruthie was alive, she had a reason to fight. When that reason was gone she'd have nothing. No hope and no support system. When you were an introvert with a job you could do from home, you didn't make many friends. Most of the people she'd even call her friends were just the moms of Ruthie's friends, not anyone she'd say she was all that close to.

What would be the point of going on without her daughter?

None.

Not a single reason that Elle could come up with.

Bright light suddenly flooded the room, and she let out a shriek, scrambling up so quickly she misjudged the amount of space beside her on the couch and tumbled off it, landing hard on the floor and banging her elbow into the coffee table.

"Sorry, thought you were asleep and you'd panic less if the lights were on when I woke you up," Rafe said as he hurried toward hers.

He wasn't the only person in the room. Five big men gathered around, obviously having filed in from the kitchen. How could she not have heard them enter the cabin? She hadn't gotten even a wink of sleep. Had she been that lost in thought? Wallowing so deep in her misery that the rest of the world had faded away?

That's how it felt living with your child snatched away from you. Bit by bit the rest of the world moved further away until it felt like you were living alone on an island with so much sea surrounding it, there was no hope of anyone ever reaching you.

When Rafe knelt in front of her and held out a hand, it felt like a lifeline, and she hurriedly reached out to grab it in case he took it away.

Pulling her to her feet, he guided her back onto the couch, frowning when he caught her rubbing at her aching elbow. "Did you hurt yourself?"

More embarrassed than in pain, she shook her head, then realized that was a silly response since it was obvious from her rubbing that she had hurt herself. "Just hit my funny bone. Sorry, the sudden light just startled me. I forgot where I was for a moment." A small lie, there was no way she could forget where she was when every inch of this place was bathed in Rafe's comforting scent. While she would have preferred one of his hoodies and his bed, the couch smelled enough like him that she hadn't mistaken this for her house.

"Totally understandable," Rafe assured her with a squeeze of her hand. Realizing he still held her hand and had taken the seat beside her had reality slamming into her like a train.

Something was wrong.

Bad news.

Why else would these men, who had to be the rest of Bravo Team, be there?

Panic tensed every muscle in her body, throwing her immediately into flight or fight mode. Part of her wanted to run and hide because if she didn't know the bad news, maybe it wouldn't be true. The other part of her wanted to drag every drop of information out of Rafe no matter how awful the information was.

"What happened? What's wrong?" she demanded, aware she was squeezing Rafe's hand far too tightly when his thumb began to sweep across her knuckles.

"It's not bad news, Elle," he quickly assured her. "It might be good news."

For a moment, it felt like the entire world had stopped spinning.

Did Rafe really just say what she thought he said?

Was she dreaming?

Imagining this?

"G-good n-news?" Excitement had her voice trembling. Heck, it had all of her trembling.

"Don't get your hopes up yet," Rafe cautioned. "These are the guys. Let me quickly introduce you and then I'll tell you what I found. This is Tank," he said, pointing to a huge man who dropped onto the other couch with a wave. "That's Trick. Don't get too close to him or he'll pull something out from behind your ear."

"Oh, you're the guy who loves the magic tricks," she said. "Andy couldn't have been more excited to tell me the things you've taught him."

"See, everybody loves magic tricks," Trick said with a grin as he took the spot on the couch on her other side.

"Sure they do," another man muttered as he sat beside Tank.

"That was Scorpion," Rafe told her. "And that's Rock. Ignore his goofy look, he just got engaged. And that's Axe." When he pointed to the man who had remained by the door, and she followed his gaze, her heart broke when she felt the sadness emanating from him.

Loss.

As great as her own.

Even though she wanted to know what was wrong and if she could help, her need to know about her daughter overrode everything else. If that made her selfish then so be it. "It's nice to meet you all. I'm so very grateful for your help finding my daughter. What did you find, Rafe?"

"Rafe?" Tank straightened in his chair.

"Doesn't mean what you think it does, man," Panther said quickly before focusing on her.

Elle had no idea what that was about, and right now, she didn't care. She was going to lose her mind if he didn't tell her what he had found out in the next half a second.

"The cops and the FBI were so focused on your security company because he had been able to get in and out of your house without setting off your alarm no matter how many times you changed the code that they didn't look into anything else. I did. There are other people with the skills to hack systems, and I just started with the most obvious. The guy who runs your website."

"Jimmy?" There was no way. He wouldn't do this to her.

The pressure on her knuckles increased as Rafe drew her attention back to him. "No guarantees, honey. Could be nothing. But a few things in his background threw up red flags. We're going to go and check them out."

"Now?" she squeaked.

"Unless you'd rather we wait."

Her head about broke off her neck she shook it so hard to refute Rafe's statement. "Now. Right now." She didn't want to wait a single second longer than she had to to get her baby back, and if Rafe was right, that could be in just a couple of hours at the most.

CHAPTER

Seven

February 16th
4:44 A.M.

Please be right.

How many times had that thought run through his head in the last couple of hours?

So many times that Panther had lost count.

There had been times before when he'd gone on a mission to rescue someone important to one of his teammates. They'd rescued Tillie from a crime boss, Ariel from a human trafficker, Jessica from a cult leader, and Stephanie from a terrorist militia. Each one of those times he'd felt the pressure. There was always pressure, but when someone was important to a member of what you considered your family, it was that much stronger. And Bravo Team *was* his family. They'd cared about him more than his parents who had shuffled him back and forth between their homes, then started new families and left him out in the cold.

But this was so very different.

This was about a little girl who might very well hold the key to his future in her small hands.

Quite simply, he couldn't fail.

If he didn't bring Elle's daughter home to her, he was terrified he was going to have to stand by and watch as she wasted away into nothingness.

She was so very strong, but everyone reached their limit sooner or later. What happened when Elle reached hers?

"She called you Rafe," Tank said as they pulled up outside a seemingly innocuous-looking middle-class house in a nice suburb.

"Doesn't mean what you think it does," Panther repeated the same words he'd used when Elle had called him by his name back at his cabin. A part of him *wanted* it to mean something, but a bigger part knew that for the foreseeable future, Elle's focus was on her child—as it should be —and not on a potential new relationship.

"It always means the same thing," Rock said, twisting from the passenger seat to look back at him.

"Her daughter is missing," he reminded them. None of them were parents, but they were close to his son. He knew they would be hurting almost as much as he would be if anything happened to Andy, so they could all empathize with Elle.

"Doesn't mean feelings can't take hold. Trust me, it's in the darkest moments when you need light the most," Trick spoke softly, making his words feel all the more powerful. If anyone knew about light in the dark, it was Trick. It was only a couple of weeks ago that he had been kidnapped by a militia based in Liberia who wanted answers that only a few people could give. It was how he'd met Stephanie, and Panther knew that neither of the couple were even remotely close to being okay after their ordeal.

But they had each other.

Clung to each other.

And somehow, that seemed to make them both okay even when they weren't.

"Right now, I just want to focus on finding Ruthie," he said, unable, maybe even unwilling, to let himself think of anything beyond that.

"Then let's get in there and pray we find that sweet little girl," Scorpion announced with a ferocity that gave Panther pause.

Of all of his teammates, he would have guessed that Scorpion and Jessica would be the last to have kids. Given how Jessica had grown up, the immense responsibility placed on her shoulders at such a young age, and that she was finally able to start prioritizing herself thanks to Scorpion's help, he knew she wasn't ready to start a family any time soon. Yet there was something in the man's voice that hinted otherwise.

"Dude, is Jessica pregnant?" he asked, making everyone freeze, and four sets of eyes fly to him then bounce quickly to Scorpion.

Dropping his head, Scorpion raked his fingers through his hair, then looked up at him. His gaze was desolate. "She's been feeling off for weeks. She was trying to hide it because it was Christmas, then New Year, everything with Beth, and then with Trick and Steph. I made her go to the doctor. She's eleven weeks pregnant." Scorpion paused and swallowed audibly. "When she was undercover, Genesis tried artificially inseminating her. She was on birth control, but obviously it failed. There's a chance the baby is his and not mine."

"Whoa," Tank muttered.

"I'm sorry, man." Rock clapped a hand on Scorpion's shoulder.

"Are you doing a DNA test?" Panther asked.

"Yeah, you can get it done from seven weeks, and she's almost twelve. We did the test yesterday, just waiting on the results," Scorpion replied.

"You should be home with her," Panther said. If he'd known, he would have insisted. The man they were looking at wasn't trained like they were, he wasn't expecting this to be difficult. If Ruthie was in that house they'd get her out and home to her mom.

"I wanted to, but Jessica insisted I come. She said she's going to be a mom, and if it were her baby who had been taken, she would want everyone there trying to find her," Scorpion explained.

"You're going to be a parent, too, that baby's father even if it's not biologically yours," Panther reminded his friend. "Genesis is dead, and even if he wasn't, he wouldn't be playing the role of daddy to that baby. You and Jessica are in love, you want to spend your lives together, DNA or not, that baby is yours, too."

"I know, man, I know," Scorpion said. "I'm going to love that baby with everything I have to give and then some. But Jess is freaked, and I don't know what she's going to do if it turns out I'm not the biological father. She said she'll keep the baby no matter what, but I don't know what it means for us. She's used to doing things alone, and I'm terrified she's going to decide it will be too much for me to have to raise another man's child and decide for the both of us to end things. It's not what I want, but I don't know how I'm going to convince her of that."

His friend looked so desperate, but Panther didn't know what to say to make things better. Truth was, Jessica was only just learning what it was like to have a team at her back, she could very easily slip back into old patterns and decide she had to handle this herself.

"One problem at a time, yeah, man?" Rock said. "First, wait to see what the DNA tests say and then you can go from there."

"I'm trying," Scorpion said. "I wanted to ask Eagle to pull strings and get a rush on the DNA results, but Jessica didn't want to. She's scared. I know she is. I just don't want her to push me away. I'm there for her. Through anything."

"Deep down she knows that," Axe said, speaking up for the first time. "You have to believe that love can overcome anything."

With that parting thought echoing in all of their heads, spoken by a man who had more reason than all of them put together to believe that, in the end, love would always win out, he and his team approached the house.

It was a two-storey brick with a neatly kept front lawn. From what they knew of Jimmy Hillier, the man was forty, single, had a good reputation as a website designer and manager. He ran his own small business with two other people working for him, had never been married, had no children, but had a criminal history dating back to his teens.

Stalking.

Four cases that Panther had been able to find including one that had led to an attempted kidnapping. Since stalking could be hard to prove, three of the cases had never gone anywhere. The fourth one Jimmy had taken a deal, get counseling and no jail time would be served. That had been back when he was in his early twenties, and there had been no more stalking charges against him since.

Didn't mean he had stopped though, just meant he'd gotten older and wiser.

Despite the security system set up, it took Panther mere moments to hack his way through it, and then they stepped inside Jimmy's home.

Cold.

The house was freezing, and in that moment Panther felt his heart drop.

Ruthie wasn't here. No one had been here in days at the least, possibly even weeks.

Had he been wrong?

Was Jimmy Hillier not the kidnapper?

Doubt and a crushing sense of failure filled him, but then someone flicked on the lights, and he knew he had his man.

Everywhere in the house there were pictures of Elle and her daughter. Not just ones he'd printed himself and stuck all over his walls like an obsessed madman. No, these were all framed and hanging on walls or sitting on furniture just like someone would display their family photos.

Which made it that much worse.

Jimmy Hillier had already decided that Elle and Ruthie were going to be his, nothing was going to make him stop until he had both of them in his clutches.

~

February 16th
5:57 A.M.

They'd been gone for hours.

It meant bad news.

Elle was positive it did.

If Rafe had found her daughter, the first thing he would have done was call her to let her know her baby was safe and he was bringing her home.

At least if he'd found Ruthie *alive*.

If he'd found her dead then … she was sure he would want to break that news in person.

Not that it would make any difference. Ruthie was all she had, neither her parents nor Ruthie's father would be all that broken up about the seven-year-old's death. More acquaintances than real friends, and no friends that she would call to come and be with her if she got the most devastating news of her life. It didn't matter where, when, or how she received the news it would still shatter her.

Call. Please call.

But her phone remained stubbornly silent.

Mocking her.

Taunting her.

As badly as she had wanted to insist that she go with Rafe and his team in case the intel he had found was correct and he'd found her daughter, she wouldn't do anything to jeopardize Ruthie's safety, and her being there, being a distraction and a liability, would do just that. Besides, Rafe had asked her to watch Andy for him, and knowing that he trusted her to look after his son when he wasn't here, even knowing she had failed her own daughter who had been snatched right out from under her nose, meant more to her than she could express.

So she was there, in his living room, pacing up and down like a caged tiger just waiting for something to pounce on.

Preferably her daughter.

Playing out how their reunion would go was something Elle had done hundreds of times over the last month. Ruthie would fly into her arms, and she'd hold her daughter tight while they both cried. She'd tell her little unicorn girl how much she loved her and how sorry she was for failing her, and Ruthie would tell her that she loved her. Whatever Ruthie wanted she would get, toys, food, clothes, or shoes, it didn't matter. Anything her baby wanted she deserved for surviving hell.

But no matter how many times she imagined it, there was always the thought niggling at the back of her mind that their reunion could be so very different.

A morgue, a small body under a white sheet, her child's lifeless body, planning a funeral, a little white coffin, and a gravestone.

That couldn't be their future.

It couldn't.

When someone knocked at the door, Elle about had a heart attack. Absolutely positive that it was Rafe about to deliver the news that

Ruthie was already dead, already gone. For a month she had lived in fear of that knock. Of that news. Of the reality it was too late to save her baby girl.

It wasn't until she remembered that Rafe would have no need to knock at his own door that she relaxed enough to check the camera feed. Before he left, Rafe had set up her phone with access to the cameras surrounding the Bravo Team compound. When she brought up the feed, she saw five women standing on the cabin's porch. Four stood together, one a little bit apart, and since she knew that access to the remote compound was limited she assumed they had to be the other Bravo team member's wives, fiancées, and girlfriends.

What were they doing here?

Had Rafe and his team contacted them and asked them to come and break the news thinking it would be better coming from women?

It wouldn't.

If Ruthie was gone, she wanted to hear it from Rafe. He understood, he was a parent, and she trusted him.

By the time she had stumbled over to the door, unlocked it, and flung it open, Elle was visibly shaking. Enough that all five sets of eyes immediately filled with concern.

"Is Ruthie dead?" she blurted out, modifying the volume of her voice only because the last thing she wanted to do was wake up Andy with hysterical shrieking.

"Oh no, honey. I'm sorry, we didn't mean to scare you," a tiny, blonde, pixie of a woman said as she stepped forward, immediately wrapping her in a hug.

"Told you we should have called first," a woman with golden blonde hair said. "I'm Jessica, that's Tillie," she pointed to the other blonde. "Ariel, Stephanie, and Beth," she added as she pointed in order to a woman with long, jet black hair, one with wild curls and healing wounds on her face and a bandage on her left hand, and the woman who kept herself slightly apart from the others. "We just thought since we were all sitting around being miserable, and you were sitting around being miserable, we may as well be miserable altogether."

"We haven't heard from the guys though," Ariel reiterated as Elle stepped back to allow them all to enter.

"Sorry, I should have known that. It's just, they've been gone for a couple of hours and I thought I would have heard from Rafe by now," she said, closing the door behind the women and relocking it. When she turned around, she froze when she saw all five pairs of eyes staring at her with a mixture of shock and curiosity. "What?"

"You called him Rafe," Tillie said like that explained everything.

Only to her it explained nothing. The other guys on Rafe's team had commented on that too, so it obviously had some significance, although whatever that was was completely lost on her. "I don't get it," she said.

"I didn't either. And no one bothered explaining it to me until way later," Stephanie said sympathetically.

"The guys only ever use their nicknames," Jessica explained.

"He told me his name and didn't seem to mind if I used it," she said, feeling defensive now. Maybe because she knew she was overstepping by hanging around Rafe's house and spending so much time with his son. The last thing she wanted him to think was that she was somehow trying to use his little boy as a substitute for her child.

"That's not it," Tillie said. "The guys use their nicknames with everyone. Except their women."

"I-I'm not R-Rafe's w-woman," she stammered. Was that the vibe she was giving off? That she was trying to use her daughter's abduction to get a man? Elle was absolutely mortified.

"No one is implying you think you are," Ariel soothed, obviously sensing Elle's distress. "It's just how these guys work. If Panther is letting you call him Rafe, then he likes you."

"Oh," she mumbled, not sure what else to say. Not sure what to feel. Needing a distraction, she took the empty armchair by the fireplace. "I know why I'm miserable, but why are you guys all up this early in the morning and miserable, too?"

All eyes turned to Jessica, who placed a hand on her stomach, her expression troubled. "I just found out I'm pregnant."

And that was bad news?

Elle had been thrilled when she discovered she was going to have a baby. Finally, she could have someone who would love her properly, the way she craved. Deep down she already knew she didn't share that kind of love with her husband. Since she didn't want to insult Jessica by implying she should love her child when there was obviously something else she wasn't aware of going on, she simply waited for more information.

"Jess was undercover in a cult, that's how she met Scorpion," Tillie explained. "Because she cares more about others than herself, she didn't stop herself from being artificially inseminated. She was on birth control, but it obviously failed, and now she doesn't know if it's a crazy cult leader or the man she loves who fathered her baby."

How awful. "I'm so sorry," Elle said, an ache of sympathy forming in her chest.

"I'm keeping the baby, but if it's not Mason's how can I ask him to raise it with me? What if he can't love him or her? I love Mason, and I already love this baby regardless of who the father is, but I don't know what to do," Jessica said, tears shimmering in her greeny blue eyes.

"You trust his love," Elle said automatically, causing the others to gape in surprise.

"How do you know he loves me enough to raise another man's baby?" Jessica asked, but the question wasn't defensive or angry, it bordered on desperate.

"Because you're here, because he stayed. He knows the baby might not be his, but he didn't tell you to leave, he wants you with him. If the baby isn't biologically his, he'll love it anyway because it's yours, and that makes it his, too. My ex didn't even stay for a child that was his because he didn't love me, didn't love our daughter, but Scorpion wants you close because you're his and he knows it. You and that little baby growing inside you." Elle might not know these people, but she was one hundred percent certain what she'd just said was the truth.

Before anyone could comment on her speech, the cabin door was opened again.

Elle flew to her feet, hope and fear warring inside her.

Six.

Six men walked inside.

No little girl.

No!

Her legs buckled, but even though he was across the room, Rafe suddenly closed the distance between them and caught her before she dropped into the chair she'd just vacated, pressing her tightly against his hard chest.

"I'm sorry, Elle," he whispered into her hair.

Those words shattered her world, her very existence.

CHAPTER
Eight

February 16th
 6:19 A.M.

Her cries of pain destroyed him.

Shredded his insides as effectively as any blade could ever do.

Failed.

He hadn't brought her daughter home to her, and the sense of failure Panther felt was crushing.

Tightening his hold on Elle, he spoke loud enough that she could hear him over her sobs of grief. "We didn't find her body, honey," he soothed, praying she hadn't misinterpreted his apology and believed him to be telling her that her daughter was dead. "Ruthie is still out there somewhere, and I will bring her home to you. I promise." Not a wise promise to make given there was no way he could actually guarantee he would follow through despite his best efforts.

But it was a promise he had to make.

Lifting her head from his chest, tear-drenched eyes looked up at him. "She's not gone?" she asked in a voice so heartbreakingly lost that he broke all over again.

"No, honey, Ruthie isn't gone. She's still out there. And now we know who has her."

Fingers curled into his shirt. "It was Jimmy? He stole my baby?" Through the tears, he saw a bolt of anger hit her, and he felt himself relax a fraction. Elle was struggling, teetering on the edge. A month of living this nightmare had taken a toll on her, but she was a survivor, a fighter, and she wasn't going to give up until she had her daughter back in her arms where she belonged.

"There were photos in his house that prove he's been stalking you and your daughter," he told her gently, keeping a hold on her as he maneuvered her to the now vacant couch. The guys had all gone to their women and whispered something to them, likely asking them to give them some time alone with Elle to talk through this development in her daughter's case since all five women had quietly left.

"It was him? He was the one breaking into my home, leaving me all those letters? He's the one who took my baby from me, who thinks he's in love with me and is going to be a family with me and my daughter?" Color was quickly draining from her face. Although the anger remained in her eyes, there was still enough pain there to fill the ocean. "I think I'm going to be sick."

Elle was shaking violently, and she'd pressed a hand to her stomach in an attempt to quell the nausea churning there. Someone—he didn't bother looking up to see who—passed him a blanket which he immediately wrapped around Elle, then shifted so he sat beside her on the couch and began rubbing her back.

"The photos were all framed, hanging on the walls, sitting on the fireplace mantle, on furniture, in every room of the house. The photos go back years, they're like a chronicle of your life for the last five years or so," he told her.

"Th-that's as long as Jimmy h-has been working f-for me," she said, the shakes making her teeth chatter. "I ... I brought h-him into our l-lives. I already k-knew this was m-my fault, but I d-didn't realize how b-badly I had m-messed up."

If his heart wasn't already breaking that would have done the job.

Her desperate words, the complete and utter grief and guilt in her words, it was nothing he ever wanted to hear fall from her lips again.

"You don't say that," he snarled, surprising everyone in the room, including himself. "I told you before and will tell you again as many times as you need to hear it. It. Is. Not. Your. Fault. Do you hear me?" He took her chin between his thumb and forefinger, pinching just hard enough that she winced, needing to be certain she was hearing him and not lost in a guilt-filled void. "Say it," he ordered.

Wide-eyed, Elle stared up at him.

"Say it," he demanded again.

"I ... can't," she whispered, sounding so defeated he couldn't not respond. Dragging her into his lap he banded his arms around her, willing her to believe the truth.

"Say it," he said again, gentler this time. "Say it's not your fault."

"How could I not know?" she asked brokenly. "How could I not know that he was a danger to me and my daughter? He asked me out the first time we met in person. I spent ages looking for someone I trusted to run my website for me. I trusted him, Rafe. I *trusted* him. I thought I wanted a woman because romance is mostly a women's genre, but he seemed smart, sensitive, enthusiastic, and I thought maybe having a man's perspective when I needed it would improve my writing."

"What did you say when he asked you out?" Scorpion asked.

"I told him he was a great guy, but I was recently divorced with a toddler to care for. I told him I didn't have time for dating, but ..."

"What, honey?" he asked when she trailed off and didn't continue.

Elle shrugged. "It wasn't just that. I just ... I don't know. I liked him and I thought he was sweet. He was good-looking and intelligent, funny, too. But ..."

"Your gut told you not to go out with him and you trusted it," Rock told her.

"What did he say when you said no?" Tank asked.

Her brow scrunched as she thought. "There was a moment when I thought he was going to blow up. Now you mention it, I remember bracing for a storm and reaching for my phone to call the cops. But then it was like he flipped a switch and he just smiled, told me I was such a great catch he had to ask, but he'd love to just work for me and be friends. I thought I imagined the whole thing and was overreacting because he was the first man to ask me out since I was divorced."

"He decided your answer wasn't a no, it was a not yet," Trick said. "He decided to wait you out, thought you would eventually come to him. Probably got tired of waiting, and since you never dated anyone else, he assumed you just needed a little push to be ready. When the notes didn't work and you called the cops, he likely got angry and decided to force your hand."

Elle flinched, internalizing Trick's words and adding them to her list of reasons why this was all on her. "I don't understand how I didn't see it. We talk often, he helps with my website, but he's also a sounding board for my heroes' points of view."

"This isn't his first time," Panther gently broke the news. "He's stalked women since he was a teenager. He was forced to get counseling, and things have been quiet with him for almost twenty years, but he didn't change, he just got smarter and better at hiding it."

"So you're sure? It's him?" she asked.

"It's him. He has the skills to hack your computer. Most of the photos were ones you had on your laptop, they weren't ones he took himself. He hasn't been home since the day Ruthie was taken. When he took her, he obviously had another place lined up and ready to take her to, probably just in case the cops looked at him as a suspect. Wherever he's holed up with your daughter, I'll find him."

"Okay," Elle agreed, although she didn't seem sure that she believed him.

"Did you sleep at all last night?" he asked, already knowing the answer. She hadn't, and she'd slept only a couple of hours the night before that, and likely every night since her daughter's abduction.

Elle gave a tiny shake of her head.

"Rock is going to give you something to help you sleep." When he looked to his friend, Rock nodded and held up a bottle of sleeping pills.

"I can't sleep now." Elle looked aghast at the very idea. "Not when we're finally making progress in finding my baby."

"Don't you see, honey?" His hands lifted, framed her face, his thumbs caressing her still-damp cheeks. "That's exactly why you need sleep. We're closer to finding Ruthie than we've been, and that means I need you on top of your game. Your *daughter* needs you on top of your game." It might be a low blow to use her missing child as a reason why she needed sleep, but the facts were, Elle was running on empty and she needed the rest before she dropped. Needed it for both her sake and her daughter's. Because when he found Ruthie and brought her home, the little girl was going to need her mommy.

"Okay," she said again, this time sounding utterly defeated. "I guess I better go home then."

"You're not going anywhere." Panther tightened his grip on her. "Jimmy Hillier might have taken Ruthie, but you're the one he really wants. He's not going to wait forever. I want you here where I know you're safe, and where I can make sure you're being taken care of."

Whatever protest she might have given faded, replaced by a soft look and a tiny smile. Whether she would admit it or not, Elle needed to know someone had her back, that she was being looked out for, and that she wasn't all alone in this nightmare. She had him and Andy and they weren't going anywhere.

Not when he brought Ruthie home, and not if the worst happened.

~

February 16th
12:32 P.M.

"Mmm," Elle moaned sleepily as wakefulness came slowly, for one beautiful moment cocooning her in a blissful bubble of ignorance.

As she hung there in a sort of state of suspended animation, she felt peace and security wash over her, and she inhaled it, trying to make it part of her so it couldn't leave, because even as she wasn't altogether sure of what was going on, she knew that this was where she wanted to stay.

But as it always did, the bubble popped, the sense of peace disappeared like it had never even existed, and reality came crushing back down.

Only for once the security lingered.

Elle was surrounded by Rafe's scent. After she had reluctantly agreed to take the sleeping pills and get some rest, he'd given her some of his clothes to wear, and told her to go and lie down in his bed.

She couldn't resist that offer even if she did want to stay by his side as he ran down leads on where Jimmy Hillier might be hiding out. Whenever she and Jimmy spent time together, they talked about work related things, and now that she thought about it, he was always asking her questions about herself she usually brushed off because she was busy and just wanted to get down to business. The little she knew about him was likely already eclipsed by what Rafe had found out.

Reality was, there was nothing useful she could do, and since she was teetering on the edge of collapse and she wanted to be there for her daughter when Ruthie came home, she had agreed to the sleep.

Now that she was awake though, she was desperate to find out if Rafe had anything new to tell her.

Unable to give up the comfort being wrapped in Rafe's clothes brought her, Elle didn't change back into her own as she padded downstairs.

"Elle!" Andy exclaimed, tossing down his game controller as he bounced off the couch and across the room, throwing his thin arms around her waist and hugging her hard. "Dad said I couldn't wake you up because you needed to sleep, but I've been waiting for you."

Warmth spread through her. Even though she missed her baby girl with every fiber of her being, it was nice to spend time with another child. Andy was such a great kid, so smart, so sweet, and even though when she played with him her heart ached because Ruthie wasn't there, there was comfort there as well. Rafe and Andy were keeping her sane at a time when she could far too easily fall apart.

"What have you been up to?" she asked, returning the boy's hug.

"Dad's working so I've been playing video games. Now that you're up though can we play?"

"Course we can." Elle gave his messy brown locks a ruffle. Being affectionate with this child was easy because he didn't hold anything back. Andy was an open book and she hoped that life didn't wind up changing that.

"After you eat some lunch," Rafe said, appearing in the kitchen doorway looking delectable in a pair of jeans and a black long-sleeve T-shirt. "After you *both* eat some lunch," he amended, giving her a pointed look.

It was weird having someone look out for her, making sure that she was eating and at least attempting to sleep. Self sufficiency and independence were her parents' mantras and she was expected to do a lot of things other kids her age weren't required to. Then in her marriage, her husband had been more like a child she had to care for than an equal partner. After he left, there was no one to help raise her daughter, and taking care of herself fell a distant third after Ruthie and work.

Having Rafe look out for her was nice.

Really nice.

A whole lot nicer than it should be given she had no idea if he was even interested in anything with her. Well, his friends had said that him letting her call him Rafe was an indication he was ... so maybe the question should be if she was interested in anything with him.

"Hey, buddy boy, what if we make some mashed potatoes for lunch? We'll make extra, pop it in the fridge to cool down, and for dinner tonight we can make potato pancakes." Before she could worry that she had overstepped, once again insinuating herself into Rafe and Andy's plans without checking with Rafe to make sure it was okay, the man smiled.

"Sounds perfect," Rafe said. "Elle, would you mind staying here with Andy for a while? I have to pop out for a bit."

"I don't mind. Is it something to do with Ruthie?" she asked, wondering if he had gotten a lead on where Jimmy was hiding with her daughter.

"Partly, but no, I haven't found her yet. I will though, I'm working on it and I won't give up until I bring Ruthie home," he promised. He'd said that to her several times, and for some reason each time he said the words she believed them a little more. Almost like in speaking them he was giving them some sort of power, sending them out into the universe to make them a reality.

"Okay," she agreed. "Don't worry about Andy, we'll have lots of fun together, won't we, buddy boy?"

"Yeah, we will," Andy agreed excitedly.

"All right, you two be good. Don't get up to mischief while I'm gone," Rafe teased as he kissed the top of his son's head.

"Mischief is the only kind of fun play, right, buddy boy?" she teased right back. It wasn't easy allowing herself to have moments of joy when her daughter was out there alone and scared and needing her mom, but these two were little lights in the dark, and their light was shining on her whether she wanted it to or not.

"Right, Daddy. Mischief is the best." Andy bounced from foot to foot in that energetic way only young children could.

Rafe laughed, then kissed his son again before moving to her. When he bent for a moment, Elle was positive he was going to brush his lips across hers. Instead, his lips pressed to her cheek, and despite the very non-sexual nature of the kiss, Elle felt her knees get weak.

When was the last time she'd kissed a man?

Maybe several months before her husband announced he was leaving.

This one little kiss, simple though it was, ignited a spark inside her.

A spark she couldn't allow to grow. Not now, not when her focus had to remain on her daughter. But maybe when Ruthie came home ... maybe ... maybe a relationship with Rafe could be in the cards.

"I won't be gone long, a couple of hours at the most," Rafe told her. "You two be good, there's mischief and then there's mischief."

Both she and Andy were giggling as they headed into the kitchen. Somehow, they kept managing to make her smile even as her heart wept.

They wouldn't be enough to save her though.

Not if Ruthie was never found. Not if Jimmy killed her because he couldn't get his hands on Elle.

But for now, they were helping her get through each day, and that was enough.

"Can I help peel the potatoes?" Andy asked.

"The peeler can be a little hard to use, and I don't want you to cut yourself, but I have an idea." Rifling through the cupboards, she found the apple corer, peeler, and spiral cutter she'd seen when she was making lunch yesterday. "How about if I put the potatoes on and you turn the handle, then I can cut them and put them into the pot," she suggested.

"Elle?"

"Yeah, buddy?" she asked as she grabbed a handful of potatoes from the bottom of the pantry and set them on the counter.

"Does Ruthie have a dad?"

"Yes, she does. Everybody has a mom and a dad whether they're part of their life or not."

"He's not part of her life?" Andy asked, taking the handle when she put the first potato on and beginning to turn it.

"No, sweetie, he's not part of Ruthie's life or mine." It should hurt more that her husband hadn't wanted to be part of raising their daughter, but it was absolutely his loss, and Elle hurt more for her child knowing her dad didn't want her, than she did for herself having her husband walk out on her.

"How come?"

"Because he didn't want to be. He left us when Ruthie was a baby."

"My mom didn't want to be in my life either," Andy said it matter of factly, no emotion, no anger or sadness like it just was what it was. Even if the boy felt like that now, at some point he would feel the betrayal of knowing his own mom hadn't wanted any part of his life.

"You know that's her loss. You're a great kid, Andy. Anyone would be proud to be your mom. I'm proud to know you and spend time with you."

"I don't miss her, I don't even know her, and I have my dad, but ..."

"But what, sweetie?"

"Sometimes I get lonely. My daddy is always busy. Do you know what I wish?"

"What do you wish for, buddy boy?"

"A mom. Not the one who doesn't want me, but a real mom, one who wants me and will love me. Elle, I need a mom, and Ruthie needs a daddy. Maybe you could be my new mom and my dad can be Ruthie's daddy."

Andy looked so hopeful at the idea, and a part of her wanted to buy into what he was selling, but the problem was, life wasn't that simple. Right now, she had no idea what the future held, getting through each second was almost more than she could handle.

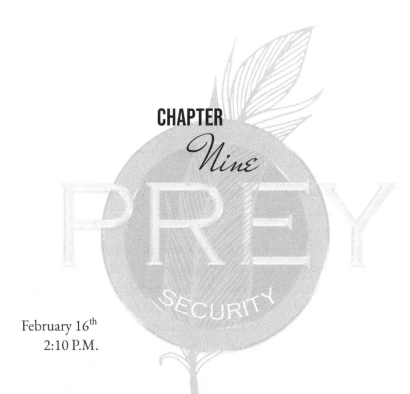

CHAPTER

Nine

February 16th
2:10 P.M.

"You sure you want to do this, man?" Rock asked.

"Never been surer of anything else in my life," Panther replied.

"You know he was cleared as a suspect," Tank reminded him.

"I'm aware." He was also aware that the cops and the FBI had made a huge mess of this entire case. From wasting too much time looking into Elle when it was clear she already had a stalker months before her daughter was kidnapped, to focusing too deeply on the security company to the exclusion of everything else.

If they had done their jobs properly, Ruthie Cavey might not still be missing. The little girl's cries for her mother had been echoing in his mind ever since the phone call Elle had received. That precious little girl should be home safe and sound with her mom right now, instead of in the hands of a madman with an obsession that wasn't going to die.

Waiting for the psycho stalker to make his next move wasn't an option. He was already strung out and could only imagine what Elle was going through. She had put her faith in the police and the FBI and both had let her down.

Not him.

Panther had no intention of letting that woman down.

"We here because you honestly believe the man could be involved or for personal reasons?" Trick asked.

They were here because they had refused to let him come alone. They were a team, meaning they supported one another whether or not they agreed.

And no one on his team had thought this was a good idea.

But his mind had been made up. Panther was coming with or without them.

"Mostly personal," he admitted. There was the smallest of chances that Bobby Beck was involved in the disappearance of his seven-year-old daughter, but Panther didn't believe he was. Jimmy Hillier had been stalking Elle, and had the skills necessary to bypass her security system and get access to her personal photos on her computer.

This wasn't really about finding clues to Ruthie's location, it was about attempting to understand how a man could walk away from his own child so easily. And maybe making sure there was no competition for Elle's heart.

Panther had grown up the child of a broken home. He knew what it was like to be bounced about from parent to parent, watching as they moved on, new partners, new kids, new families, leaving him out in the cold alone. If he was going to attempt anything with Elle, he had to know that he wasn't going to be the guy who broke up Ruthie's family. The child had been through enough, and as much as he liked Elle, if there was even a chance that Ruthie could have both parents together then he wasn't going to stand in the way.

"At least you admitted it," Scorpion muttered.

When they pulled up outside a construction site, it didn't take him long to spot the man he was looking for. Half a dozen guys were working, one was leaning against the fence, a can of soda in one hand and his cell phone in the other.

"Don't do anything stupid," Tank reminded him as they all piled out of the car.

"Don't intend to," he assured them. He hadn't come here to defend Elle's honor and beat up her loser of an ex. He had to make sure that Bobby wasn't in any way involved in Ruthie's kidnapping, that he hadn't wanted his family back and decided to go about it any way he could. No stone was being left unturned in his hunt for Ruthie, and if her father was responsible for hurting the child and her mother, he would make sure that Bobby was punished to the fullest extent of the law.

It wasn't until he was almost upon the man that Bobby even looked up from his phone long enough to register that someone was approaching him. A glint of nervousness in the gray eyes told Panther that even if Bobby wasn't involved in Ruthie's abduction, he was up to no good, and he was glad the man was out of Elle's life so he couldn't drag her down with him when he eventually crashed and burned.

"Who are you?" Bobby asked, straightening and casting a nervous glance toward his colleagues who were all now watching with interest.

"Your worst nightmare if you're involved," Panther growled, letting every ounce of disdain and contempt he felt for this man seep into his voice.

"Involved?" Bobby repeated, clearly nervous.

"Are you?" he demanded. While he hadn't really believed the man was involved, his cagey attitude sparked all sorts of concerns in Panther. If this man had put the fear and pain in Elle's eyes that made his stomach fill with lead every time he looked into them, then Bobby would be lucky if Panther left him to be handled by the law instead of inflicting his own breed of punishment.

"I'll p-pay it b-back, I s-swear," Bobby stammered, his gaze darting from Panther, to each of the five huge, intimidating men standing at his back.

"Pay it back?" Panther repeated. That's what Bobby was worried about? The man probably had a gambling addiction and had resorted to taking money from loan sharks to feed that addiction. If Ruthie had been taken and a ransom demand made then he would have been positive Bobby was the cuprite, but the man didn't even seem to care that his young daughter was missing. "That's what you care about right now?"

Confusion swirled in the man's eyes, eyes he knew from studying her pictures that were the same as Ruthie's. All the little girl seemed to have inherited from the man who couldn't have cared less that she was in danger, alone, scared, and suffering.

"You're not here to collect?" Bobby asked.

"Do you even care?" Panther snarled.

"About what?"

"Ruthie!" he bellowed. "You know her? The child you created, your seven-year-old daughter who was kidnapped and has been missing for a month."

If there was one thing the man could have done that would have set off Panther's temper like nothing else, it was relax at the outburst like he'd just been let off the hook. Any man who thought his own problems were more important than those of the child he had fathered was no man as far as Panther was concerned.

Just before he could pull back and slam his fist right into Bobby Beck's relieved face, Axe caught his elbow, stilling him. Panther knew he ought to be grateful that his friend had stopped him from doing something that would have tied up his time dealing with the cops when it could, and should be better spent searching for Ruthie, but he couldn't seem to find it in him.

"You are a despicable excuse for a man," he snarled. "She's your daughter, don't you care about her at all?"

"I signed away my parental rights," Bobby said as though that explained everything.

"Doesn't change the fact that she's your daughter," he growled, completely unable to comprehend the man's blasé attitude to his young child's abduction. Regardless of whether he was legally Ruthie's father, she shared his DNA, she was a part of him, and he seemed unable to dredge up even an iota of concern.

"I told the cops I didn't have anything to do with it," Bobby said as though that was what they were here for.

"Did you also tell them that you're up to your eyeballs in debt from illegal gambling?" Panther sneered. Given the man's attitude, he wasn't above going home, getting on his computer, digging up proof of Bobby Beck's illegal gambling activities, and handing it over to the cops.

"I ... I ... you can't ... I'm not ... there's no ..."

Disgusted, Panther shook his head. "You know what? She's too good for you, you don't deserve that little girl. I'm glad you walked away from her, showed her and her mother what kind of man you are. They need a real man. One who puts their needs first, takes care of them, and protects them. They need someone who isn't so wrapped up in his own problems he can't spare an ounce of sympathy for what his own child and her mother are going through."

Obviously taking more offense to being told he wasn't good enough than in being called out on not caring that his daughter had been abducted, Bobby stiffened. "What? You think you're better than me? You think Elle and Ruthie would be better off with you?"

"I don't think it. I know it," Panther said. Because he really did want to put Elle and Ruthie first, he turned his back on the man who had thrown them away like they were nothing instead of the precious gifts they could have—should have—been.

Beating up this lowlife loser, while satisfying in the moment, wasn't what was important. Finding that child, bringing her home, and helping her and her mother heal, that's where his focus needed to lie.

∼

February 16th
  8:28 P.M.

"Elle, you do the best voices. I wish you could read to me every night," Andy said, giving her a sleepy smile as she set the book on the nightstand and made sure the covers were tucked up to his chin.

She cast a quick glance over her shoulder to where Rafe was sitting on the floor of his son's room, listening as she read bedtime stories, to make sure he wasn't going to call her out for overstepping. Try as she might, Elle couldn't seem to shake the worry that Rafe would think she was using his son as a substitute since she couldn't have her daughter.

While she couldn't deny that being with Andy helped a little when it came to soothing the ache in her heart because of her missing child, it was more than that. She genuinely liked the child. There was real affection there, he was a great kid and she enjoyed spending time with him. Would still enjoy it even if Ruthie was there with them.

"Couldn't agree more, kiddo. Elle's voices are second to none," Rafe agreed with a lazy smile as he pushed to his feet and walked over to kiss his son's forehead. "Sweet dreams, my favorite son."

"Sweet dreams, my favorite daddy," Andy said on a yawn.

Tears stung her eyes. Their sweet bedtime routine made the ache in her chest grow as she thought of her own bedtime routine with her daughter, and the pain that came from knowing she wouldn't be tucking Ruthie in tonight.

Or maybe ever again.

"Sweet dreams, my favorite Elle," Andy said.

A single tear leaked out before she could stop it. "Sweet dreams, my favorite Andy," she replied before hurrying out of the room. How could spending time with this child feel so good, and yet hurt so much all at the same time? Ice-cold fear and sweet warmth warred inside her, and suddenly exhausted, Elle sank back to rest against the wall.

That was where Rafe found her a minute later when he closed the door to Andy's room and turned to face her.

"Reading him bedtime stories is always something I do when I'm home, it's my favorite part of the day with him," Rafe said.

Guilt lanced through her chest.

She'd intruded on his special time with his son.

"I'm sor—"

A finger to her lips silenced her. "I don't want an apology, Elle. He asked you to read to him, and I loved every second of listening to you do it. It may be my favorite part of the day, but the way you read to him, it's obvious books are your passion."

"Mine and Ruthie's both," she said, another tear trickling free and winding its way down her cheek.

"Oh, honey, I'm so sorry."

Rafe scooped her up, and she didn't fight him as he carried her downstairs, just curled into him and clung on like he was the only thing keeping her sane. Because it was absolutely true that without this man and his son, she would have lost it by now. There was no way she could have handled that phone call from Ruthie without their steady, comforting presence.

"Seeing you with my son makes my heart hurt for you. You're such a good mother, and you've been doing it all alone, I hate that I haven't brought your baby home to you yet."

Something in his voice told her he'd met her ex. The hatred simmered beneath the respect as he mentioned her raising her child alone. "Today, when you went out, did you go to Bobby?"

"Not going to lie to you, Elle. Yeah, that's where I went."

"Because you thought he was involved?" Elle sighed, hating to admit the truth about the man she had married and intended to spend her life with. "He's not. He doesn't care enough about Ruthie to want to be part of her life or mine."

The arms wrapped around her tightened. "He's a loser and a jerk who threw away the two best things to ever happen to him. Your ex is something else, I wouldn't have believed his complete apathy in relation to his abducted child if I hadn't seen it with my own two eyes. But I didn't go because I thought he was involved."

"Then why?" she asked, unable to come up with another plausible reason.

"Are we going to beat around the bush or be upfront and honest?"

Rafe's blatant question surprised her, and she lifted her head to meet his serious golden-brown eyes. The fact that he wasn't going to beat around the bush and confront the elephant in the room warmed her. With her ex, it was always about lies and half truths, now that she was free of the situation and looking back, she knew he had put in just enough work to keep her happy without ever giving her all of himself. That would have been too much work and Bobby was all about avoiding effort whenever and wherever he could.

"Up front and honest," she whispered. Honestly, they were both too old and had too much at stake to be anything but. Elle knew she was taking one gigantic leap of faith here, laying her already bruised and shredded heart out on the table where it could so very easily be broken beyond repair. But if Ruthie's abduction had taught her anything, it was that life was way too short to hold back anything.

Relief filled his eyes and the sweetest smile she'd ever seen curled up his lips. "I went because I wanted to make sure there was nothing between you and your ex."

"There's nothing," she said quickly. It had been over between them for long enough that even her resentment and anger had faded. Now she was just relieved she'd dodged a bullet and was no longer married to Bobby, and grateful he'd given her the single best thing she'd ever had in her life in their daughter.

"Needed to be sure because I don't think I'm imagining this thing between us." Although he was being open with her, she detected the tiniest bit of doubt in his eyes. Rafe had been hurt, too, and like her, he had a child to protect.

"Not imagining it," she assured him and felt his entire body relax like she had lifted a weight from his shoulders. After everything he was doing for her and Ruthie, it felt good to be able to do that one teeny tiny thing for him.

"What are we going to do about it?"

If Ruthie had never been kidnapped, and she wasn't terrified that she wouldn't get her back alive, that would be an easy question to answer. But right now, with her life how it was, there was no way she had the mental or emotional energy for anything other than focusing on Ruthie. "Rafe ... it's not that I don't like you because I do. Andy too. But right now, with Ruthie—"

"I know she's your priority at the moment, honey, I would never ask or expect anything different. I'm not asking you for any sort of commitment right now, I just hope that you'll keep letting me and Andy be there for you, that you won't shut us out when we *want* to be there for you. And when Ruthie comes home, you'll let us continue to be there for the both of you. After my ex left, I thought Andy was all I needed. I didn't think anything was missing from our lives, but these last few days with you here, I realized something was missing. You. You filled a hole here I didn't even know existed."

Everything inside her went soft and warm. Never once in their four-year relationship had her ex ever said something that sweet to her. Dating hadn't been off the table, she'd just never had the time or inclination to do anything about it. It all seemed like too much work, but the thing was with Rafe it didn't feel like work, it felt effortless. They just seemed to slot together so very easily.

"Thank you," she whispered, touching her lips to his jaw in a featherlight kiss.

"For what?"

"For understanding that Ruthie is my priority. For taking care of me, sharing your son with me, and offering me a future I thought had died when I got divorced. For knowing and embracing that a future with me doesn't just come with me but with a traumatized seven-year-old. For doing more in a few days than the cops and the FBI combined was able to do in more than a month. For caring enough to track down my ex just to make sure you wouldn't get in the middle of anything. For caring more about my daughter than her father ever has. For being here right now not just holding me in your arms but holding me together."

Placing a finger underneath her chin, he nudged her face up so he could brush his lips across hers. "Thank you for giving me a chance. Thank you for trusting me to find your little girl and bring her home to you. Your faith, your trust, your willingness to still believe in happy ever afters, it's humbling. I promise you, Elle, I won't let you down like your ex did. I won't walk away from you unless its your choice. From you or Ruthie."

Thing was, she believed that wholeheartedly.

Offering her damaged heart up to anyone was a huge gamble, but she believed Rafe would never take advantage of that and hurt her.

CHAPTER Ten

February 17th
  10:17 A.M.

Was that what he thought it was?

Panther clicked on the file, opened it, and stared at it as though it were suddenly going to start shouting answers.

Maybe it wasn't shouting, but the file was whispering them.

Going through Jimmy Hillier's life with a fine tooth comb was harder than it sounded. The man's life appeared to have three completely separate parts. As a young child, Jimmy was intelligent, had a good sense of humor, worked hard in school, had lots of friends, and was described as sweet and caring.

Up until the age of around fourteen, then all of a sudden seemingly overnight things changed.

Going through puberty had done something to him, or there had been an unreported trauma that had altered the young man's life dramatically. Grades started slipping, he lost his place on the football team, and kids started distancing themselves from him because he was displaying erratic and violent tendencies. School counselors recommended he speak with someone, concerned about the possibility of mental illness, but none of the doctors Jimmy was sent to were able to diagnose anything.

For eight years, he moved from one obsession to another, culminating in the attempted kidnapping that finally got him charged.

Despite no diagnosis, a judge sent him to receive treatment, believing that Jimmy could be rehabilitated and would have a better outcome in a hospital than in prison.

To all appearances it worked.

When he was discharged two years later with a degree in computer sciences, there were no more stalking instances. The man set up his own business, developed a good reputation with clients, and now ran a company with several other employees working for him, and enough income to live more than comfortably.

But Jimmy hadn't turned a corner, he hadn't changed in his time in the psychiatric hospital, he'd just gotten smarter, more patient, and better at hiding who he truly was inside.

Evil.

That's what he was.

While he was receiving treatment, there was one doctor in particular who worked with Jimmy the most. An older woman, who appeared to have become a sort of mother figure to Jimmy. Even after he was discharged she kept in touch with him, and he with her. In fact, it looked like he kept up more communication with her than with his own family, even though both his parents and three siblings had all stood by him through his legal issues.

Was it possible that Jimmy was using the woman even now?

According to records, Dr. Francis Wells had retired around ten years ago at the age of seventy-three. Widowed at just twenty-six she had never remarried, had no children, no siblings, and no other close family. Although from what he could find, she had lived an active life up until around five years ago, when she seemed to just disappear.

Five years ago was right around the time Jimmy met Elle.

Had he been planning all along to abduct Elle and her daughter? Had he decided that no one would think to look for him at the house of his elderly doctor?

So far, this was the best lead Panther had been able to dig up and he wasn't going to let it pass by. Best case scenario, he and his team checked out the house, found and arrested Jimmy, and brought Ruthie home to her mother. Worst case scenario, it was a dead end and he got Elle's hopes up for nothing.

There was a part of him—a big part—that didn't want to tell her about the lead until he knew whether or not it was going to pan out. Especially after last night when they had both acknowledged the attraction simmering between them, and decided to do something about it once Ruthie was back home where she belonged. Sleeping with Elle snuggled against him had soothed old lingering hurt about not being wanted by his parents, and his wife walking out on him. It filled him with a protectiveness that would fuel his hunt for her daughter for as long as it took to find the little girl.

Elle had to know, he'd promised her he'd tell her anything he found because it was what she wanted. What she needed.

"Guys, I might have a lead," he called out, shoving away from his desk. Today, he was working in his office in the main building on the compound, while Elle and Andy played at his cabin. She had yet to leave, although he had asked one of the guys to go to her house and pack her a bag so she had more than one outfit to wear. Kind of a shame though because he liked seeing her in his clothes when she was sleeping or washing her own. What was with that? Some kind of caveman-like satisfaction seeing your woman covered in your scent he guessed.

"What did you find?" Tank asked, sticking his head into the office. While Panther worked on finding Ruthie, the others did another pass through all the intel they had on Leonid Baranov. It wasn't their second go through the information, wasn't even their tenth, had to be about the twentieth time they'd laid everything out and reread it all, hoping that something new might pop out at them this time around.

"Possible location where Jimmy might be hiding out. House of the doctor who worked with him while he was hospitalized. She was elderly, kind of abruptly fell off the grid right around the time Jimmy met Elle."

"You think he killed her so he could get access to her house?" Scorpion asked.

"So far, he hasn't been violent, just obsessive. He could have escalated or maybe he's just keeping her there drugged so she can't resist him," Panther replied.

"All right, let's gear up," Axe said.

"We going to call in the cops?" Rock asked.

"Hell no," Panther said vehemently. The cops had failed Elle and Ruthie, bungled the entire case, and then all but given up on the missing child, marking it a cold case just a month after the little girl had been abducted. "They gave up on Ruthie. We're not bringing them in now so they can try to claim the glory if we're right. Eagle can smooth over any ruffled feathers if there are any." Eagle Oswald, former SEAL, billionaire powerhouse, founder and CEO of Prey, had never met a problem he couldn't solve.

None of the guys offered any protests to that plan. They all knew the cops didn't have a leg to stand on. They'd turned Elle away and told her there was nothing else they could do. She was well within her rights to seek help elsewhere. And even if they did try to cause trouble for Prey, Eagle would handle it, the man had too many connections to let something like this ruffle a single one of his feathers.

"I'm going to update Elle then we can leave," he informed the guys. Usually, they walked around the compound, although roads connected all the buildings. Today Panther wished he'd driven over to the main building because then he could drive back and get to Elle quicker. Since he hadn't, he took off at a run toward his ten acres and the cabin where his son was hanging out with his woman.

When he approached his cabin, he could see the two of them bundled up in a ridiculous amount of clothes, chasing each other through the remains of the slushy snow left on the ground. Spring was a few weeks away, and there was still a bite of cold in the air, would likely be well over a month before there was any real warmth. Not that the cold had deterred these two. They were so engrossed in their game that he was almost on them before Elle finally noticed him.

Immediately she froze. Fear warred with hope on her beautiful face.

"Rafe?" she asked as he closed the remaining distance between them.

Damn, he loved the sound of his name on her lips. Who knew it was so intoxicating to have the woman you were interested in call you something different than everybody else? He'd never gotten why the guys loved hearing their women use their given names until now. Until Elle.

"You asked me to keep you in the loop," he said as he placed his hands on her shoulders, gently kneading the tight muscles.

"I did. And ...?"

"I might have a lead on where Jimmy is holed up with Ruthie," he told her.

Her knees buckled, and he quickly shifted his hold from her shoulders to her elbows, keeping her from collapsing into the cold slushy snow. "Y-you really think R-Ruthie is there?"

"I don't know, honey. But even if she's not I won't give up on her. Won't give up on you," he promised.

"I believe you. If anyone can find my daughter it's you, Rafe. It's only you. Please find her, please bring my baby home to me."

Tears shimmered in her eyes, and the trust that she was placing in him humbled him like nothing else ever had. He was a father, he knew how he would feel if their roles were reversed, and he understood that she was putting her faith in him to protect the most precious thing in her life.

Leaning down he touched his forehead to hers. "I'll bring Ruthie home to you."

~

February 17th
11:42 A.M.

"Again?" Elle groaned.

Andy giggled, and she couldn't not smile. Was there any sweeter sound on earth than that of a child's laugh?

"Maybe you'll win this time," the little boy said, a small, encouraging smile on his face, and her own smile grew.

"Yeah, maybe, but I won't get my hopes up too high." Giving an exaggerated mock sigh to make Andy laugh again, Elle went to the cupboard filled with games. "What do you want to play this time?"

"Hmm ... maybe Monopoly?"

"Monopoly?" This sigh was completely genuine. She sucked at Monopoly. Andy might only be eight, but there was little to no chance she was going to beat him. "Which one, you guys have like a dozen different variations?" she asked with an amused chuckle. Just because board games weren't her thing didn't mean she wasn't more than happy to spend the morning playing them with the little boy. Anything to put that smile on his face.

"The Pokémon one," he replied immediately.

"Pokémon Monopoly it is." As she pulled the game from the stack in the playroom cupboard and carried it back over to the table, she heard her phone ring in the other room.

Rafe?

Wherever he had gone, she didn't think he would have had time yet to find Ruthie and rescue her, but since she didn't know exactly what the lead was she didn't really know. Maybe he already had her daughter in his arms. Maybe he was climbing into a car to bring her home.

"Be right back, 'kay, Andy?" she said as she set the game on the table and hurried into the kitchen where she'd left her phone.

"'Kay. I'll get everything set up," Andy called after her.

"Sure thing, buddy boy." When she reached the kitchen table where she'd left her phone, she saw that it was an unknown number calling.

Dread took hold deep in her stomach.

Rafe hadn't just programmed his number into her phone but the numbers of his teammates as well. If there was some reason Rafe himself couldn't call, one of the other guys would, and their name would currently be on her screen.

She had all the numbers for the detectives and agents assigned to Ruthie's case as well, and it wasn't any of them. Wasn't her agent or anyone else she worked with.

Unknown.

Danger.

Her stomach cramped painfully with tension, and if Rafe was there she would have called out to him and asked him what she should do.

But he wasn't there.

Just her.

Hand shaking so badly she almost dropped her cell phone, she lifted it to her ear and accepted the call. "H-hello?"

"Why haven't you been home?" a voice demanded angrily.

Now that she knew who had taken her daughter, she knew this was Jimmy, and from the sounds of things he wasn't just angry he was boiling mad.

What should she say?

What should she do?

What if she said the wrong thing and stoked his rage making him hurt or even kill her daughter?

The pressure was too much, her knees buckled under it and she grabbed the table with her free hand just in time to stop herself from collapsing.

Wherever Rafe had gone he'd been wrong. Her daughter wasn't there because if he'd been right then Jimmy wouldn't be calling her right now.

"I thought you understood," he continued, seemingly not caring that she hadn't offered an answer to his question. "I thought you would be here waiting for us when we got home. You said you needed time and I've given you plenty, but time is up. I'm ready for the three of us to be a family."

"A family?" she squeaked. When family was mentioned in the same sentence as her, Ruthie, Rafe, and Andy it sounded so perfect, like being wrapped up in a warm fluffy blanket, all cozy, safe, and happy. But family in the same sentence as her, Ruthie, and her stalker it made her feel frozen inside.

"I'm done waiting," Jimmy snapped. "You come home now or the kid dies. I didn't want to hurt her—I didn't want to hurt anyone—but I've been patient, and she's not essential to our happiness. We can always have more children and this one doesn't even belong to us. I was only keeping her around because I love you and she's important to you. Come home, Elle. Now."

"H-home?" Did he mean her house or his? Or some place entirely different that he had bought or rented for the three of them to live in together.

"Yes. I have a fire in the fireplace, and the table is all set for a special dinner, I used your good china, I didn't think you'd mind."

Okay, so her house. She'd been to Jimmy's once and knew it didn't have a fireplace, and she doubted he'd gone to her place just to pack up her china.

"I expect you hear within an hour," he added.

One hour?

Even leaving now and forgetting the speed limit that was pushing it. An hour wasn't long enough for her to call Rafe, find out what she should do, and get to her place.

"One hour. Oh, and, Elle. I'm inside your phone, I want it destroyed before you leave. I don't want anyone messing with us. We need family time, and after the kid goes to bed you and I need time alone together. I've waited a long time for you and I've made sure everything is going to be perfect. I won't let anything ruin it. I'm hanging up now and if I don't see on my end that your phone is disabled I kill the girl."

With that, the call ended, leaving Elle with nothing but her fear and panic.

There were no other phones in the house for her to use to call for help.

How could she leave Andy there alone?

She had to tell the boy to go to the closest cabin. How was she going to explain that to him? And she had to leave him with some sort of message that would tell Rafe where she was so that when he came home he could come for her and Ruthie.

"Andy?" she called out as she picked up the phone, threw it onto the floor then stomped on it as hard as she could. Scooping up the pieces she dumped them in the sink and turned the tap on. Hopefully, that destroyed the phone.

"What are you doing?" he asked as he came into the room.

Before she could ask him to put on his coat and go to Trick and Stephanie's cabin, the front door was thrown open, and the other women came bursting in, all big smiles and bright laughter.

"Mason is going to be so mad, but I can't wait until he gets back to tell everyone else first," Jessica called out as the women practically ran into the room. "Guess what?"

From the smile on the other woman's face it was pretty obvious. "You got the DNA results back," Elle said.

"Yep. And Mason is the father. Mason is the father," Jessica said again, this time her smile fading and she burst into tears.

Everyone rushed to comfort the soon-to-be mother, and Elle ached to join them, but she had to put her daughter first. Ruthie's life was on the line, she could apologize to Jessica later for not being more supportive.

As badly as she wanted to tell the others about the phone call, if she did they would try to stop her from going. If she wasn't there soon then Jimmy would kill Ruthie. Elle didn't have a single doubt that he would follow through on the threat.

Already she'd wasted more time than she should.

Dropping to her knees she pulled Andy against her. "My favorite Andy, can you remember one thing for me. It's really important, okay?"

Serious hazel eyes stared back at her as the child nodded.

"There's no place like home. Remember that, please. Tell your daddy when he gets home. There's no place like home. There's no place like home. There's no place like home." If only she could be like Dorothy and simply click her heels together and turn up at her house.

"There's no place like home," Andy echoed.

"Perfect, thanks, buddy boy." Standing, she approached the others. "I'm sorry to do this. I'm supposed to be watching Andy but I'm not feeling well and need to go and lie down."

Tillie stepped forward, took her hand and squeezed it. "Don't worry about it, we got him. We got you, too, okay?"

Lying felt awful, but Ruthie was always going to come first, Elle was a mother before anything else.

Whispering her thanks, she hurried up the stairs to the bedroom to grab her purse. Then she snuck back downstairs, thankful everyone was still in the kitchen so she could slip unnoticed out the front door. Her car was in Rafe's garage, and she was sure the cameras would capture her leaving the property, but she didn't have time to try to sneak off unnoticed, already she'd wasted almost five minutes of her allotted time.

I'm coming, Ruthie, just hold on for me. Mommy is coming.
Rafe, please come after us.
We need you.

CHAPTER

Eleven

February 17th
  12:40 P.M.

"Five minutes," Jimmy growled as he stalked up and down across the living room.

Ruthie cowered in the rocking chair in the corner of the room, making her as far away as she could get from the scary man while still doing what he'd told her to do.

If she didn't obey him he got angry.

When he got angry, he screamed so loud it hurt her ears.

When he got *real* angry he punished her.

Sometimes, he wouldn't give her any dinner. Sometimes, he'd leave her alone in the room he told her was going to be her new bedroom for days and days without letting her out, not even to watch TV or play in the backyard. And sometimes, he spanked her.

Her mommy *never* spanked her.

Not ever.

Not even one time.

Not even when Ruthie knew she was being naughty but did whatever she wanted anyway. Her mommy's punishments didn't hurt, but Jimmy's did.

She didn't know why they'd come back home. Ruthie had been away from her mommy for a long time. It was hard to keep count even though math was one of her favorite subjects at school and she could count real high—all the way to one thousand—because sometimes he put her in the basement and there were no windows down there.

How could she count the days when she didn't know when it was morning and when it was night?

Every day, she'd wished she could come back home. When he kept her in the bedroom upstairs she would wait by her window every night for the stars to come out so she could make a wish.

Starlight, star bright, first star I see tonight. Wish I may, wish I might, grant the wish I wish tonight.

Sometimes she and Mommy would play that game, but when she made those wishes they were just for toys, or treats, or things she wanted to do with her mom.

They weren't real important.

But this was.

This wish was the most important one she'd ever wished in her life.

Ruthie missed her house, she missed her backyard, and her bedroom with her white princess bed. She missed her toys, especially her very special teddy bear that her mom had given her when she was first born.

Most of all, she missed her mom.

Now that they were home, her mommy wasn't here, and she'd heard Jimmy on the phone tell mom that if she didn't come home he was going to kill her.

Would Jimmy kill her?

She thought he would.

She didn't want to be dead. Being dead was for old people like grandmas and grandpas. Only Ruthie knew that wasn't always true. She'd had a friend in kindergarten who got really sick and died, and they were only five. Now she was seven, seven was bigger than five, which meant she could die.

A surprised squeak came out of her when Jimmy stopped right in front of her. She knew better than to speak to him if he didn't ask her a question. He didn't like little girls and had told her lots of times that children should be seen and not heard. At first, she would speak to him anyway, beg him to take her home to her mommy, but after enough punishments she learned.

Only this time, she'd forgotten.

Shrinking into the rocking chair, she wished she could turn invisible so he wouldn't see her.

"One minute. If your mother isn't here in one minute I'm going to kill you," Jimmy snarled down at her.

Even though she knew he didn't like crying, Ruthie couldn't stop a couple of tears from rolling down her cheeks. The man was scary, and she knew she'd made a mistake going to him that day. Only he worked with her mom, and she thought it would be okay. When he appeared at the side gate and said her mom wasn't answering the door and could she give her the files, she'd said yes.

It was her fault he'd gotten her.

She'd opened the gate to get the files he said he had, and that was how he'd grabbed her.

Ruthie hadn't even understood what was happening until it was too late. Until she was in the back of his van and he held something that smelled sweet up to her face. The next thing she knew, she was waking up in a bedroom that looked like her room, only it wasn't and her mom wasn't there.

"I want my mommy," she whimpered, too close to full-on crying.

When he reached out to wrap his large hand around her neck, Ruthie cried louder and harder, trying to pull his much bigger hand away. "I want your mommy, too, but it seems she doesn't want you, doesn't it now? I told her what would happen if she wasn't here in one hour and she didn't show up."

Her mommy loved her. Ruthie knew that. Her daddy wasn't around, he had left her and her mom when she was a baby, but she didn't need a dad, her mom was enough. Her mom was everything. She cooked and cleaned, worked real hard, and still ensured she always had time for Ruthie. They played dolls, tea parties, and fairies. They drew pictures, and colored, and did crafts. Every night before bed, her mom would read her the best stories and make such funny voices.

"My mommy loves me," she said, a bit of anger coming through all the sad and scared. Jimmy was mean, and she was scared of him, but he didn't get to say her mommy didn't love her. That was a lie and her mommy said it was wrong to lie. Ruthie tried her best not to tell fibs, but sometimes she couldn't help it. If she didn't want to get into trouble, she sometimes said things that weren't true.

But she wasn't going to let this man say things that weren't true about her mom.

Her mom was the very best mom in the whole entire world.

In the whole entire universe.

"Your mommy doesn't love you, if she did, she'd be here. But she's not. Time is up. That means you die."

The hand wrapped around her neck started to tighten. It hurt, and she couldn't breathe.

Her fingers clawed at the man's hand, but it was too big, he was too big, and she knew she couldn't make him let go of her.

Tears continued to fall down her cheeks, but it got harder and harder to scratch at the hand around her neck.

Like someone had switched out all the lights, her eyes started to darken.

"Ruthie!"

The sound of her name being screamed made the world a little lighter again, or maybe it was because the hand around her neck suddenly wasn't squeezing so tight.

"Let go of my baby!"

Mommy.

That was Mommy's voice.

She was here, she'd come. Ruthie had told Jimmy that her mommy loved her.

Something crashed into Jimmy, and he let go of her neck, swatting at something that had grabbed onto his back like you swatted at a fly.

No, it wasn't something it was her mom.

Mom was holding onto Jimmy's back, her arms around his neck, and he was jumping about trying to throw her off.

But her mommy wasn't letting go.

"Ruthie, run!"

That was the voice her mom used when she expected Ruthie to obey without arguing, only this time it also sounded scared.

The only time she'd ever seen or heard her mommy be scared was when Jimmy made her call mommy's cell phone. Jimmy had been so mad at her after the call because she hadn't said the things he wanted her to say. He'd spanked her so hard her butt had hurt for days.

Scrambling to her feet, she scurried toward the front door while Mommy fought Jimmy.

Her hand was on the door handle when she heard a thump and a cry of pain.

Even though she knew she shouldn't, Ruthie stopped and turned around, saw her mommy lying on her back trying to push herself up off the floor. There was something red on her mom's cheek.

Blood.

"You walk out that door, Ruthie, and I'll hurt your mom," Jimmy warned, and she knew he meant it.

Crying, she ran toward her mom, throwing herself into Mom's arms. "Mommy," she cried.

"I'm here, my baby girl. I'm right here. Oh, my baby. My baby. I thought I was never going to see you again." Mommy was crying, too, as she crushed Ruthie in a hug that hurt, but even though it hurt she didn't want her mom to let go.

Didn't want her mom to ever let go of her again.

Not ever.

No matter how big she got.

She wanted to stay here in Mom's arms forever.

"Finally." Jimmy smiled as he stood over them. Bloody scratches were on his arms and face, but he didn't seem to care. "We're all here together. A family. Now the three of us can be together forever."

That forever scared her and Ruthie curled deeper into her mom's hug. She was a big enough girl to know that even though her mom was here, that didn't make everything okay this time.

Mommy couldn't save them from Jimmy.

Nobody could.

CHAPTER

Twelve

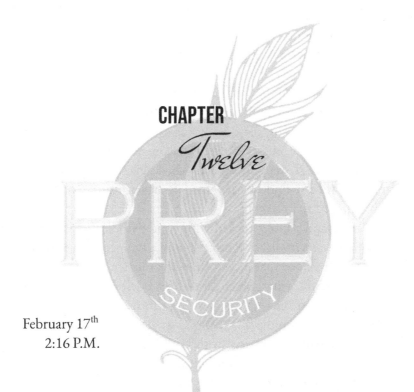

February 17th
2:16 P.M.

Panther's heart was heavy as he and his team drove into their compound.

Failed.

He'd failed once again in finding Elle's daughter and now he had to tell her he still hadn't found her little girl. Seeing the pain and heartache on her face as he broke the news was going to shred him to pieces. Even though he knew she had to know that Ruthie hadn't been at the house they'd gone to search because he would have called her immediately if he'd found her child, she was still going to be holding out hope.

Wouldn't be able to help it.

And he was going to dash that hope to pieces.

How many more times could she survive believing she might get her daughter back only to have to once again face the possibility that her child was gone forever?

Each time it would destroy another piece of her, and he was afraid that even if Elle got Ruthie back, she would have lost too many pieces of herself to still be the same woman she had been before.

If she didn't get her daughter back ... Panther wasn't ready to go there yet.

So close.

They had been so close this time to finding Ruthie and Jimmy. He'd been right. The house of his old doctor was exactly where Jimmy had been hiding out. There was evidence that someone had been there recently, although there were no signs of Dr. Francis Wells. While he wouldn't be surprised to find a body buried in the backyard, it had been the living he'd hoped to find there.

With a fridge and pantry stocked with child-friendly food, a little girl's bedroom upstairs similar to Ruthie's room at home, and a room in the basement with a door that locked from the outside it was obvious that a child had been staying there. Clothes were left behind, and the sheets on the bed weren't clean, there was a toothbrush in the bathroom cabinet, and dirty dishes in the sink. Panther was sure that DNA would be found and that when compared with both Ruthie and Jimmy's, it would prove that both had been in the house.

But that didn't solve the question they needed answers to.

Where were the pair now?

Panther sighed as he climbed out of the car and walked toward his front door. As much as he didn't want to do this, it was best to just do it and get it over and done with.

Excited chattering filled the room as he opened the door, and the second the girls spotted them, Jessica was flying across the room and throwing herself into Scorpion's arms. "It's ours. It's our baby," she repeated over and over again.

Clutching her to his chest like she was the most important thing in the world, Scorpion buried his face in her neck and sank to his knees, tears unabashedly streaming down his cheeks and he rocked her from side to side. "It's our baby? Yours and mine?"

"Yours and mine," Jessica echoed. "I'm sorry, I know I should have told you first, but I was so happy, so relieved I couldn't hold it in, and I didn't want to distract you while you were raiding a house. But it's ours, Mason. Our baby. Yours and mine."

Pulling her back so he could see her face, Scorpion framed it with his large hands, his thumbs catching her tears. "It was *always* ours, Jess. Always. I would have loved that baby with everything I had to give. But knowing there's no part of that monster growing inside you, that you don't have to be scared and stressed, and try to be all noble and do this alone, that's what I care about. You're free, which means our baby is free."

"I love you so much," she exclaimed, pressing her lips to Scorpion's.

"Love you more, sweetheart," Scorpion whispered against her mouth.

"I did save one thing to tell you first," Jessica said, pure love and adoration shining in her eyes that right now were the brightest blue he'd ever seen. "It's a girl. We're having a daughter. A sweet little baby girl who is going to have her daddy wrapped around her little finger before she even makes her big entrance into the world."

Fresh tears streamed down Scorpion's cheeks. "I'm having a daughter? You hear that, guys, I'm going to have a little girl." There was so much pride and love on Scorpion's face that Panther couldn't not smile despite the heaviness in his heart for the news he had to deliver.

As everyone offered congratulations to the happy couple, he scanned the room looking for Elle.

Only she wasn't there.

Andy was bouncing on the couch, catching all the grown-up's excitement, but there was no sign of his girl.

"Guys, where's Elle?" he asked, a bad feeling settling in his gut.

"Oh, I'm sorry, Panther, I think I upset her," Jessica said, the smile falling from her lips, replaced by an anxious frown. "I was so excited I came bursting in here to tell her the news about Mason being the baby's father, and I think I reminded her of Ruthie. I mean, not that she doesn't think of her daughter every second of every day, but I think I made it worse. She said she wasn't feeling well and went upstairs to lie down. I'm sorry."

"Don't be sorry, Jess. I'm so thrilled for you." Panther went to her and kissed her cheek. "For both of you," he added, giving his friend a one armed hug. "I'm so relieved everything worked out the way it should have. I'm just going to go up and check on her."

"You didn't find Ruthie?" Jessica asked, one hand moving almost absently to caress her stomach.

"No, but she was there. We just have to find where Jimmy took her when he left," he said as he headed for the stairs. He completely understood why Elle had needed some time to herself. Sweet and loving as she was, it had to be hell for her to see Jessica's joy over her pregnancy and know that her own daughter had been snatched away from her and might never come home.

Taking the stairs three at a time, he bypassed Andy's room and Mrs. Pfeffer's room, knowing that if Elle needed to feel safe and comforted she would have sought his bed.

At least, that's what he thought, but when he opened the door to his room his bed was empty.

"Elle?" he called out as he headed for the ensuite.

There was no answer and the bathroom was empty as well.

That gnawing in his gut that said something was wrong grew as he ran back into the hall, throwing open the doors to the other two bedrooms and the other bathroom.

All of them were empty.

Elle wasn't there.

"She's gone," he called out as he ran down the stairs. The room went instantly silent.

"What do you mean?" Tillie asked. "She went up there to rest."

"She's not there and the bed hasn't been touched since it was made this morning," he said.

"So she left?" Ariel looked confused. "Why would she tell us she was going up to lie down but leave?"

"Daddy," Andy said, tugging on his hand.

"In a minute, bud. What did she say exactly?" he asked the women who were the last ones to see his girl before she just vanished.

"But, Daddy—"

"In a minute, Andy," he repeated, more firmly this time.

"She just said she was supposed to be watching Andy but was feeling sick and needed to lie down," Tillie said.

"She wouldn't just leave though," Tank added.

"Something must have happened," he said, raking his fingers

through his hair. Why would she leave without telling him? She knew he would do whatever it took to bring her daughter home.

"He phoned her once already, right?" Rock said. "So maybe he called again."

"Daddy," Andy said, reaching for his arm.

"I said hold on a minute, Andy. Yeah, he called once, but if he called again I don't know why she wouldn't tell me."

"Maybe she couldn't," Trick reminded him. "Maybe he threatened her. Maybe she thought her only chance was to follow his instructions."

"Handing herself over to the man who's obsessed with her on a silver platter isn't the answer. Elle is smarter than that," he shot back, frustrated mostly because he hated this feeling of helplessness.

"She's a mother," Jessica said softly, her hands on her stomach as she leaned into Scorpion's side. "This little one isn't even here yet, and I would do whatever I had to in order to protect her. Elle would do the same for her daughter. If he threatened Ruthie, Elle would go to him."

"Damn it," he roared as the helplessness soared. Elle absolutely would do anything to keep her daughter safe, but just going off without at least leaving him a clue so he could come after her was still reckless, and it wouldn't keep Ruthie safe for long. Jimmy wanted Elle not her daughter, and sooner or later once he had Elle, Panther was sure he would wind up disposing of the little girl.

"Daddy!" Andy yelled in a voice he hadn't heard his son use before. "Elle told me I had to tell you something. She said I had to tell you, there's no place like home."

No place like home.

He should have known better than to think even for a second that Elle would just leave and not give him a way to find her.

Snatching up his son he hugged Andy hard. "Sorry, buddy, should have listened to you. I think you just saved Elle and Ruthie's lives."

At least if he could get to them in time.

February 17th
4:40 P.M.

. . .

What happened next?

Elle was terrified that she already knew the answer to that question.

Her face throbbed where she'd hit it against the side of the table when Jimmy threw her off him earlier, and her ribs screamed with every breath she took because she'd hit them, too. But it was fear for her daughter that left her almost paralyzed.

Every time she saw the hand-shaped bruises on Ruthie's slender neck, she was forced to confront how close she had come to losing her only child.

She'd been late, and Jimmy had been in the process of following through on his threats to kill Ruthie when she burst into her house. No matter how long she lived, whether Jimmy wound up killing her or she died of old age, she would never forget seeing his big hand wrapped around her child's small throat.

But Ruthie was alive, and currently huddled against her side. The feel of her daughter's tiny frame was the only thing keeping her strong. Ruthie's life was in her hands and she wasn't going to mess up.

She couldn't.

Messing up meant losing her child and that wasn't going to happen.

Jimmy nodded approvingly as Elle put the final dish away in the china cabinet. True to his words, he had the table set and ordered her to cook them a roast meal like the kind you'd have for Christmas day. After they'd finished eating, she and Ruthie had washed all the dishes by hand while he sat in a chair and stared at them in the creepiest way imaginable.

Like he was undressing her with his eyes, and Elle had a sinking feeling that she knew exactly what was going to happen next.

Where was Rafe?

Why hadn't he come?

She was sure he would have made it back to the compound by now. Wherever he went to look for Ruthie, her daughter hadn't been there and she knew that Rafe would want to break the news to her himself. Andy was a smart little boy, and she had no doubts that he had told his father exactly what she'd asked him to.

So why wasn't Rafe there?

Had he not understood the clue she left with Andy?

That seemed to be the only logical conclusion because Rafe would come after her, she knew he would. There was no way he would leave her and her daughter alone with a lunatic for a second longer than he had to.

Was he out there right now? Planning the best way to enter the house without getting her and Ruthie killed in the process? If he was out there, or if he'd hacked into the house's cameras, he would have seen that Jimmy had a weapon on him.

Writing romantic suspense was one thing, but living it was another. Elle wasn't cut out for this. She was so sick of being shaky and scared all the time, of the pressure in her chest, and the weight in her stomach. She didn't want to live balancing on a knife's edge any longer, terrified that at any second she would slip and slice herself open.

"Perfect." Jimmy nodded as he pushed away from the table.

When he stepped toward them, Ruthie pressed closer against her side, and Elle wrapped an arm protectively around her daughter's shoulders shifting slightly so she was between Jimmy and Ruthie.

"Time to put the kid to bed so the two of us can have some alone time."

Shivers danced up her spine at the way he looked at her when he said it. She knew exactly what he meant by alone time, and her entire body rebelled at the notion.

Just because she didn't want this man to touch her, if it was the only way to protect her child, to buy time until Rafe could come for them, then she would absolutely allow him to do anything he wanted to her.

Ruthie was her priority.

Ruthie was her everything.

Any sacrifice was worth it if it ensured that her daughter lived.

"Bedtime? Mommy, it's not dark yet," Ruthie said, her sweet little voice music to Elle's ears.

Quickly, before Jimmy could say anything, she leaned down and picked up Ruthie. At seven, she was really too big to be carried, but Elle wanted her daughter close and to protect her from Jimmy. "It's okay, baby. Sometimes we need an early night, and I bet you're really tired after today, it's been a big day."

Giving a nod, Ruthie snuggled closer, resting her head on Elle's shoulder and she relaxed. Jimmy nodded approvingly, and she knew she had averted a crisis. It was clear that Jimmy didn't care about Ruthie at all, so while theoretically Elle should be safe enough with him for the foreseeable future, her daughter was not.

Carrying Ruthie up the stairs to her bedroom, she quickly got the little girl into her pajamas and tucked into bed with her favorite stuffed unicorn. For weeks, Elle had dreamed of this, of having her little unicorn girl home, of tucking her into bed like she always did, reading to her, singing to her, and kissing her goodnight.

But it wasn't supposed to be like this.

The man who had stolen her daughter wasn't supposed to be standing in the doorway with a gun tucked into the waistband of his jeans.

Her little girl was supposed to be safe once she came home, but Ruthie was no safer now than she had been for the last month.

Since she didn't want to risk Jimmy's anger, Elle didn't read to Ruthie, but she did sing to her, stroking her daughter's hair as she held the little girl close against her breast. She didn't care that the added weight of the child against her cracked or broken ribs hurt so badly she had to fight back tears, all that mattered was that she was holding her daughter again.

When she sensed Jimmy getting antsy behind her, Elle laid Ruthie back against her pillows, and kissed her forehead. "I love you, little unicorn girl, so very much," she whispered.

"Love you, Mommy," Ruthie's teary but brave voice whispered back.

Letting her daughter go was the hardest thing in the world when all she wanted to do was keep her little girl glued to her side, but somehow, she managed to straighten, turn on the nightlight, make sure the covers were tucked up to Ruthie's chin, and walk out the door, closing it behind her.

Left alone with Jimmy, it took all her willpower not to scream and try to run away. But with her daughter in the house and Jimmy armed, she couldn't do anything without risking Ruthie's safety, and that was the one thing she wouldn't do.

So when Jimmy took her hand and led her down the hall to the master bedroom, she let him. And when he opened the door, and she saw rose petals strewn about and lit candles on every available surface, she fought her instincts to run.

Just like she fought them again when he guided her into the middle of the room and stood there staring down at her like he couldn't wait to devour her. And again when he began to undress her.

Afraid that at any second she would break, lash out, and do something that would get her daughter killed, Elle allowed her mind to drift away and find a place to hide. It hid itself in Rafe's rustic cabin, up in his big bed, surrounded by his scent.

Rafe was coming, she believed that with every fiber of her being. All she had to do was hold on until he got here.

When he had her naked, Jimmy's hungry eyes roamed her body, his hands seemingly everywhere at once. They touched her breasts, tweaking her nipples painfully. They skimmed her hips then swept all the way up until they circled her neck, squeezing just enough to hurt before sweeping down again.

They brushed up the inside of her thighs, and when he touched her between her legs, Elle wasn't strong enough to stop tears from leaking out.

You can do this.

For Ruthie, you have *to do this.*

Be strong.

Your daughter needs you.

Anything for Ruthie.

The internal pep talk was the only reason she didn't fight him as Jimmy pushed her back onto the bed, then unzipped his jeans. His length sprung free as though it had a mind of its own and had only one goal.

As he climbed onto the bed, covering her body with his much larger, much strong one, Elle turned her face away. If she had to do this to keep Ruthie safe she would, but she couldn't look at him while he raped her.

"Eyes stay on me," Jimmy growled as one of his hands grabbed her face, squeezing her cheeks painfully as he turned her head so she had no choice but to look at him.

If he even noticed she was crying he didn't say anything. She felt him lift his hips, and she prepared herself for the intrusion that would forever change who she was even if by some miracle she and her daughter survived.

CHAPTER
Thirteen

February 17th
5:05 P.M.

Fury like he had never experienced before flooded Panther's body as he
eased open the door to Elle's bedroom, and saw her naked on the bed
with Jimmy Hillier's body on top of her.

If it were any other victim in any other op he was working, he might
have tried to reason with the man, might have tried to talk him down,
convince him to give himself up. But this wasn't any other victim, and
with the weapon on the nightstand, well within Jimmy's reach should
he try to lunge for it, Panther didn't hesitate.

A single shot was all it took to end the life of the man who had dared
hurt Elle and her daughter.

At the sound of the gunshot, and the weight of the now dead man
crushing her into the mattress, Elle didn't make a sound, and panic had
Panther sprinting to the bed and literally throwing Jimmy off her,
paying no attention to the man's body as it hit the hardwood floor. Was
she hurt? Was she conscious? Was she dead?

The questions ran through his mind in a rush as he leaned a knee against the bed and reached over to angle Elle's face toward him. Her eyes were open but vacant, and even though he could see she was in fact alive, he needed the added reassurance of touching his fingertips to her neck so he could feel her pulse thumping against them.

There was blood on her pale skin that he assumed came from Jimmy since he couldn't see any open wounds. On her face, there was a small gash on her left cheekbone and the beginnings of what was going to be one hell of a bruise. The anger inside him grew and he wished he could kill Jimmy all over again, only slower this time, and much more painfully.

Somehow, he managed to keep his touch gentle as he ran his hands over Elle's body in search of injuries. As he touched her ribs she flinched, the first voluntary movement she'd made since he found her, and he relaxed a tiny bit.

"Elle?" he spoke softly as he cupped the non-injured side of her face. "Honey, it's Rafe. Can you hear me?" Since he had no idea of how far Jimmy had taken things before he'd gotten there, he had no idea if there were internal injuries as well or if Elle was just in shock.

After a slow blink, her eyes cleared and she bolted upright, her hands grabbing fistfuls of his clothes, twisting them between her fingers. "Ruthie, where's Ruthie?"

Panic was evident in her expression, her voice, and the desperate way she clung to him, and he ached to soothe it away. "She's down the hall in her bedroom with Scorpion," he replied. As soon as he knew where Elle had gone, he'd hacked into the security system at her house. Forced to watch as Elle cooked a meal while keeping her daughter at her side, the three of them ate at the table together like a family, the only thing stopping him from bursting in was that Jimmy was armed.

Knowing the man would rather kill Elle than let her go, and with a seven-year-old in the crosshairs, they had decided to wait until Elle and Ruthie were separated before making their move. It had been hell waiting, but as soon as Ruthie was tucked safely into bed they entered the house.

Since Panther knew that Elle's priority would be her daughter, they had secured Ruthie first before he'd continued down the hall to Elle's bedroom.

"I need to see her, I need her here, Rafe. I need my baby," she babbled, growing increasingly hysterical.

As badly as he wanted to tell her that her daughter shouldn't see her like this, that he needed to have Rock check her over before Ruthie came into the room, he knew if their positions were reversed and it was Andy who had been taken, the only thing in the world that would make him feel better was seeing his son.

"Okay, honey, hold on just one second for me, okay?" he said soothingly, reaching out to take the blanket Rock brought him. Since Elle had been raped, or come as close to it without actual penetration, he didn't want to do anything she wasn't comfortable with. To help remind her that she could say no at any time, he talked through what he was doing before doing it. "I'm just going to wipe this blood off you so it doesn't scare Ruthie okay?"

Only after Elle nodded her consent did he take the wet towel from Rock and carefully clean away the blood. He didn't care about cops and lawyers and evidence at this point, between Elle and Ruthie's statements, there was no doubt that Jimmy was the kidnapper, and he doubted anyone would care that the man was dead. All he wanted was to get his woman to her daughter as quickly as he could.

"I'm going to wrap you in the blanket and carry you down the hall to Ruthie's room so she doesn't have to see the blood and the body, okay?" he asked. At her nod of assent, he tucked the blanket around her and scooped her up. "The two of you are going to go to the hospital to get checked out, okay?"

Expecting an argument, Panther was surprised when Elle merely nodded and clung to him as he carried her down the hall. The second he opened the door to Ruthie's room the child scampered off the bed where she'd been huddled, refusing to allow any of them—who were just more scary big men to the traumatized seven-year-old—to get too close to her.

"Mommy!"

"Ruthie!" Elle shoved to get out of his arms, and the second he set her on her feet she yanked her daughter into her arms and sunk onto the floor, rocking her baby on her lap.

Watching the two clinging to one another, both crying, both

holding on for dear life, Panther felt his own eyes sting. There was no way for him to watch the mother and daughter and not think of his own son and how it would feel to finally be reunited with his boy after going through such a long, horrific ordeal.

"Mommy, is Jimmy going to hurt us again?" Ruthie asked.

Elle looked up at him for reassurance, and when he shook his head, she turned back to her daughter. "No, baby girl. Jimmy is *never* going to hurt you again."

"Do you promise?"

"I promise," Elle vowed as she tucked her daughter against her body, continuing to rock her as the two sat together on the floor.

"Ambulance is here," Tank said quietly from behind him, and Panther nodded.

Crouching beside the pair, he laid a hand on Elle's shoulder. "Ambulance is here," he told her when she looked up at him.

She nodded, but when she tried to push to her feet, still holding onto her daughter, her exhausted body couldn't make it.

"I got you, honey," he murmured as he lifted both mother and daughter into his arms.

Downstairs he found medics already inside and waiting for them, so he set Elle down on the living room sofa.

"Look at Ruthie first," she insisted even though it was clear to all of them that she was the one with injuries while her daughter appeared to be physically unharmed.

Wanting to give the two space, uncertain now about his role in their lives, just because he and Elle had talked about giving a relationship a go after Ruthie was found he wasn't sure it was still what she wanted, Panther turned to walk away. Wasn't sure that even if she did want it that she had the emotional energy to expend on anything else but her daughter and herself right now. Or for the foreseeable future.

It wasn't that he didn't understand or respect the fact that Ruthie was her priority, he just ached to be there for the two of them. But right now, Ruthie was afraid of big men like him and he didn't want to make her recovery any harder than it was already going to be.

"Rafe," Elle's panicked voice stopped him in his tracks.

"Yeah, honey?"

"Where are you going?"

"Was going to let the EMTs do their thing and get you two to the hospital."

"Y-you're l-leaving us?" Elle stammered.

His heart thudded in his chest at Elle's obvious distress at the idea of him leaving. Maybe he was wrong, maybe she and her daughter didn't need or want space while they worked on processing their ordeal. Maybe all they needed was unconditional support. Support that he and his son wanted to offer.

"I thought maybe it was what you wanted," he replied honestly.

She shook her head hard enough to make herself wince. "It's not what I want." Elle looked down at her daughter in her lap. "It's because of you I have her back, that she's safe and sound in my arms again, where she belongs. I want you to stay with us. Please."

"Oh, honey, you don't have to beg. I want to be here, for both of you." Sitting down on the couch beside her, he pulled her sideways so Elle was in his lap, with Ruthie in her lap. "Nowhere else I'd rather be."

∼

February 17th
   7:31 P.M.

Fatigue weighed heavily down upon Elle's shoulders, but she couldn't wipe the smile from her face.

Ruthie was here.

In her arms.

Safe.

Home.

Right where she belonged.

True to his word, Rafe had stayed right by their side. He'd ridden in the ambulance with them, he'd held her hand while a doctor examined Ruthie, and caught her weight before she could collapse and scare her daughter when the doctor said there were no signs of sexual abuse. Somehow, he'd even managed to win enough of Ruthie's trust that she had allowed him to hold her while Elle had been examined. It was obvious her daughter was now afraid of all big men who bore any kind of resemblance to Jimmy.

All except Rafe it seemed.

Even now as they waited for discharge papers so they could leave, Ruthie seemed content to sit on the bed sandwiched between her and Rafe.

Relief that her daughter wasn't terrified of Rafe wiped away a little of her exhaustion. She needed Rafe, but if it was too much for her daughter, she would have asked him to give them space and time.

Ruthie had to be her priority.

Just because her daughter had come out of her ordeal physically unharmed didn't mean she wasn't hurting. Elle had already set up an appointment for her daughter with a child psychologist who specialized in childhood trauma, and whatever the woman suggested she would do. Whatever it took to help her daughter heal.

"Mommy?"

"Yeah, sweetie?" Never again would she take for granted the simple pleasure of hearing her child call her mom.

"Are we ... do we have to ... where are we going when we leave?" Ruthie asked in a small voice Elle wasn't used to hearing her daughter use.

Honestly, she hadn't thought that far ahead. Between the cops asking them questions, and she and Ruthie being examined, there hadn't been time to think more than what happened next. But Ruthie was right, she had to figure out a plan. "We'll probably stay at a hotel tonight, sweetheart, then when the police say we can go back home we'll go there."

"No, I don't want to go back home," Ruthie cried, bursting into tears. Even as a baby Ruthie hadn't been a big crier, and seeing her sweet little girl so lost and scared was heartbreaking. She was the mom, she wanted to fix it, make everything better, and soothe every hurt, but this wasn't something she could just use her mom magic and fix.

Her daughter wasn't the only one who didn't want to go back to that house. From here on out, every time she walked in there, Elle knew she would see Jimmy with his hands around Ruthie's neck. But it would take time for her to put the house on the market and hunt for a new home, and right now, her daughter needed one hundred percent of her time and attention.

"I guess we can stay at a hotel for a while," she soothed. It wasn't ideal, Ruthie needed to be somewhere she could feel safe, where she could rebuild her sense of stability, and a hotel wasn't the place for that. But beggars couldn't be choosers and they didn't have family they could go and stay with.

"Don't want to overstep, but Andy and I would love to have the two of you stay with us," Rafe spoke up.

"We can't impose on you like that," she said the words even though there was nothing in the world she would rather do than take her baby out to that cabin in the quiet, peaceful woods. It was the perfect place for her daughter to heal, but just because Elle felt peace out there didn't mean Ruthie would.

"Not imposing if we want you there," Rafe refuted.

"Who's Andy?" Ruthie asked, the first hint of curiosity in her inquisitive daughter showing itself.

"Andy's my son. He's eight," Rafe told her.

"Where do you and Andy live?" Ruthie asked. Her daughter looked so small sitting next to Rafe's huge frame, and she liked knowing that Rafe could and would do whatever it took to protect her child. As long as Rafe was there they were both safe.

"We live in a cabin out in the forest. It's still winter, but in the spring we have deer, and rabbits, lots of birds and butterflies, and sometimes we get the occasional bear."

Ruthie loved animals and any mention of them was enough to garner her interest. "I like bird, and butterflies, too. Everything that flies."

"I have a friend who lives out in the woods with me and she loves butterflies so much that her fiancé made her a butterfly house."

At the sound of that, Ruthie's eyes grew so wide that both she and Rafe chuckled. "Wow, that's cool."

"The coolest," he agreed. It was no surprise that he was completely at ease with the seven-year-old since he had a son around the same age. Still, Elle felt her heart warm listening to them bond.

"Who else lives with you in the woods?" Ruthie asked.

"Well, me and Andy live together in one cabin. Sometimes Mrs. Pfeffer stays with us, too, she looks after Andy when I'm not home. Then there's Ariel who has the butterfly house, and Rock, her fiancé. There's Tank and Tillie, they live together, Trick and Stephanie live together, and Axe and Beth. And lastly there's Scorpion and Jessica, they live together, too, and they're going to have a baby."

Her daughter's eyes lit up at the mention of a baby. Ruthie was *dying* to be a big sister. "Why do they have such funny names?"

"They have regular names, too, but they're our special names, our nicknames."

"What's your nickname?"

"It's Panther."

Ruthie giggled, and tears filled Elle's eyes. It was the first time her daughter had laughed and it gave her hope that one day Ruthie could go back to the carefree child she'd always been.

"That's a great nickname," Ruthie enthused, then she grew serious. "Are your friends the men from our house?"

"They are."

"They're scary," Ruthie said with a shudder.

"They're big and can look kind of scary, but they're not really scary when you get to know them. We help people like you and your mom who need help, we save people, we protect people, and we would never *ever* hurt anyone."

After considering this for a moment, her daughter turned to her. "Can we stay with Panther and Andy?"

"If you think you'd like to, baby, we can stay." It probably wasn't the wisest move, deciding they would give a relationship a try didn't mean they should jump straight to the moving-in-together stage. But truth was, it was the only place she would feel safe, and the only place she would feel safe having Ruthie stay.

Both Rafe and Ruthie smiled at her, and her heart eased a little. Her daughter was home, and she had an amazing man and his amazing little boy offering to be there for both of them. What more could she ask for?

A few minutes later, a nurse came in with discharge papers and then she was carrying Ruthie through the hospital halls and outside to Rafe's vehicle. Her daughter's weight made her cracked ribs ache, but Elle didn't care, this was exactly where she needed her child to be.

The car's rocking motion lulled her off to sleep as she sat in the backseat with Ruthie snuggled against her side, and the next thing she knew, Rafe was stroking one hand down her hair and the other down Ruthie's.

"Wake up, sleepyheads," he called softly.

"Rafe?" she murmured.

"Panther?" Ruthie mumbled at the same time.

"You can call me Rafe if you want," Rafe said to Ruthie. "That's what your mom calls me."

Now that she knew the significance for these guys of having someone call them by their first name, Elle felt tears well in her eyes. The only good thing to come out of this whole ordeal was meeting Rafe and Andy.

"Rafe," Ruthie agreed, sounding sleepy.

"Come on you two, Andy has a surprise all cooked up for you inside," he said, nodding over his shoulder to where Andy was standing.

Scrambling forward, the little boy wriggled past his dad. "Elle, I did 'xactly what you told me. I told Daddy what you said. There's no place like home," he said as he wrapped his thin arms around her.

"You did amazing, buddy boy. You saved our lives." She hugged the child tightly, forever grateful for his help. No matter what happened between her and Rafe, she'd like to maintain a relationship with the boy.

"Are you Ruthie?" Andy asked. "I told Elle that my dad would save you. He's a superhero and won't let nobody hurt you again. I won't let nobody hurt you neither," he declared in the same exact tone she could imagine his father would use.

Ruthie smiled shyly at Andy. "My mom and I are going to stay here."

"I know." Andy looked and sounded excited by the idea. "Me and Beth got Mrs. Pfeffer's room all ready. We put up fairy lights everywhere so it wouldn't be too dark, and we put lots of pillows and blankets on the bed so it's all snuggly. We put the TV in there and Beth is making hot chocolate right now. After you have a bubble bath, we're all going to get in the bed and watch movies till we fall asleep. Beth said that's what she does when she can't sleep."

Elle knew enough about Beth to know the woman had been rescued by Rafe and Bravo Team, and had eventually fallen in love with and married Axe. Only then she had been taken, missing for months, and when she returned it was with no memory of who she was or who the people around her were. It was sweet that the woman had wanted to make a safe place for Ruthie even when she had her own issues to worry about.

"You thought of everything, huh, bud?" Rafe asked, ruffling his son's hair.

"Yep."

Once Andy had scrambled back out of the car, Elle went to reach for Ruthie, only to have Rafe stop her.

"I got her, honey. Your ribs are hurting you, let me carry her."

She would have asked Ruthie if she was okay with Rafe carrying her inside, but her daughter had already unbuckled her seatbelt and held up her arms to Rafe to allow him to pick her up.

Andy grabbed Elle's hand as soon as she was out of the car, and as she followed Rafe and Ruthie inside, she prayed she wasn't making a mistake allowing the two boys to care for her and her daughter. Because Rafe was already her security blanket, and if she allowed him to become Ruthie's as well and things didn't work out between them, then she was setting both herself and her daughter up for a huge fall.

CHAPTER
Fourteen

February 18th
1:29 A.M.

The sounds of screams tore him from sleep.

Since Panther had been tossing and turning, sleeping lightly because he already knew that sooner or later his girls were going to need him, he woke instantly and came fully awake immediately.

Mrs. Pfeffer had insisted that Elle and Ruthie make use of her room for as long as the two would be staying with him and Andy, so he threw open his bedroom door and hurried down the hall. As much as he would have liked to have Elle sleeping in his bed beside him, he had completely understood her need to stay with her daughter. Ruthie was understandably clingy right now, and honestly, Elle was just as bad.

It had been a long month for both of them, and the only way they could heal was by being together.

Just as he reached the closed door to Elle and Ruthie's room, Andy's swung open and his sleep rumpled son stumbled out. Exhausted, both Elle and her daughter had fallen asleep within minutes of finishing their hot chocolate and snuggling under the dozen or so blankets Andy and

February 18th
1:29 A.M.

Beth had piled onto the bed. Leaving the two to sleep, Panther had sat down with his son and had a long talk about some of the issues Ruthie would be facing, including the fact that she might have nightmares and wake up screaming or crying. The last thing he wanted was to freak his son out by being woken by screams in the middle of the night.

"It's okay, bud, go back to bed, I've got it," he told Andy.

Looking so very grown up, Andy shook his head. "No, Dad. I'm going to help."

Proud as he was of his boy and his desire to support and protect, he could hardly ask his eight-year-old to take on the responsibility of helping a traumatized child heal. Andy knew the basics, that Ruthie had been kidnapped, and he was old enough to understand what that meant. But he was still a child, Panther's child, and he wanted to shield his son from the harsh realities of life for as long as possible.

"It's not going to be easy, Andy, and it's going to take time." Maybe the reassurance was as much for his benefit as it was his son's. He genuinely liked Elle, admired her strength in enduring hell with her daughter missing, loved how natural and at ease she was with Andy, and thought she was the sexiest woman he'd ever laid eyes on. The desire to fix this problem for her was strong, but there was nothing he could say or do to ease either her trauma or her daughter's.

Slipping his hand into Panther's, Andy squeezed. "They just need us to be there for them, Dad. That's what Beth said. She said when you're scared and you feel all alone, all you need is for people to be there. She said it doesn't matter if you know them or not so long as they're there."

"Beth said that huh?" Poor Beth had been through so much, yet she was the sweetest, most caring and compassionate woman. It killed every single member of Bravo Team that they couldn't wave a magic wand to return her memories. "All right then, let's get in there and show our girls that we're there for them."

Knowing it was way too soon to be calling Elle and Ruthie his girls didn't seem to stop him from doing it. From wanting to do it. If he'd had any doubts about what he wanted he wouldn't have invited the two to stay with him. All he would have done was ensure that Prey had them covered, that they would be well taken care of and would have access to anything they needed.

But this was where he wanted them. Right here where he could make sure they knew they were safe and protected, where he could make sure Elle was taking care of herself as well as taking care of her daughter.

Together, he and Andy opened the door and walked into the bedroom. With all the fairy lights Beth and his son had strung up, there was plenty of light in there, and the TV was still on. He'd left it on when he and Andy snuck out because he wanted some background noise, hoping it might help stave off nightmares.

In the middle of the bed sat Elle with her arms wrapped around her sobbing daughter. Panther wasn't sure if it had been Elle screaming in her sleep, or Ruthie, or whether they had both been plagued by bad dreams, but both of them were currently crying. While Panther hesitated a moment, even as Elle's big brown eyes turned to him imploring him to do something to make her feel better, safer, reassured her daughter was home, Andy had no such hesitation.

His son just jumped up onto the bed and crawled over to the crying girls, wrapping his arms around them. With all his eight years of sweet innocence, his little boy just came right out and asked what he wanted to know. "Did you have bad dreams?"

Lifting her tear-stained face from her mother's neck, Ruthie nodded. The little girl had taken instantly to Andy, and Panther was relieved that she seemed to have taken to him as well, even though she was scared of men right now. There was no shadow of doubt in his mind, if Ruthie hadn't been okay with being near him then she and Elle wouldn't be there.

"What did you dream about?" Andy asked.

"I dreamed about Jimmy, he was hurting me and my mommy," Ruthie whispered.

Andy patted her shoulder. "Jimmy isn't here, and even if he were, me and my dad wouldn't let him hurt you."

When did his son grow up this much? When had he gotten so smart and intuitive?

"In my room I have a special ring," Andy told Ruthie, and Panther smiled at the mention of the ring that had been a lifesaver when his son was younger.

Like most small children, Andy had gone through the stage of being scared of the dark. To help out, Panther had found a superhero ring. It had a little light to turn on and you could flip through several super-heros and it would project their picture up onto the ceiling, making it seem like they were watching over you while you slept. It had been a couple of years now since Andy outgrew the ring and its uses, but he wasn't surprised that his son had kept it.

"You can use it if you want, it will keep you safe, and you know my dad is the best superhero of all, he won't let anyone hurt you," Andy said confidently.

"How does your ring keep people safe?" Ruthie asked, obviously curious about the idea.

"It has all the superheroes inside it, and you can choose which one you want. There's Batman, and The Flash, Hulk, and Ironman," Andy said excitedly.

"Supergirl is the best superhero," Ruthie said, all full of seven-year-old sass.

"Supergirl is in the ring. You want to go see? I have bunk beds in my room, you can sleep on the top one if you want, that way you can have Supergirl and me keeping you safe," Andy offered.

"Can I, Mommy?" Ruthie asked.

Panther could tell Elle didn't want to say yes. She wanted to keep her daughter close and be able to see and touch her. Ruthie might have been the one who had been kidnapped, but both of them had suffered equally just in different ways.

Despite her hesitation, Elle nodded, and smoothed a lock of hair off her daughter's wet cheek. "If you want to sleep in Andy's room, you can."

"Thanks, Mommy." Ruthie kissed her mom and then bounded off the bed with Andy and the two children ran off hand in hand to Andy's room.

The second Ruthie was out of sight Elle just broke.

Watching her battle to keep her sobs silent so she wouldn't upset her daughter broke his heart. She'd been so brave, so strong, and she knew she had to keep being brave and strong because her child needed her to be.

Reaching for her felt like the most natural thing in the world.

Panther hauled her onto his lap and Elle came without hesitation. Her arms wrapped around his neck, her fingers curling into his bare shoulders as she clung to him. Tears wet his skin as she pressed her face into his neck, and her entire body shuddered as he held and rocked her, while murmuring soothing words in her ear.

"I was almost too late," she whispered through her tears. "I was one minute late and he had his hands around her neck as I walked into the house."

Even though he'd already heard her give her statement to the cops, hearing it again, so raw and painful, broke his heart. She'd been one minute late because she was here with his son. If Ruthie had died because Elle had been with Andy he never would have forgiven himself.

"But you weren't late, honey. You saved your daughter's life, you did everything you had to to make sure you both stayed alive until I could come for you. I will always come for you, Elle. For you and Ruthie. Whatever you need, I'm there for you."

～

February 18th
  2:03 A.M.

I'm there for you.
  Those words sounded so wonderful ... almost magical.
  When had anyone ever offered her their unconditional support?
  Certainly not her parents. Their support was conditional upon her following the path they had chosen for her. And certainly not her ex. His support had been non existent. In his mind, she should take care of the house and him, all while earning a good living for the both of them.
  It was something Elle was used to, being strong for herself and her daughter, taking care of everything by herself, but now as she sank deeper into Rafe's embrace, she felt a knot inside her loosen and unravel.
  She wasn't alone.
  Rafe was here.
  Even though they both knew she could take care of herself and

Ruthie alone if she had to, she didn't have to. Because Rafe was right there offering his unwavering support so she didn't have to do this alone.

This was her safe place, a place where she didn't always have to be strong and have it all together. Which was why she felt free now to cry out her pain, knowing she wouldn't be judged for it, something she wouldn't have allowed herself to do with anyone else.

Uncurling her fingers from where they were pressed much too firmly against Rafe's bare back, she lifted her hands and placed them on his shoulders. They were so broad, Elle was sure there was no limit to what he could carry. But if they were together she would never make him carry the load alone. They'd be partners in every sense of the word.

"I want you, Rafe," she whispered, allowing the need and desire brewing inside her to shine through.

Echoing desire flared in his golden-brown eyes making them look like two glowing gold orbs, but his touch when he palmed her cheek was light as a feather. "I didn't ask you and Ruthie to stay with me because I expected sex, Elle."

"I've wanted you since the second I saw you, but I couldn't even let myself think about it because my daughter was missing and that was my priority. I couldn't have sex with a stranger while she was in danger."

"I'm still a stranger," he said softly, the fingers of the hand cupping her cheek never ceasing to caress her skin.

"You don't *feel* like a stranger." Crazy, but the truth. It reminded her of the song in Disney's Sleeping Beauty, where Aurora knew about Prince Phillip from her dreams. It was like there was a part of her soul that recognized Rafe. Never before had she experienced anything like it. Not with any of the boys she'd dated in high school, and not with her ex-husband.

"You're vulnerable right now, Elle, and I don't want to take advantage. I don't ever want to be something you regret, and I want our first time to be special."

His words only made her want him more. Everything he said, everything he cared about, everything he stood for, it was everything she had craved in a partner. Bobby had been a mistake, part of her knew it at the time, but he'd offered her an out of the life her parents were trying to force her into and she'd taken it.

Nothing about Rafe could ever be a mistake.

"This is the most amazing day of my life. I got my baby back alive, and it's all thanks to you. I want you, Rafe. I need you. Make love to me, please." Elle didn't want to beg, and if he said no she would respect that, couldn't not when he thought he was doing the right thing, but she knew herself, knew this was what she wanted, it wouldn't be taking advantage.

"You're hurt," he reminded her, but she could see his resolve weakening.

"So we'll go gentle, and I'll let you be in complete control, I know you won't hurt me."

Fire burned in his eyes, lust mixed with desire. "Oh, honey, I don't know if you want to make me that offer. I like control in the bedroom and it's been a long time for me."

"Me too. Not since my ex. After the divorce I didn't have the time or the interest in sex. I'm clean and I'm on birth control."

His other hand lifted to frame her face and he studied her gaze carefully. "You're positive? Because I'm not going anywhere, this can wait until you're ready."

"I'm ready now."

"All right, honey, then I got you. You want to do this here, on neutral ground, or in my room?"

"Your bed," Elle replied without hesitation. She didn't want neutral, she wanted to be completely surrounded by Rafe. "That's where I want to be. I want to be completely surrounded by your scent."

"Oh, honey, you'll be covered in it," Rafe promised with a wink as he scooped her up and carried her down the hall to his bedroom.

Without her even having to ask, he paused at the door to Andy's room, balancing her in one arm so he could ease it open and they could both see their children asleep in the bunk beds, a projection of Supergirl on the ceiling. As shocked as she was that Ruthie had been willing to sleep anywhere but in her arms, Elle was glad that her daughter felt comfortable enough there, and with Andy specifically, that she was okay sleeping in the little boy's room.

Once they reached Rafe's room, he set her on her feet and stared down at her for a moment. Then he leaned down and touched the softest of kisses to the bruises covering most of the left side of her face.

"So brave," he whispered as he reached for the hem of her tank top. Carefully, he maneuvred it off her, doing his best to cause her as little pain as possible. Then once the top was off, discarded on the floor, he leaned in and kissed the bruises forming on her chest. The sweet touch made the cracked ribs more than bearable.

The tenderness emanating from Rafe as he kneeled before her, nuzzling the stretch marks on her stomach as though they were the most beautiful thing in the world, had heat pooling between her legs.

When had a man ever made her feel this sexy? This alive?

Never.

While she wouldn't say the sex she'd had before was bad, it wasn't the passionate, all-consuming experience she wrote about in her books. In her books, the heroes worshiped the heroines, they made love to them in the most exquisitely perfect ways, in the way she had always longed to be made love to.

In the way Rafe was slowly inching her fuzzy pajama pants down her legs.

Because her ribs had been sore when she'd changed into pajamas, she hadn't bothered with underwear, and now she was glad she hadn't. As soon as he had stripped her of the pants and tossed them aside, Rafe pressed his face to the apex of her thighs and breathed in.

The puff of air that escaped as he breathed back out again tickled her already throbbing bud and Elle sucked in a breath of her own.

"So beautiful, so strong," Rafe whispered, brushing his fingertips over her bruises as he stood. "So very brave. My gorgeous warrior woman."

That he respected her and found her bravery in doing what she could to fight for her and her daughter's lives as attractive as he found her body had to be the sexiest thing ever. Attraction was one thing, but she wanted so much more.

She wanted the soulmate, forever kind of love she wrote about.

Elle just hadn't thought it was in the cards for her.

Now she wondered if it was.

"You're my gorgeous warrior man, what you did for me and Ruthie, I can never repay you for that." Elle knew that if it hadn't been for this man, her daughter would have been lost to her forever. She would have gone into that house alone, the cops wouldn't have come in time to save her from being raped, and her faith in them was low enough that she believed they would have bungled the whole thing, possibly getting her or her daughter killed.

"Don't want you to repay me, honey," Rafe said as his hands curled around her backside and he lifted her. His huge length strained against his sweatpants, held like this it settled snugly against her center making her already aching core grow wetter.

Laying her out on the bed, he shucked his pants, and then nudged her legs apart, settling between them.

That first swipe of his tongue was pure heaven.

Then he latched his mouth onto her bundle of nerves and sucked and licked, driving her wild. Elle's fingers curled into the sheets, and her body began to writhe as pleasure built inside her, and then it just ... stopped.

When she lifted her head to find Rafe moving up her body, she looked at him in confusion. He was just going to leave her hanging on the verge of what she already knew would have been the best orgasm of her life?

"Trust me, beautiful," Rafe said just before his mouth closed around one of her nipples and she lost the ability to think of anything but the attention he was lavishing on her breast.

Time was nothing as she lay in Rafe's bed, her body his to do with as he pleased. It could have been minutes or hours before his mouth left her right breast and touched the softest of kisses to her left nipple before his hands went between her legs.

Her already sensitive bud throbbed when he rolled the pad of his thumb over it, and she was so wet that his finger slipped easily inside her. He pumped it in and out at a leisurely pace, pausing to play with her bundle of nerves, then added another finger. With every thrust he made sure he grazed a spot inside her that Elle hadn't been entirely convinced existed even if she did include it in the spicy scenes in her books.

Just as she could feel an orgasm begin to shimmer to life inside her, Rafe withdrew his hands.

"Rafe," she whined, hating how needy she sounded, like she was begging him for pleasure. Only she was so close, so desperate for release that she was prepared to beg even if she didn't like it. "I need—"

"I know what you need, gorgeous, and trust me you're going to get it. By the time I let you come its going to be so big it will devour you."

His mouth ravished her breast again, and then he kissed her as his hand went back between her legs, stroking, thrusting, rolling her bud between his thumb and forefinger. Elle felt like a mindless, throbbing, needy mess of sensations, she was so desperate to come and yet, at the same time, she loved the sweet torture he was inflicting on her body.

With each touch, each kiss, he was showing her how much he cared, how much he wanted to bring her pleasure. After all, she had no one to blame but herself for her delayed gratification, letting Rafe be in control was her idea.

"Are you ready, beautiful?" he asked as he settled between her spread legs again.

"Yes, Rafe, please, please let me come."

"You'll be coming all right." This time, when his mouth swiped across her center, delving deep inside her when his fingers spread her open, then latched onto her bud there was a fervency to his touch. Her pleasure wasn't the only one he was delaying, and when they both did come Elle had no doubts it was going to be out of this world amazing.

It was building quickly, her body already so sensitive it wasn't going to take much to push her over the edge. Her fingers clutched the sheets tight enough they ached, and her head moved restlessly on the pillow.

Crescendoing faster than she could have believed, when Rafe sucked hard on her bundle of nerves and flicked his tongue at the same time he thrust his fingers inside her and brushed against that special spot, the explosion hit.

It rocketed through her with the force of a tornado, tossing her about until she had no idea which way was up.

She couldn't think, all she could do was feel, and it felt so big, so strong, that it almost scared her.

"Rafe," she whimpered, needing him to join her on his crazy journey.

Aftershocks were still rippling through her when he plunged inside her in one smooth move.

"Come again for me, gorgeous," he commanded.

"Can't." Her body was too strung out, too wiped out by the intensity of her orgasm that she was positive she couldn't come again so soon.

Rafe, on the other hand, was positive of the opposite. He thrust in and out of her, balancing his weight with one hand while his other began to touch her where their bodies were joined. Her overly sensitive bud still buzzed but Rafe just took it, worked it between his fingers and in mere seconds he had another orgasm building.

This one somehow managed to be even more intense, perhaps because Rafe found his release at the same time she did, and Elle clung to him as pleasure fired through her body, burning every single nerve ending, her heart, and her soul.

Branded.

That's how she felt. Like Rafe had branded her tonight in a way she would never be able to forget, never be able to outrun, never be able to escape.

Which was perfect because she didn't want to escape what was growing between them.

CHAPTER

Fifteen

February 18th
9:33 A.M.

This was as close to perfect as Panther thought it was possible to get.

For some, perfect might be freedom, no strings, or hot sex and naked breakfast in bed with a gorgeous woman. For him, it was sitting around the kitchen table serving homemade pancakes to his son and his girls.

Okay, so he'd had hot sex with a gorgeous woman last night, but he would so much rather have family breakfast than naked breakfast in bed. Even though he'd never been sure that he wanted to be a guy with strings, it was forced on him at a young age when his girlfriend became pregnant. Strings hadn't been as bad as he thought. At least until his wife up and left.

Now strings were exactly what he wanted.

In fact, he wanted to find all the string he could and tie himself to the two beautiful girls sitting at his table.

While they had agreed in principle to take things slow between them and keep the focus on Ruthie's recovery, in practice, they had kind of jumped several steps ahead. Elle and Ruthie were living in his house, his son had already appointed himself the little girl's protector. Ruthie was sleeping in Andy's room, Elle was sleeping in his bed, and they would be spending pretty much every second of the day together.

Yeah, they weren't taking things slow at all, they'd gone right into overdrive.

Last night, when he'd gotten Elle and Ruthie home, the two had been too exhausted to do much but take a bath, drink the hot chocolate Andy and Beth had made for them, and fall asleep. Starting today, there would be no more skipping meals. Three a day no matter if they felt like eating or not and as many snacks in between as they wanted. Showers in the morning, clothes on, facing each day and its challenges, baths in the evening if they wanted them, and plenty of sleep. Both Ruthie and Elle needed a routine to feel safe again, grounded, and there was plenty of fresh air and open spaces out there for the two of them to find their peace again.

Taking care of these two girls was his job for the foreseeable future. Eagle had grounded Bravo Team, claiming they all needed the time off. Since last time he'd enforced a vacation, Scorpion had joined a cult to save the sister of an old friend—a sister who turned out not to need saving—this time he was ensuring that nothing came up.

Nothing other than a lead in Beth's case, because grounded or not, Panther wasn't going to stop running leads.

"I'm stuffed," Elle said, leaning back in her chair and placing her hands on her stomach.

"What about you guys?" he asked the kids. Andy had eaten four pancakes, but Ruthie had only managed one, and despite her claim of being full Elle had eaten only two. Stress had stolen both their appetites but they would rebuild them. They had time, all the time in the world.

"I'm full," Ruthie said. There was still a little hesitation in the girl when it came to him being too close to her. She would instinctively stiffen, but then it was like she reminded herself he wasn't going to hurt her and she'd relax.

"Me too," Andy agreed.

"Are you sure? There's still plenty left."

"That's because you made way too many, Dad," Andy said with a giggle.

Following Andy's lead, Ruthie giggled too. "He made enough for a hundred people."

"A *thousand* people," Andy said.

"A *million* people," Ruthie countered.

"A *billion* people," Andy said, one-upping the little girl with the sweetest smile he'd ever seen in his life.

"A *trillion* people," Ruthie said proudly, beaming at Andy like he was her hero. It was weird, but the way the little girl looked at his son was the same way Elle looked at him, only in a childlike version. If he'd had any worries about the kids bonding, he shouldn't have. It was like they had known each other all their lives.

You don't feel like a stranger, Elle had said to him last night. Guess Andy and Ruthie felt the same way about each other.

"A ... Dad, what comes after trillion?" Andy asked.

"Umm ... a four-illion?" he guessed.

"That's not a word," Elle said with a laugh, her eyes twinkling. "It's quadrillion, then quintillion, sextillion, septillion, octillion, nonillion, and then decillion."

"My mommy knows *every*thing," Ruthie said proudly.

"My dad thinks he knows everything, too," Andy said, and Panther wasn't quite sure if that was supposed to be a compliment or an insult. "Dad, we're going to go outside and play."

While Andy jumped out of the chair, Ruthie hesitated, the smile falling from her face and anxiety taking its place. "Mommy, am I allowed to go outside and play?"

Elle seemed surprised by the question, but recovered quickly. "Course you are, little unicorn girl. You'll have to wear one of Andy's coats, though, since we don't have yours. Beanie, scarf, and gloves, too."

Ruthie nodded, and climbed off her chair, following Andy out of the kitchen.

"I'll need to go by the house today, pack up clothes for me and Ruthie, and some of her toys. Do you think I'll be allowed back in?"

"No need to worry, the guys are heading over there this morning, probably already left. They're going to pack up everything they think you two will need and bring it over here. I hope I wasn't overstepping in organizing it, but I thought of it last night, and you were already asleep, so I just texted them and asked."

There was that hero smile again, just like the one Ruthie had been giving Andy. Elle pushed out of her chair and came around to where he was standing by the stove. She wrapped her arms around his waist and stood on tiptoe to touch a kiss to his jaw. "Thank you for thinking of that for me. Thank you for taking care of me and my daughter."

"Always, honey." Hooking a finger under her chin, he nudged her face up so he could lean down and kiss her properly.

The sound of the front door closing indicated the kids had gone outside, and he felt Elle stiffen. She wasn't comfortable with Ruthie being too far away from her.

"How about we clean up this mess later and go outside with the kids?" he suggested. "I'll loan you my coat," he added to coax her because he already knew that she loved being wrapped up in his clothes. "And you can take your laptop out, sit on the porch, and get a little writing done."

Elle seemed surprised by the idea. "I haven't written anything since Ruthie was taken," she admitted.

"Then now's the perfect time to start again. I'll play with the kids."

After a brief hesitation, she nodded, and they both bundled up and headed outside to where the kids were running about in the snow.

"Dad, push us on the swing," Andy called out, grabbing Ruthie's hand and pulling her toward the swing hanging from a huge oak tree.

"Mommy, can I go on the swing?" Ruthie asked.

Again, Elle stiffened at the question, but her voice was even when she answered. "Sure thing, sweetheart."

Leaving Elle to set herself up on the porch, Panther ran over to the kids just as Andy helped Ruthie onto the wooden seat.

"You go first, Ruthie, I'm going to make a big pile of snow for you to jump off into," Andy said excitedly.

"You good with that, princess?" he asked the little girl.

Looking over her shoulder at him, she chewed on her bottom lip. "Am I allowed?"

Didn't take a genius for him to figure out that the child was asking permission to do everything because Jimmy had likely not allowed her to do anything unless he told her it was okay.

Smiling reassuringly, he nodded. "Yep, you sure can. But you don't have to jump off if you don't want to."

"I want to," she said with a shy but brave smile.

"You want me to push you or you going to push yourself?" he asked. Ruthie was old enough to do it herself, but he'd loved standing out here with Andy when his son was very small, pushing him on the swing he'd made himself. Nothing would make him happier than creating those memories with this little girl, but he absolutely was not going to do anything she wasn't okay with. For over a month the child had had zero power and control over her own life, he wanted to give that back to her.

"Umm, you can push me," Ruthie answered with another shy smile.

"All right then, hold on tight," he said as he started pushing. "Andy, is there enough snow to make a safe pile to land in?" Andy loved jumping off the swing and landing in snow, he'd been obsessed with the game this winter and the previous two, ever since he learned how to kick his legs and push himself. But it was getting to the end of the season and there wasn't a whole lot of snow left.

"Plenty," Andy replied as he ran about, gathering armfuls of snow and dumping it all a short way from the swing.

Not quite as convinced as his son, Panther pushed the little girl higher and higher, his smile growing bigger with every delighted squeal the child gave, but when Andy announced that the pile was ready for jumping into, he slowed it down a bit so Ruthie wouldn't hurt herself when she landed.

"Ready, Ruthie?" Andy called out.

The girl dragged in a breath, but nodded. "I'm ready."

"On three," Andy said. "One. Two"

"Three," Ruthie and Andy said in unison, just as Ruthie let go of the ropes and jumped. For a second, the little girl seemed to hang in the air and then she was coming down, landing with a muted thump in the pile of snow Andy had collected.

A half second later the child jumped to her feet, a huge smile on her face. "I did it," she exclaimed proudly.

Panther could feel Elle's eyes on them, feel her pride in her daughter for being willing to try new things even after what she'd been through.

"Course you did, princess," he told Ruthie, wanting her to be sure of this from the very beginning. "Not anything you can't do. The only thing that will ever stop you from flying high is if you lose faith in yourself. Believe in yourself and you can do anything. And, Ruthie, if you ever feel yourself slipping, you have your mom, and Andy, and me to catch you."

Slow or fast it didn't matter how they got there, the outcome was going to be the same. The four of them were a family now, and nothing was ever going to change that.

～

February 22ⁿᵈ
11:47 A.M.

"Mommy, am I allowed to go in Andy's treehouse?" Ruthie asked.

Elle froze, hating the way her daughter asked for permission for even the tiniest of things before she would do them.

Trauma.

She knew that.

Her daughter was doing as well as could be expected given her ordeal, but she hadn't come out of it unscathed. Nightmares Elle had expected, and they'd settled into a pattern. She and Ruthie would start the night in Mrs. Pfeffer's bedroom, then bad dreams would come for one or both of them, usually waking them in the early hours of the morning.

When they did, Rafe and Andy were always there for them. Andy would take Ruthie to his room where her daughter's favorite unicorn sheets were now on the top bunk, her clothes shared the wardrobe, and her toys sat on the shelves. Ruthie would put on the superhero ring, and with Supergirl watching over them the kids would go back to sleep.

It was in those moments, alone with Rafe, that Elle would allow her own pain and fear to come out. He would hold her while she cried, never complaining about her emotional outbursts. Then once she was finished, he would carry her to his bed, make love to her, and then she would fall asleep in his arms.

During the day Rafe would cook breakfast, the kids would help with lunch, and she would cook dinner. In between, the children played board games and video games, built Legos, had tea parties, and played with Ruthie's dollhouse. Then they'd play outside, running in the snow, playing on the swing, laughing, and being regular children.

But every time Ruthie looked up at her with scared eyes to ask permission to do something, Elle was reminded that her little girl wasn't a regular child anymore.

Her ordeal had changed her, and as Ruthie's mother, Elle wanted nothing more than to soothe that pain away.

It sucked that she couldn't make this better for her daughter. Ruthie was still young, and while she was old enough that a kiss could no longer take away pain like it could when she was a toddler, she was still young enough that she needed her mom to make her world safe.

Instead, Elle had brought danger to them.

It was five days since she'd gotten her daughter back and her guilt was only growing. It felt tight beneath her skin, like it was a physical being that lived inside her, and although she went through the motions and tried to keep up a smile for Ruthie and Andy's benefit, she was struggling every bit as much as her daughter was.

Maybe more.

Because while Ruthie was an innocent victim, Elle couldn't help but feel like she was part perpetrator which gave her no right to be suffering. Suffering should be all for Ruthie. The focus should all be on her daughter, yet she was so aware of the fact that Rafe worried over both of them and made sure to take care of them. As much as she loved him for it, she also wished he would stop and treat her like the villain she truly was.

"Yep, you absolutely can play in the treehouse," she answered. Elle wanted to tell her daughter that there was no need to ever ask for permission to do anything ever again. That anything she wanted she could have. But Ruthie's counselor had pointed out that the little girl still needed boundaries, that she would heal from her ordeal, and that in a few short years Ruthie would reach her teens, and the last thing Elle would want was a child that believed she was in charge.

So instead, Elle just gave her permission, and hoped the therapist was right and that soon her child would start feeling safe enough to know she didn't have to ask to be allowed to do the simplest things.

True to Rafe's word, his friends had dropped off carloads of boxes of her and Ruthie's belongings. While she had expected a suitcase each filled with clothes and a few of Ruthie's toys, the guys and their women had gone above and beyond. Both her entire wardrobe and her daughter's had been boxed up, and their towels and bed linen. Photos of her and Ruthie now hung on the walls alongside pictures of Rafe and Andy, and at least eighty percent of her daughter's toys now lived in the playroom and Andy's room.

It made Rafe's house feel like their home, too, and she loved that.

Turned out she wasn't all that keen on moving slow after all.

Bundling the kids into their coats, scarves, beanies, and gloves as they ran outside, she and Rafe pulled on their own coats.

"I can't get over her always asking if she can do things," Elle whispered to Rafe as she watched Ruthie skip along after Andy toward the treehouse.

"It'll pass," Rafe assured her.

"Ruthie is a great kid, she was usually obedient, and it wasn't like she never asked if she could do things. But she was never like this. She didn't ask if she could play with her toys, read her books, or go outside. She knew the house rules and she just followed them. I hate seeing her so afraid of doing something wrong and being punished. I want her to feel safe again." Elle knew that the first time Ruthie did something without asking she was likely going to break down in tears because it would be the first step in Ruthie's journey to healing.

"It will happen when she's ready, it's only been a few days, honey."

"It hurts to see her hurting."

"I know." Rafe pulled her against him, using his bigger body to curl around her almost like a protective shield.

"It hurts worse knowing that her hurting is all my fault."

"Oh, honey, when are you going to stop doing that? Stop blaming yourself? Jimmy hurt both of you, he stalked you, he kidnapped your child, he hurt you, he almost raped you. This wasn't Ruthie's ordeal, it was *yours* and Ruthie's. You need to heal, too, I'm worried about you, I want you to talk to someone. A professional."

While it seemed like the most natural thing in the world to get her daughter help, Elle couldn't accept that she needed help, too.

She didn't feel like she deserved it.

What kind of mother put her own child in danger like she had?

She should have done more and fought harder to get the cops to take the stalking seriously. Gone to Sparrow earlier and asked for Prey's help. Something. Anything. What she had done hadn't been enough, and her daughter had paid the price.

Before she could tell Rafe that, Ruthie's scream tore through the air.

Both she and Rafe turned to see Andy sitting in the treehouse, and Ruthie halfway up the ladder, dangling off it, obviously having slipped as she climbed up.

Elle was moving, running toward her daughter before she even realized what she was doing. Why had she said yes to the treehouse? It was high in the tree, and while Ruthie had a good head for heights it was cold out and had rained overnight, the wooden planks nailed to the tree trunk would be slippery.

Seemed she failed her daughter no matter what she did.

Rafe overtook her and reached the tree first, but she was only moments behind, fear giving her extra speed.

Dangling six feet off the ground, Ruthie was high enough that on her own Elle wouldn't really be able to help much other than attempting to guide her daughter's feet back onto the wooden stairs, but Rafe was tall enough to just reach her, pick her up, and set her on the ground. She was about to demand he do just that when Andy spoke.

"It's okay, Ruthie. You can do it," the little boy said, all calm and confidence. "All you got to do is give me your hand." Andy was lying on his tummy on the treehouse floor, about two feet above Ruthie, his hand held out to her.

There wasn't even any hesitation, Ruthie just reached out and grabbed the offered hand.

"All you got to do now is put your feet back on the stairs, you just slipped is all," Andy said, still calm.

Listening to her friend's advice, Ruthie stopped wriggling her feet wildly, and instead, focused on what she was doing. One foot found a step, and then the other, and then with her hand still in Andy's she scrambled up the final steps and into the treehouse.

Heart still hammering in her chest, Elle couldn't help but be proud of her little girl. Even with nothing but air beneath her feet, nothing solid to get a footing on, she hadn't hesitated to reach out and take the help offered to her.

Yet Elle herself had been going to turn down whatever offer of help Rafe had been going to give her before Ruthie's screams.

"I did it, Mommy, did you see? And I only needed a little bit of help from Andy." Ruthie beamed down at her.

"You did awesome, sweetie. I'm so proud of you, even though you were scared you figured out what you needed to do."

"It was easy," Ruthie said, the same confidence that had been in Andy's voice now in hers. "Rafe said I could do anything. He said I just had to believe it. And I did. I believed. Because Rafe said that if I slipped he would catch me, or Andy would catch me, or you would catch me. And I had all three of you there so I knew I couldn't really fall."

Innocent words spoken by a child who had been through so much put Elle to shame. She hadn't been taking advantage of her safety net. Sure she was staying in Rafe's house because she felt safe there, and she cried in his arms each night, but she wasn't really letting him help her. She wasn't trusting that if she slipped—when she slipped—he would be waiting right there to catch her.

That was going to change.

CHAPTER
Sixteen

February 28th
11:53 P.M.

Panther hated this part of the night the most.

The waiting.

Waiting for the terrified screams of his girls to echo through the house.

Eleven days had passed since he and the rest of Bravo Team had crept into Elle's home and he'd opened that bedroom door to find her naked on the bed and seconds away from being raped. A lot had changed over that time. Elle and Ruthie had both put some lost weight back on and looked healthier. The four of them had grown close and felt like a family even if nothing was official yet. Andy and Ruthie had quickly become more than siblings, they were best friends, and Elle's daughter was never more at ease than when she played with his son.

Things with Elle were going better, too. She had agreed that she needed help, too, and although he knew it had been hard for her to admit—he knew she blamed herself for the whole ordeal and on some level likely always would—he knew she'd done it for her daughter. Ruthie needed her, and Elle wasn't going to let her down.

Everything felt so perfect. Almost *too* perfect.

Everyone on the compound was doing so well. Tank and Tillie were busy planning their spring wedding, Rock and Ariel would be following them with a wedding in the summer, and Scorpion was adamant he wanted to marry Jessica before their baby arrived in six months. Trick and Stephanie were still suffering from the ordeal in Liberia, and he completely understood how his friend felt seeing the shadows that haunted the eyes of the woman you would do literally anything for. But Stephanie was strong, a fighter, and with Trick's unwavering support, she was slowly recovering.

If they could just find and take down Leonid Baranov once and for all, then Panther was sure Axe and Beth could find their way back to one another, and then everything truly would be perfect for the people he cared about.

A high pitched scream filled the quiet house, and Panther quickly threw back the covers, closing his laptop and setting it on the night-stand. As much as he would love to have Elle spend the entire night in his bed, he knew she needed to fall asleep holding her daughter.

Andy met him in the hall like he did every night. Didn't matter how many times Panther told his son that he didn't have to get up when Ruthie or Elle had nightmares, the little boy had appointed himself Ruthie's protector and he never failed to be there for her.

In the bedroom—a room he hoped one day might become Ruthie's —his girls clung to one another on the bed. They were bathed in the warm light of the fairy lights, and even through their tears they both smiled when he and Andy entered the room.

"Our heroes," Elle said, making Ruthie giggle.

The little girl scrambled off the bed. "I want the Hulk watching over us tonight," she exclaimed.

"How come?" Andy asked, sounding surprised since Supergirl was Ruthie's favorite and she always felt safest when the superhero watched over her at night.

"Cos he's your favorite, silly," Ruthie replied like it was obvious.

Both children were giggling as they scurried off to Andy's room, and

Panther turned to Elle, ready for her to break down in tears. These stolen moments in the middle of the night when she knew her daughter was safe and happy with Andy in his room were the only ones she allowed herself the freedom to cry.

Only tonight, no tears brimmed in her big, brown eyes.

"Are you okay?" he asked, startled by the change in their routine.

"I ... think I am," Elle answered slowly. "I mean, I'm not. I won't ever really be okay again because those memories of the month my daughter was gone are always going to be with me. But you keep catching me every time I slip, and ... I think ... no ... I *know* that I'm going to be okay."

"Always, honey. I will *always* be there to catch you when you slip. Nothing could ever keep me away from you. From either of my girls."

Elle's face transformed into the most breathtaking smile. "I love it when you call me and Ruthie your girls. It's just been the two of us for so long. My ex never really cared about me, not the way you do. I didn't want to see it at the time, but now, with you, it's so obvious he never loved me. He didn't even love his own daughter. But you're so good with her, and she likes you so much. You make her feel safe, but you also make her feel brave, and you already care about her so much more than her father and that means the world to me."

"She's a special little girl, just like her mommy. That you trust me with the most precious thing in your life means the world to me. I won't break that trust."

Climbing onto her knees, she crawled toward him. "I know you won't and that makes me like you even more. You know I would never do anything to hurt Andy either. I love him. He was everything I needed when Ruthie wasn't here. I felt guilty at first, almost like I was using him, but what I feel for him is genuine, real, separate from what I feel for Ruthie. I love him for him, for the amazing, sweet, generous, thoughtful, kind, intelligent, funny boy he is."

"You're perfect, you know that?" The love Elle shone so brightly on his son was the exact opposite of what the boy's own mother had felt for him. To Marcia, Andy had been a responsibility, one she didn't want and had abandoned, but Elle just loved him because she wanted to.

"So you keep saying." Elle giggled. "Want to show me?"

"You bet I do." Scooping his woman into his arms, he carried her back to his bed, and like he did every night, he stood her on her feet and kissed the now fading bruises on her face. Then he stripped off her tank top and kissed the still dark bruises littering her chest.

Normally, he liked to take his time, bring her to the edge of orgasm and then pull back before building her up again and pulling back, repeating the process until he knew the orgasm he gave her would consume her mind, body, and soul. But tonight felt different, tonight he felt the need to hurry up and be inside her.

"You up for being on top tonight, honey?" With her cracked ribs they'd been taking things easy. He still made her come several times, but he always made sure he did all the work so she didn't hurt herself.

Tonight he wanted to watch her take what she needed from him.

"I'm up for any way you want me," she said with a smile that if he wasn't already rock hard would have done the job in an instant.

Stripping her out of her pajama pants, he shed his own and then lay down on the bed, leaving her to do what she wanted. For a moment, Elle just stood there staring at him. Panther wasn't one for fake modesty, he worked hard for the cut body he had, but he loved the way Elle's gaze roamed it, so greedily like she didn't know what to touch first.

Turned out to be his jaw. A gentle fingertip trailed along it then down his neck, tracing his pecs and every line of his six pack. She circled his erect length without touching it and then climbed onto the bed, straddling his thighs.

Then she touched.

Greedily.

Hungrily.

Her fingers curled around him, settling him in her palm as she ran her hand up and down his length, slowly at first but then faster, and he wondered if she was going to play with him like he played with her. Bringing him right to the edge without letting him tumble over it.

But it seemed his girl didn't have the same patience he did because when she could feel his length twitch at her touch, she moved so she was positioned above him. When she sank down she took only his tip inside her, rolling her hips a few times before sinking down to take another inch.

So Elle had a little more patience than he'd thought because she took him one inch at a time. She paused after each inch to roll her hips, enjoying the feeling of him and the way he grunted and groaned and had to curl his fingers into fists so he didn't just grab her hips and slam into her until he filled her up.

Another inch, and then another, and finally he was buried deep. Panther was about a half second away from coming but his woman wasn't quite there yet. Reaching between them, he gathered some of her juices and smeared them over her bundle of nerves. Then as Elle lifted her hips up until just his tip remained inside her, then sank down again to take all of him, he made good use of his fingers on her bud, working her until her breathing grew ragged, her skin flushed, and her internal muscles quivered.

Still, Elle kept the pace slow, steady, torturous.

Since they had been together enough times for him to know exactly what she liked and how to get her to come even when she thought she couldn't because he'd already made her orgasm several times, Panther cheated a little to speed things up. Rolling her bud just the way she liked it, Elle tossed back her head and moaned.

It only took one more tweak of her bundle of nerves between his thumb and forefinger and her orgasm exploded inside her. When her body clamped around him, he allowed himself his own release, exploding inside Elle.

One day soon, when the time was right, he hoped he and Elle would create a baby together, the final piece of their little family, making them and their lives complete. But as he pulled his woman down to rest against his chest, keeping himself inside her, not ready to break that connection yet, he knew that the time wasn't right yet. Now was a time for healing, for exploring this relationship, and growing and building a steady foundation.

Still, he couldn't wait until the day when he pressed his hand to her stomach and felt the life they had created moving inside her. He'd missed out on a lot when Marcia was pregnant with Andy, but he wasn't going to miss a single second when Elle was pregnant with his baby.

Hindsight was definitely twenty twenty because, looking back, he knew he had never loved Marcia the way he ought to have because the feelings he'd had for her didn't even come close to what he already felt for Elle.

She sighed and snuggled closer against his chest as sleep took her under, and he took the opportunity to say the words when he knew they wouldn't have to discuss them. They were true, but Elle might think it was too soon and he couldn't mean them yet.

But he did.

"I love you, Elle," he whispered against her forehead, then he pressed his lips there in a soft kiss before holding his woman tight and allowing sleep to come now that he had her in his arms.

Right where she belonged.

~

March 9th
   2:37 P.M.

"Mommy, look!"

At her daughter's excited squeal, Elle looked up from the sandwiches she was setting up on the picnic blanket. "What's wrong?"

"Nothing, look!" Ruthie squealed again, this time holding out the apple she had been snacking on because to quote, she was dying of hunger. Embedded in the apple was one of Ruthie's front teeth. The tooth had been loose for a week, and although she'd told her daughter to stop fiddling with it, every time she looked at the girl she could see that Ruthie was working that loose tooth with her tongue, dying for it to fall out.

"Oh, wow, your tooth came out," she exclaimed, remembering how much fun that had been as a child. Now watching her daughter tug on the tooth, bending it backward and forward, poking at it with her tongue made her feel a little queasy, even as she remembered doing the exact same things when she was a kid.

"That means you get to leave it out for the tooth fairy tonight," Andy said, dropping to his knees beside Ruthie, his voice just as excited.

For a moment, the smile fell off Ruthie's face and she looked thoughtful. Elle knew she wasn't worried about the tooth fairy, this wasn't the first tooth her daughter had lost, so she wondered what was running through her little girl's head.

She didn't push though. Over the last couple of weeks she had learned to respect Ruthie's need to process what she wanted to say before she said it. While there was a part of Elle that wished her impulsive, vivacious, bubbly daughter would come back, she also admired Ruthie's strength and bravery, and admitted that even though she didn't like it, the ordeal had forced her daughter to grow up a lot and much too quickly.

"Mom?"

"Yeah, sweetie?"

"Do you think it would be okay if I went to sleep in Andy's room tonight?"

Elle stilled. She wanted to yell that it wouldn't be okay, that she needed the reassurance of feeling her daughter's small body snuggled against hers, but this was a big milestone for Ruthie and she wasn't going to ruin it or take it away from her. If Ruthie felt safe enough in Rafe and Andy's home—a place that now felt like their home, too—then she was so proud of her for finding the courage to fight her fears.

"If you want to sleep in Andy's room, that's fine with me," she answered.

"Are you ..." Ruthie trailed off, hesitating. "Are you going to be okay to sleep without me?"

How perceptive her intelligent little girl was.

But this wasn't about Elle. This was about Ruthie. And if her daughter was ready to go to sleep for the first time since being rescued without her mom by her side, then Elle had no choice but to be ready to take this leap as well.

Reaching over, she grabbed Ruthie's arms and tugged until her daughter was in her lap. "I will be okay, little unicorn girl. I promise.

And you know I'll be right down the hall if you change your mind or you need me."

"In Dad's bed," Andy added like he already knew and accepted that she and his dad were together, and if Elle wasn't going to sleep in Mrs. Pfeffer's room with Ruthie then it was a foregone conclusion that she would be sleeping in his father's room.

Ruffling the boy's hair, she smiled at him. "Yeah, in your dad's bed."

They hadn't sat the kids down and given them a talk about the future, but they also hadn't tried to hide that they were together. That was probably going to have to change. She and Rafe had jumped right into the deep end, focusing on Ruthie's healing, but they'd done it together as a team, a team she never wanted to break up. So it was time to sit the kids down and make sure they understood what was going on and had a chance to voice any questions or concerns.

"Mom, can I go put the tooth under my pillow now?" Ruthie asked. As well as her daughter was doing, she still hadn't reached the stage where she could do things without getting permission first.

"Sure can," she replied, even though letting the kids go back to the cabin meant they would be out of her sight for a few minutes at least. "But straight there, straight back."

"Okay, Mom," Ruthie agreed as both kids bounced to their feet and ran off toward the house.

"What are those two up to?" Rafe asked from the grill where he was busy barbecuing.

"Ruthie lost a tooth, she wants to put it under her pillow ready for the tooth fairy. Under the pillow in Andy's room." She sighed and fought back tears, torn between her fears of not having her daughter in her arms, and her pride and awe of her little girl and her strength.

Knowing how hard this was for her, Rafe set down the tongs and came to pull her up and into his arms. "She's healing, honey, you are, too. It's okay to be scared about not having her with you when you go to sleep, but she'll be just in the next room, and you can check on her as many times as you need to. And I'll be right there with you, holding you, making love to you, and keeping you safe in my arms."

Snuggling closer into his embrace, Elle forced herself to let go of the anxiety. She couldn't keep Ruthie glued to her side for the rest of the girl's life, and she didn't want the ordeal to shape every part of Ruthie's future. She wanted her daughter to learn, to do the things she enjoyed, to graduate high school and go off to college, to fall in love one day and get married and have a family of her own.

She wanted Ruthie to have a normal life, and that meant taking this first step toward her daughter getting her independence back.

"Have I told you today how grateful I am to have you in my life?" she asked, looking up at Rafe.

He smiled down at her. "Nope, but you can show me tonight after we tuck the kids in."

Middle of the woods or not, kids returning at any second, the rest of Bravo Team joining them at any moment, Elle would have thrown all caution to the wind and made love to her man right there if throats hadn't cleared behind them, and she turned to see all of Bravo Team standing there.

"Everything okay, love birds?" Scorpion teased, his smile so big and wide as he held his woman close to his side.

"Perfect," Elle replied.

"Perfect," Rafe echoed.

"Where were the munchkins off to in such a hurry?" Trick asked.

"Ruthie lost a tooth," she explained. "And apparently couldn't wait to go and get it all ready for the tooth fairy tonight."

"Tooth fairy," Jessica murmured then tears filled her eyes and began to trickle down her cheeks.

Scorpion rolled his eyes, but his gaze was tender as he tugged Jessica in front of him and wrapped his arms around her. "Don't mind her, apparently now that she knows she's pregnant she's being hit by the pregnancy hormones all at once. Cries about *everything*."

"I do not." Jessica sniffed through her tears, swatting at her boyfriend's shoulder.

"Sure you don't, honey," Scorpion said with just enough mocking in his tone to tease his woman. "Just so you know, guys, the crying gets evened out by the increased sex drive during pregnancy."

"Mason!" Jessica exclaimed. "Don't say that."

Scorpion just laughed. "It's true. We've already had sex three times today," he said, making Jessica groan and bury her face in her hands.

"Huh, didn't know about that," Tank said thoughtfully, eyeing his fiancée.

"Don't go getting any ideas, mister. I want to focus on the wedding before we add in anything else. The wedding that is only four weeks away," Tillie said, a hint of anxiety in her tone.

"It's just a party," Tank said with a shrug, making his tiny fiancée slug him in the stomach.

"Did you just call our wedding a party?" Tillie demanded.

"All I care about is making you my wife, the rest is just stuff to make you happy," Tank replied, and Tillie softened, grabbing his shoulders and pulling him down for a kiss.

"I'm glad you're getting married first," Ariel piped up. "That way Sebastian and I can just steal all your ideas."

"Doesn't matter to me, I just want the next five months to hurry up and go on by so I can finally make you my wife," Rock told his fiancée.

"I wish the baby was due in the fall instead of late summer." Jessica sighed. "I love when the leaves change color, and I would have loved to get married out here surrounded by nature. But Mason insists we have to be married before the baby comes."

"Damn right I do," Mason muttered.

"Maybe you guys could do a fall wedding," Jessica said hopefully to Trick and Stephanie.

"Hold up there, darlin', I haven't even proposed to her yet," Trick said, obviously amused.

"Yet," Jessica added. "There's time. Tank and Tillie have spring covered. Mason and I will probably join Rock and Ariel for a summer wedding, then you two can have fall, and those two should be ready to get married by winter," she teased, pointing to her and Rafe.

Maybe that should make her nervous, already thinking about marriage, but the thing was it didn't.

Elle had learned what true fear felt like, and the idea of marrying Rafe didn't even fill her with a hint of anxiety. Children's giggles told her the kids were coming back, and with Rafe's team all around her it felt like being surrounded by a huge family who teased one another but who had each other's backs no matter what.

She'd never had that before and she liked this.

Liked it enough to have a spark of excitement flicker to life inside her at the thought that one day she might stand in these woods and marry Rafe. Or stand in a church, or on a beach, it didn't matter because their kids would be there with them, along with this big extended family, and finally Elle would find her place in the world.

CHAPTER
Seventeen

March 19th
8:25 A.M.

"You can't do that," Ruthie said staring at him incredulously.

"Sure can," Panther shot back, hiding his grin at the look of complete and utter shock on the little girl's face.

"I've never seen you do it," Andy piped up.

"Just because you haven't seen me do it doesn't mean I can't," he told his son.

"I don't think you can. I don't think *anyone* can," Ruthie said adamantly.

Elle watched the exchange from the table, an amused smile on her face. She had no idea where he was going with this but she knew he was up to something.

She was right, teasing the kids was so much fun and he knew he was going to prove them both wrong.

"Well, maybe not anyone can, princess, but I can," he told her as he grabbed the butter from the fridge. Breakfast time was his favorite time of the day. Usually, they ate lunch and dinner at the table as well, but breakfast was his meal to cook and he liked taking care of his family.

"Prove it," Andy said, looking every bit as doubtful as Ruthie did.

"I'll do just that," he said confidently, grabbing peanut butter from the pantry and setting it and the butter beside the toaster and the four plates waiting for their toast.

"You can't cut the toast into a dinosaur shape, it can't be done," Ruthie insisted adamantly.

"Totally can't," Andy added.

"About to prove you both wrong, kiddos," he told them.

"But, Dad, you're not so great at drawing," Andy said gently like he was breaking bad news Panther might not be aware of.

"Never said anything about drawing, bud," he reminded the boy.

"But if you can't even draw a dinosaur how can you cut one with a knife in toast?" Andy asked, perplexed.

"I'm better with a knife than a pencil." He shrugged, making Elle snort her tea and choke herself. "You okay, honey?" he asked, filling a glass with water and delivering it to her.

"What *are* you up to?" she asked, taking it and drinking the water to clear her throat.

"Just making the kids breakfast. Not my fault they asked for their toast cut in an interesting shape and then insulted me by telling me I can't do dinosaurs," he teased, making both kids giggle. Elle and Ruthie had been there for just over a month, long enough that Ruthie no longer stiffened instinctively when he was too close, long enough that she was comfortable with him, knew when he was teasing, and that she wasn't going to get in trouble and be punished.

Every day he felt the bond he was building with the little girl, and the one with her mother, growing stronger, and he loved it.

Toast popped up and he went to the cupboard to grab his secret weapon. The kids were watching with interest as he hid what he was carrying on his way back to the toaster. Buttering all four slices, he added peanut butter to the kids' ones, and blackberry jam to Elle's. Then he opened the container of cookie cutters, found the dinosaur, and cut all four slices.

"See, dinosaurs," he said as he balanced the three plates in his hands and delivered them to the table.

"Dinosaurs," Ruthie breathed in amazement, but his son eyed it suspiciously.

"How did you do that? They look too good," Andy said, obviously not caring about sparing his dad's feelings.

"Ta-da," he said, picking up the cookie cutter and setting it in the middle of the table.

"Dad, that's cheating." Andy looked aghast, but both Elle and Ruthie burst into laughter.

"Not cheating at all, bud. You said you wanted your toast cut in the shape of a dinosaur. Voila, dinosaurs."

"But you're supposed to cut the toast with a knife," Andy protested.

Putting four more slices in the toaster, Panther grabbed his plate and joined the others at the table. "Na-uh," he said. "You never specified that I had to use a knife, you just said you wanted the toast cut like a dinosaur, and that's exactly what I did."

"Still think it's cheating," Andy grumbled as he picked up his dinosaur toast and took a bite.

"I think it's amazing," Ruthie piped up. "Can you do a princess next?"

"Don't have a princess cookie cutter, sorry, princess." Although as soon as breakfast was done he would hop on his computer and find a place that sold them and order one. "But I do have a crown. Would my princess like a crown for her next slice of toast?"

Ruthie beamed at him, and he felt that smile down to his soul. Damn, he was falling in love with this kid right along with her mother. They were the sweetest pair. So similar in so many ways, and other than Ruthie's eyes having her father's blue gray color, she was her mother's absolute mini.

Nothing he had ever done in life, other than loving his son, had ever been easier than falling for the mother daughter pair. They just made it so easy.

"Yes please," Ruthie exclaimed, picking up her dinosaur and taking a huge bite, clearly in a hurry to get it eaten so she could have her crown.

"Does Mommy also want a crown, my queen," he asked as he started eating his toast.

"If Ruthie's a princess, and Elle's a queen, then that means I'm a prince," Andy said, his annoyance over being tricked with the cookie cutter forgotten.

"Sure does, my prince. It also means I'm the king." Panther made a big show of pretending to put a crown on his head, making the others laugh.

"But we can't really be kings and queens," Ruthie said, sounding disappointed.

"Why not?" Elle asked.

"Because what are we kings and queens of? We don't have a country. I mean, we do but it's just regular old America. If we were real kings and queens we'd have our own country," Ruthie explained.

"Hmm, I guess that is a problem." He tapped his chin thoughtfully. "I suppose we'll have to make up our own country then. We'll be the kings and queens, princes and princesses of ... Cabinland."

The kids giggled like he hoped they would.

"Cabinland?" Andy groaned. "Dad, that's a terrible name for a country."

"You think you can come up with something better?" he asked.

"The dinosaur toast could come up with something better," Andy shot back. Sometimes, like right now, like this whole last month when his son had been such a support to Ruthie, his little boy seemed so grown up. Two more years and he'd hit double digits, then the teenage years would be right around the corner.

It was going too fast.

A knock on his cabin door had him pushing away from the table. He gave a low bow. "I will leave my subjects to determine the name of our kingdom while I go see to whoever is at the door."

"Hey, I'm not your subject I'm the queen," Elle called out to him, so he was laughing as he pulled open the door.

Assuming it was going to be one of the guys or their women—not that anyone had texted to say they were stopping by but who else would it be—he was already bowing as he flung the door open. "Welcome to the kingdom of Cabin—" The words died on his lips when he saw who was standing there.

No.

Impossible.

In fact, it was so impossible that Panther actually pinched himself, positive he must be dreaming because that was a much more plausible option than admitting who was standing before him was really standing before him.

"What are you doing here?" he asked, not even bothering to hide his shock or irritation. When he found out who had allowed her onto the compound, some not so pleasant words would exchanged.

His ex-wife could not have gained access to the compound without someone letting her in. She hadn't been part of his life for well over seven years, she didn't know the code to the gate.

"I ... came to see you ... and ..." Marcia trailed off, not even able to speak their son's name.

Panther didn't want anything to ruin the fun he'd been having, but his ex was like a bucket of ice water. She took the fun out of everything. Nothing she could say would convince him she had really come, after all this time, just to pop in and say hi to the ex-husband and son she had abandoned so casually.

"Sure." He gave a mocking laugh. "Course you did. And what possible reason could there be for you to make time in your busy schedule to come and see the boy you gave birth to?"

If you'd asked him, he would have said nothing could have made this day any worse than it had become.

He would have been wrong.

"I came because I realize I made a mistake walking away from the two most important men in my life. I came because I want a second chance. I came because I want you and Andy back."

The shriek of the smoke alarm told him he'd forgotten about the toast, and so had the rest of his little kingdom.

Only it wasn't his kingdom anymore.

It had just gone up in smoke.

～

March 19th
  9:04 A.M.

"What about Poopyland?" Andy said with a grin, causing both children to burst into fits of hysterical laughter.

Elle rolled her eyes.

Poopyland, could anyone other than a little kid think that was a good idea? Maybe a teenage boy would agree it was funny, although a teen would probably have made it a little cruder.

"I am not going to be the queen of a place called Poopyland," she told the kids, using her best royal voice.

The kids just giggled some more, and then the smoke alarm began to blare, and she looked over to see smoke coming out of the toaster. The toaster she had completely forgotten about because usually Rafe made breakfast and he took care of everything.

"Rafe, the toaster is smoking," she called out as she hurried over and unplugged the appliance. "Oops, your kingdom got a little distracted," she added when she heard him enter the kitchen.

Everything suddenly got really quiet.

The kids stopped giggling.

Rafe must have switched off the alarm because it was no longer shrieking at them, but he hadn't said anything.

A bad feeling settled in her gut.

Something was wrong.

Call her a coward, but a huge part of her didn't want to turn around and find out what it was. She wanted to stay right there in her happy little bubble, pretending to be queen of her happy little kingdom.

But hiding wouldn't change anything.

So she pulled herself together and turned around to find an attractive woman standing beside Rafe. She didn't have to ask the woman's identity, she knew exactly who she was because she had the exact same hazel eyes as Andy.

This was Andy's mother.

Or at least, the woman who had given birth to him since Elle hardly believed you could call yourself a mother when you abandoned your baby for seven years and made not a single attempt to make contact with him.

"What's going on?" she asked, dismayed when her voice came out strangled and filled with anxiety. Rafe had been so sweet to her and Ruthie, he'd promised them that he would always be there for them, but now he had his ex in his home and she didn't know what to think. Elle definitely knew she felt stupid, almost like she had been played this whole time.

Only that wasn't possible.

Rafe hadn't lied to her. He wouldn't do that.

"Elle, this is Marcia. Marcia, this is Elle and her daughter Ruthie," Rafe said so formerly that whatever hope she had been clinging to vanished.

He was speaking about her and her daughter like they were strangers. People who just happened to be in his house at nine in the morning, like they hadn't spent every day for the last month there. Like she hadn't spent the last month sleeping in his bed, making love to him, playing with his son, cooking and cleaning, and doing laundry.

Like they hadn't spent the last month living like a family.

Whether Ruthie sensed her distress or her daughter just suddenly felt as uncomfortable as she did, the little girl scrambled out of her chair, ran over to Elle, wrapped her arms around her waist, and pressed herself close.

There was pain in Rafe's eyes, but he didn't comment on Ruthie's sudden shift in behavior. Just nodded to Andy who was sitting at the table staring at the woman in shock.

"Marcia, this is Andy. And Andy this is—"

"I know who she is," Andy cut in, using a voice she'd never heard the boy use. Andy was sweet and even tempered. Sure, he was eight years old and he sometimes pouted and complained, but he was such a happy child that hearing him sound so angry was a shock.

Taking a hesitant step toward the boy, Marcia gave him a smile. "Hi, honey. I'm your—"

"No." Andy shook his head violently. "You're not my mother." The little boy's gaze cut to her, and Elle felt every bit as tossed into the stormy ocean as he did.

While nothing was official, she had thought she and Rafe were building a future. She had already begun to think of him as Ruthie's father, the same way she had started to think of herself as Andy's mother. With neither other biological parent in the picture, it was easier to feel yourself step into the role because you weren't worried about stepping on someone else's toes.

"I don't know you," Andy said firmly.

"I was kind of hoping we could get to know one another," Marcia said uncertainly.

Elle kept waiting for Rafe to say something. To tell the woman that she'd had a chance to be Andy's mom and his wife, and she'd thrown it away. But he didn't say anything. He just stood there like he was in shock, not saying or doing anything.

Although, really that told her everything she needed to know.

Andy was his son, and Marcia was the boy's mother. If it came down to a choice between Andy and Marcia, or her and Ruthie, then she knew what he was going to choose.

She couldn't even really be angry with him about it. Because if it was a choice between her child and someone else she would choose her daughter every time.

Only ...

Since she had already begun to think of Andy as hers, she wasn't sure she could toss him aside like it seemed Rafe wanted to do to Ruthie.

Maybe she couldn't be angry with him about choosing his ex over her, but she sure as heck could be upset about it. Her daughter had been through so much, and Elle had thought that she and Rafe were building a safe place for Ruthie. A place to heal, to feel safe, to find herself again.

Rafe wouldn't rip that away from the little girl.

She was overreacting.

Sure, he'd had a shock, but that didn't mean he was throwing her and her daughter away.

"Rafe?" she asked, bringing Ruthie with her as she walked toward him. She needed him to tell her that everything was going to be okay, that Marcia was leaving and she wasn't coming back. That she'd lost her chance to be his wife and Andy's mother.

Instead, he took a step back as she approached, holding up a hand to halt her.

Right there, in that very moment, her heart broke into a thousand pieces. A million pieces. A decillion pieces.

"It's over," Elle said, not sure if she was asking him, or telling him, or telling herself.

"No, damn it, Elle." Rafe looked agitated as he dragged his fingers down his face then speared them through his locks. "I just ... I need some time."

"Time?" she echoed. He was telling her to leave, she knew that, she was just having a hard time comprehending it. Ruthie didn't want to go home, she didn't want to go home, this had become their home, but now in an instant it was all gone.

"Please. I need to talk to Marcia and Andy. I need to figure out what's going on. I need to figure out what's best for my son and what I want."

It was the last one that hurt the most.

Because she already knew what she wanted, and even if her ex was to walk back into her life and tell her he wanted her and Ruthie back, she would tell him no. That it was too late, that she was already in love with another man and had never really loved him. If he wanted access to Ruthie she would allow a court to figure that out, the last thing she would want was for her daughter to resent her cutting her biological father out of her life.

But she would never tell Rafe to leave.

Never.

Ever.

If there was a problem they would face it together because that's what you did when you had a partner. Only what did she really know about having a partner? All her life she'd been left to fend for herself, parents who only wanted a prodigy to continue their work, and a husband who only wanted a slave to take care of him. She had never really had a partner and it looked like she still didn't.

First sign of trouble and Rafe was sending her away.

Since words were beyond her right now, and she had no idea how she was going to pack up all their belongings and take them all back with her, she simply gave a single nod of her head. Of all of Ruthie's toys that were there, the only thing she really needed was her stuffed unicorn that she slept with and it was already downstairs on the couch from when the kids were watching cartoons earlier.

Taking her daughter's hand, she walked out of the kitchen with her head held high, grabbed her purse and the unicorn, and walked away from the fairytale future she thought was going to be hers.

A future that was now forever stained with the sour smell of burned toast and all that it represented.

CHAPTER
Eighteen

March 19th
    9:16 A.M.

This couldn't be happening.

Yet the finality of the sound of his front door closing confirmed that it was indeed happening.

No going back.

Panther was all too aware that he might have just ruined the best thing to ever happen to him outside of his son and lost Elle and Ruthie for good.

Anger flooded through him.

How dare Marcia come back now. She'd had seven years where she could have decided that she was sorry she'd walked out on her husband and son without discussion, without warning, seemingly without regret.

So why was she there now?

Not for one second did he buy that she truly wanted a second chance. If she loved Andy the way she was supposed to, there was no way on earth she could have just walked away from him and stayed away. If it was just about their marriage, about her not wanting to live the military lifestyle anymore, she could have just divorced him, there had been no need to sign away her parental right.

Parental rights she said she wanted back.

If he believed her.

Which he didn't.

"What's this all about, Marcia?" he demanded, doing his best to ignore the sound of the car engine turning on outside. The car that would take Elle and Ruthie away from him, away from where they belonged.

It was on the tip of his tongue to call them back, to tell them he couldn't bear for them to leave.

But then he glanced at his son and ... he couldn't do it.

All Panther had wanted as a child was for his parents to be together. He'd hated the stress of the divorce, hated being bounced between houses, hated that his step-siblings spent more time with his parents than he did, and hated when new babies had come along and he'd felt left out and unwanted.

How could he do that to his son?

There was no way he could allow history to repeat itself, and cause his son the same pain he had lived with, the feelings of being unwanted and unimportant. As much as he hated to send Elle away, he had to be sure he was doing what was in his son's best interest.

"I missed you," she said, batting her big hazel eyes like she used to do when they were young.

Only they weren't teenagers anymore and too much time has passed. One thing he knew for certain was that he wasn't in love with this woman and never had been. Back then, he'd believed that he was, but now that he'd experienced the depth of feelings he had for Elle, how strong they were already, he knew that it had been a whole lot more lust than love with Marcia.

Giving a humorless laugh he rolled his eyes. "Yeah. Sure. I totally believe that. Seven years, Marcia. It's been seven years since you walked away, I'm going to ask you again, what is this all about?"

Tears shimmered in her eyes, and she wrung her hands together in front of her. "I *did* miss you guys, okay? I finally realized that I made a mistake and I came back to rectify it. I want to be your wife again, I want to get to know my son."

"I'm not your son," Andy snapped in an angry tone Panther had never heard come out of his sweet little boy's mouth. There had been plenty of times Andy had been angry, thrown tantrums, grumbled and complained, but nothing like this.

"Andy," he warned. Regardless of whether or not his son was hurting, this was the woman who gave birth to him and he needed to show her due respect.

"What?" Andy turned his glare from Marcia to him. It was more than obvious his son was angry, hurt, and confused, and for the first time Panther realized it might have been a mistake to have Elle and Ruthie move in with them so quickly.

Everything had gone at breakneck speed given the situation with Ruthie's abduction. Elle had needed the support, hadn't been able to stay alone any longer, and he'd been filled with a need to take care of her. Then Ruthie had been afraid to go back home, and he'd wanted the two of them there where he could watch over them.

At the time it had seemed so simple, but now he realized that they might have moved too quickly because he'd just thrown Elle and Ruthie to the wolves. Sent them home alone without the support system they had been used to.

"You show your mother respect," he told his son.

"Why? She didn't show me no respect when she left. Why did you make Elle and Ruthie leave?"

"Because this is your mother. We were married, I need to sort things out with her." His son was young and didn't understand about grown-up relationships, but Panther knew how attached he was to Elle and her daughter so he was prepared to explain himself.

"Work what out?"

"Work out where we go from here." Did he believe that Marcia had suddenly had a change of heart and wanted to find a way to get back to where they had been before? No, not completely. Even if she did want to rekindle their relationship, was he interested in doing that? No, not at all.

His future was with Elle, Panther believed that wholeheartedly, but there was no way in good conscience he could not make absolute sure he was making the right choices for his son. If nothing else, Andy should have some sort of relationship with his mother if it was what she truly did want.

Andy tossed a glare Marcia's way. "I don't want it to work out with her. I want Elle and Ruthie back. Ruthie will be scared tonight because she doesn't have the ring, and if Elle has bad dreams then you won't be there."

"Elle and Ruthie will be okay," he soothed, even as guilt soured his gut. This was their safe place, he knew that, and he had just ripped it away from them, without warning, without explanation. Panther had always felt like he wasn't the bad guy when it came to his relationship with Marcia and the way it had fallen apart, but when it came to his relationship with Elle he was absolutely the bad guy.

"They won't be okay because we're not there," Andy yelled, then he ran from the room, his footsteps thumping on the stairs as he ran up them, presumably to his bedroom.

This was going from bad to worse. The last thing he wanted to do was upset his son, he was trying his best to do the right thing for Andy.

Seemed like he was hurting everyone.

"Sorry about that," he said as he scrubbed his fingers down his face, wishing he could just go back in time just an hour ago to when everything was perfect. When he was waking up with the woman he was falling in love with in his arms, when they came downstairs to the sounds of the kids giggles as they watched cartoons, when they were all around the table laughing and having breakfast together.

A hand tentatively touched his shoulder, but he shrugged it off.

He didn't want Marcia's touch, didn't want her comfort, or her presence messing up the perfect life he was building.

Maybe if she had come back earlier before he'd realized the lack of feelings he'd had for the woman he had married, then maybe he would have taken this opportunity for a second chance. But things had changed and he didn't want to go back, he wanted to go forward, and going forward didn't include restarting a relationship with his ex.

"I didn't know you were ... involved," Marcia stammered.

"If you had, would you have come back?"

While she hesitated for a moment, she still nodded. "I wanted to see you and my son. I'm sorry to have ruined whatever you had with that woman, but this is my family and I can't be sorry for fighting for them."

Irritation had him turning his back on her. "Too little too late, Marcia. I won't stand in the way of you spending time with Andy and getting to know him. But he doesn't know you. You want to see him, you do it here where he feels safe. But just picking things back up like the last seven years never happened, that won't happen."

"I want you back, Rafe," she said softly. "I want it all. I won't settle for just a relationship with our son, I want him to have everything. I hate that I stole what should have been a perfect family life for him. The kind of life neither of us were given by our parents. I can't go back, I can't erase my mistakes, but I can rectify them. I can fight for my family. I can fight for my son to have the life he should have had all along, with his parents together, raising him as a team. If you don't object, I'll come back tomorrow morning to spend some time with Andy. And you."

With that, Marcia walked past him and out of the cabin leaving him standing there feeling trapped. He didn't want a future with Marcia, but more than anything he wanted his son to have what he had never had.

A happy family with his mom and his dad.

Problem was, he also wanted a future with Elle and Ruthie, and he couldn't have both.

∽

March 19th
8:41 P.M.

"I don't want to go to bed, Mommy," Ruthie yelled.

Her daughter was distraught bordering on hysterical, and honestly, Elle couldn't say that she was doing all that much better herself.

The little girl wasn't the only one who dreaded going to sleep. It was one thing to know that if nightmares came for you while you were vulnerable that someone would be there to hold you while you wept, to soothe and comfort you. It was completely another to know that if those nightmares came for you, you would have to face them alone.

But neither she nor Ruthie had a choice.

This was their reality now, and the sooner they got used to it the better. For both of them.

It had been a long day. They'd stopped off at the mall on the way back to their house—a house which was no longer home in her mind but just a building—and stocked up on everything they would need to get through the next few days. Clothes, toiletries, food, and toys. Elle didn't care what it cost to buy stuff they didn't need so long as she didn't have to talk to Rafe or anyone else on Bravo Team until she had her composure back in place.

Of course, she knew the conversation was inevitable, she wasn't going to leave behind all her photos and mementoes of Ruthie's life, but she could live without those things for a little while. Once she felt back in control, she'd call one of the women and ask if they could help her organize boxing up all her and Ruthie's things and deliver them to the house.

Problem was, the one thing both she and her daughter needed the most was the one thing they couldn't have.

Rafe and Andy, and the safe place they had been creating there.

With that safety net ripped away from them, Elle knew both she and her child were floundering, left adrift with no life ring in an ocean that would absolutely toss them about and drown them.

Well, it would try to drown them, but she wasn't going to allow her daughter to go under. Whatever happened she would make sure that Ruthie was okay. That would be her entire focus, and maybe then, she wouldn't have to think about the huge gaping hole Rafe had left in her heart when he sent her away.

Doing her best to cling to a calm she most certainly was not feeling —Elle absolutely wanted to yell, scream, and cry just as Ruthie had done all day—she stroked a hand down Ruthie's tangled locks. "I know you don't, my sweet little unicorn girl, but you need sleep and its already past your bedtime."

"But what if a bad man comes? Rafe isn't here to save us, and Andy isn't here, and I don't have the ring and Supergirl." Ruthie sobbed helplessly.

Never before had Elle felt so ill-equipped to deal with her own child.

Sure, there had been a whole lot of challenges, especially in those early months when she was still learning about a baby's needs and how to care for one. But as Ruthie grew older, Elle's confidence grew along with her. Every challenge she faced confident in the knowledge that she loved her daughter and that was what mattered the most.

Now her confidence was shaken.

Knowing that she was responsible for her daughter's ordeal and her current state of hysteria made Elle feel not only incompetent but dangerous to her child. She should have known better than to allow two people she hardly knew to so quickly become so important to her seven-year-old daughter.

Selfish.

That's what she'd been.

She had agreed to stay with Rafe because it was what *she* needed.

In putting her needs before her daughter's, there was no one else responsible for Ruthie's pain other than herself.

Unable to fight back her own tears, they trickled down her cheeks and she didn't bother to wipe them away, didn't bother to pretend that she was a grown-up and that grown-ups could handle anything.

This wasn't something she could handle.

"I'm scared too, baby," she whispered.

Ruthie stilled. "You are?"

"Yep. I've never been more scared in my life than when I went out into the backyard and you weren't there. Every day that you were gone I was scared. I'm sorry that I brought Jimmy into our lives," she gave her daughter the apology she owed her.

Thin arms wrapped around her with a strength that belied their small size. "No, Mommy. It's not your fault. It's Jimmy's fault. I hate him and I'm glad he's dead," Ruthie said with a coldness that would have scared her if she hadn't felt the exact same way.

"I know I'm not Rafe, or Andy, or Supergirl, but I promise you, sweetheart, I will not let anyone hurt you."

Snuggling closer and crawling into her lap, Ruthie rested her head on Elle's shoulder. "I know you won't, Mommy."

Something inside Elle settled at her daughter's trust. Maybe that was what she had been afraid of the most all along. That the ordeal that she would forever blame herself for no matter what anyone else said, would have irrevocably damaged her relationship with her child. Ruined it in a way that meant it would no longer be just the two of them against the world.

Ruthie was the only person she could count on to show her unconditional love, how would she survive without that?

"Mommy?"

"Yeah, baby?"

"Will you sing to me?"

"Of course I will." Wrapping herself around her child, Elle settled back against the pillows in the guest bedroom—unable to face her bedroom and what had happened there she and Ruthie had agreed to share this room for now—and began to sing.

For almost half an hour she sang, every song she could think of, over and over again, and slowly Ruthie's cries began to diminish, eventually dying out.

Still she sang and rocked her daughter, cherishing every single second of the slight weight in her arms. Her daughter was home, alive, in one piece, struggling to process all she'd been through but so darn brave it filled Elle's heart with pride.

They would make it.

Together the two of them would rebuild their lives.

Maybe they'd move away somewhere else. With her job, she could live anywhere in the world and she wasn't anywhere close to being ready to allow Ruthie to go back to school. She could move somewhere quiet and remote, hire a tutor and homeschool her daughter so she never had to let Ruthie out of her sight again.

Her voice began to grow hoarse, her throat ached, and in the end Elle had to give up singing only because she had no other choice. Sleep was the furthest thing from her mind. It was one thing to wake her daughter with screams climbing out of her nightmares when she knew that Rafe and Andy were there to have her back. But it was another to risk waking Ruthie with screams when it was just the two of them.

How long could she go without sleep?

Elle had no idea, but she was going to find out. Because she had already put her daughter through so much and she wasn't going to make it worse.

Ruthie needed to feel safe, so whatever she had to do, whatever sacrifices she had to make in order to build that safe place for her daughter Elle wouldn't hesitate to do.

The muted buzz of her phone indicated she had a new message, but Elle didn't bother to look at it.

She already knew who it would be.

Rafe.

She'd barely made it home when the first message came. An apology for asking her to leave and a question asking how she and Ruthie were doing.

While her heart had soared with hope at first, praying he chose her and Ruthie over his ex, she had quickly squashed it. Rafe was doing what he thought was best for his son, and she couldn't blame him for that. But nor could she allow her daughter to be hurt, and mixed messages from Rafe were going to do just that.

Rafe had made his choice for better or worse, and so she now had to make her own. Already she had caused her daughter so much pain, but no more. She would never allow anyone else to enter their lives, it would be just the two of them because that was the only way to keep them safe.

The two of them against the world, mother and daughter, safe together.

Elle knew that one day Ruthie would grow up, most likely fall in love and have a family of her own, leaving Elle truly alone.

But loneliness was a price she was well and truly prepared to pay for her daughter's peace of mind, and if that meant she would grow old and die alone then so be it. No way was she risking another broken heart.

Her stories always had a happy ending, they wouldn't be romance without them, but it looked like her own life wasn't going to turn out the same way.

CHAPTER

Nineteen

March 22nd
  3:24 P.M.

Damn.

She still hadn't replied to a single one of his messages.

Should Panther be surprised that Elle didn't want to answer his messages given the way he'd asked her to leave without even talking to her about it first?

Probably not.

Was he?

Yeah. Honestly he was.

He'd thought ...

Shame bubbled inside him as he thought about how he'd handled things. In the moment, he had believed he could ask Elle and Ruthie to leave, sort out this thing with Marcia and figure out if the best thing for Andy was for his parents to attempt to try making a relationship work, then go back to Elle after he knew what he was going to do. In the meantime, leaving her and her traumatized daughter hanging while he got himself and his life sorted out.

What kind of idiot was he that he thought she would still be there waiting for him if and when he decided he wanted her?

Talk about selfish.

It would have been thoughtless and careless enough to have done what he had if both Elle and Ruthie weren't recovering from a horrific ordeal, but to know they were, and that they needed him and he'd walked away ... that had guilt eating non stop in his gut.

"I don't want to see her," Andy growled behind him as his son stomped into the kitchen.

Over the last few days, the sweet little boy he'd always known had morphed into an angry child who argued over everything and wasn't shy about making his feelings known. Not that Panther wanted Andy to lie to him, he just thought that he owed it to his son to give the boy a chance to get to know his mother. Thing was, he'd expected Andy to have stopped resisting this by now and started to forge some sort of bond with Marcia. With Elle, he'd bonded with her instantly, but when it came to his own mother the boy seemed to want to have nothing to do with her.

"Nonetheless, she's going to be here in a couple of minutes, and the two of you are spending the afternoon together. She wants to cook you dinner so I'll be back before bedtime," he told his son as he turned to face the angry child.

"You're leaving me alone with her?" Andy asked incredulously.

The last few days Panther had stayed while Marcia visited with Andy, but Andy refused to engage, and he'd wondered if he wasn't there then maybe the two of them would be able to start bonding.

"She's a stranger," Andy growled.

There was no bother pointing out that Elle had been a stranger and Andy had had no problem at all being left alone with her. No bother pointing out that Panther had had no problem leaving his son alone with her although the thought of leaving his son alone with the boy's own mother left him anxious and unsettled either.

"Mrs. Pfeffer will be here," he assured his son. He wasn't trying to be the bad guy, given his own past he just couldn't not try to see if things with Marcia could be salvaged. But he wasn't going to leave his child alone with someone the boy wasn't comfortable with. Andy loved Mrs.

Pfeffer and the woman would make sure that he was okay while he was spending time with the mother he didn't know and didn't seem to want to get to know.

Ten minutes later, Panther was walking out his front door leaving a nervous Marcia, a confused Mrs. Pfeffer, and an angry Andy inside, and trying to figure out what he was going to do for the next few hours. Part of him wanted to get in his vehicle and drive to Elle's place, check for himself how the two of them were doing even though Sparrow had assured him that they were hanging in there several times already over the last few days.

It wasn't a good idea, he knew that. What would he say to them? Sorry I kicked you out when I promised I would always be there for you, but this was something I had to do?

That wasn't going to help anyone. Not his girls, not himself, not his son.

His girls.

Still how he thought of Elle and Ruthie. Dragging his fingers down his face, Panther sighed. None of this was turning out the way he wanted it to, and he was no longer sure he was doing the best thing for anyone.

In fact, he was starting to feel like he had done the *wrong* thing for everyone.

Whatever plans he was deciding on were halted as he walked down the porch steps and found his team standing there waiting for him.

Not a single one of them looked happy.

Join the club.

These last few days had been amongst the most miserable of his life. He missed Elle and Ruthie with an ache, like a part of himself had been amputated and lost to him, possibly forever. If his friends were just here to make him feel worse about the situation then he wasn't in the mood.

"What do you want?" he muttered as he stalked past them and out into the woods where just a week ago his son and Ruthie had been running around playing and having fun.

"To understand," Rock said gently. "Trust me, I'm the king of messing up a good thing, so there's no judgment here. Not from any of us. But we've never seen you more miserable."

"Honestly, you weren't this miserable when Marcia left you a single dad of a baby, bro," Trick added.

"You were happy with Elle," Tank said. "You and Andy both. Happiest we've ever seen the two of you."

"You think I don't know that?" he roared out his frustration.

"Then why did you ask her to leave?" Scorpion asked. "I'm going to be a father now so I can get that you have to think of Andy and his needs above everyone and everything else. But you could have seen whether your ex was serious about wanting a relationship with her son without kicking Elle and Ruthie out."

"No I couldn't," he insisted. They just didn't get it. You only got one childhood, and every child wanted their parents to be together. How could he not give Andy a chance at the happy childhood with both parents together every kid wanted and still call himself a good father? If he didn't do this, he'd be proving he was every bit as selfish and self-centered as his own parents had been.

"None of us get why," Trick said.

"You don't have to get it," he muttered. No one needed to understand his choices, he didn't owe anyone an explanation. Anyone except Elle and he hadn't done that. If this didn't work out with Marcia—and there was a huge part of him that didn't want it to—then how could he expect her to ever trust him again? It was like he'd set her on the back-burner and just expected her to be there waiting if and when he returned.

There was no doubt about it, he *had* ruined the best thing to ever happen to both him and his son. Elle was everything that Marcia wasn't, everything he wanted his son to have in a mother.

"My parents split when I was six. I hated it, begged them to stay together but they told me they didn't love each other and were divorcing. Mom remarried first, I was eight. Guy she married was divorced with sole custody of his three kids, kids she was excited to step up and mother. Dad remarried two years later, the woman was a widow with two kids of her own, and my dad fell head over heels for all three of them. Two families, neither of which I ever felt like I belonged in. I was the only one being bounced about between homes, the only one always on the outside."

The worst thing a child could ever feel was unwanted, and that was exactly how his parents had made him feel.

They loved their step kids more than they loved him, Panther had always been positive of that. Back then as a child and now as an adult.

"Both of them had another two kids each with their new partners. That was a lot of kids in each home. I was the one who wasn't always there, so I was the one who slept on the pull out bed in the study at my mom's, and had a tiny room in the attic at my dad's. Family vacations were expensive so they took them when I was with the other parent because that was one less kid to pay for. I hated it, hated them, hated my step-siblings and half-siblings who had the family I wanted. I wished on every birthday candle, asked in every letter to Santa, and begged and pleaded with God, to give me my family back so I could be wanted again. How can I put my son through that same kind of life? Shuttled about between two homes, never feeling like he belonged?"

Axe stepped forward and met his gaze directly. "You're looking at it all wrong. You're trying to invent problems that aren't there. Trust me, there is only one thing in life that's truly important, and that's keeping the people you love close because you never know when you could lose them forever."

If there was anyone who knew about losing loved ones it was Axe. Even now as his wife slept in his home she wasn't truly with him. Beth might never get her memories back, and Axe would have to live the rest of his life having his wife nearby but not having her *close*.

His friends weren't wrong when they said this was the happiest they'd seen Andy. Under Elle's love and attention, his already happy, intelligent child was blossoming.

Was a family really all about DNA?

Wasn't it about love?

Elle had filled their home with love, support, attention, care, and understanding. She had been acting like Andy's mother. If he and Marcia weren't together, and Marcia proved she could be a stable influence in their son's life and they wound up sharing custody, then who said Andy had to feel left out? Panther knew for a fact that he and Elle would never make Andy feel like he wasn't wanted, like he was an extra in the family. They would shower the boy with love and attention when he was with them. Andy would have his own space, he would always be included in family vacations, and they would both make sure he knew that it was his home and not just a house he stayed in sometimes.

With Elle he could have given Andy the stable home he himself had lacked as a child, and instead, he'd ripped it all away from his son.

Turned out Panther was worse than his parents had been, he wasn't just selfish but a coward as well. He'd let his own fears from the past ruin the best thing to have ever happened to his son.

~

March 25th
9:21 A.M.

Why was this happening to her?

Hadn't she been through enough?

Elle's thoughts were quickly plummeting from shock to downright despondency.

Of all the things she thought would ever happen to her again this one had to be right down at the bottom of the barrel.

This was ... impossible.

After her husband had walked out on her when Ruthie was just a baby, the last thing she ever wanted to do was put a child through knowing a parent didn't want them. It wasn't the raising that child on her own—hard though that was—that made her get herself on the pill immediately, it was that her child would grow up feeling the same way she had. Unwanted. A burden.

So ... this ... this had to be impossible.

The pill made it impossible.

It wasn't true.

A false positive.

Had to be.

Nothing else would make sense.

Only ...

Elle lifted the hand that wasn't clutching the pregnancy test and brushed a fingertip over the mostly healed cut on her cheek. The cut she'd gotten when she attacked Jimmy, stopping him from killing her daughter. At the hospital, after cleaning the wound and using butterfly bandages to close it, she'd been given a shot of antibiotics.

Antibiotics could mess with the pill's effectiveness.

Not that it was one hundred percent effective anyway.

It wasn't that she was opposed to the idea of having more kids, and she knew Ruthie would be over the moon about becoming a big sister, but she didn't want it like this.

Alone again.

Unwanted.

Not good enough.

No matter how hard she tried, she always seemed to fail. Failed as a daughter by not becoming what her parents wanted. Failed as a wife even though she knew she had been the best wife she could be. Failed as a mother bringing someone unsafe into her daughter's life and almost getting her killed. Failed as a girlfriend to Rafe who tossed her away without even talking through where he was coming from and his fears and concerns.

Failed.

Always a failure.

Now she had another little person she was going to fail because, once again, she wasn't going to be able to give this baby the happy home she'd always dreamed of giving any children she would have.

Rafe had already made his choice and it wasn't her and Ruthie. Why would she think that would change now that she was pregnant with his baby?

Did she think he would abandon the child?

Absolutely not. Elle knew without a shadow of a doubt that once he knew she was pregnant—and she would never hide that from him no matter how much he had hurt her and her daughter—that he would step up and be there for their child.

Problem was, she didn't want him to want to be with her because she was having his baby, for once in her life she wanted someone to appreciate her enough to *want* to be with her. Not put up with her because as parents you had a legal obligation to provide for your child. Not put up with her because she cooked and cleaned and paid the bills. Not even put up with her because she was their mom.

But want her for her.

Want her because living without her was like living with a piece of yourself missing.

The ringing of her phone had her head snapping up. She was still in the bathroom, right where she'd been for the last hour or so, ever since she realized she was late and that she better take a pregnancy test in case it wasn't just exhaustion and anxiety messing with her periods. Thankfully, Ruthie was in front of the TV, having a Disney movie marathon and hadn't come looking for her.

Now, she picked up the phone and answered only because it was Sparrow's name on the screen. She had grown closer with the other woman over the last few days. Actually Sparrow had become a godsend. The woman checked in on her several times throughout the day and had even brought her kids over to play with Ruthie a few times and sat and kept Elle company even though she knew she wasn't very good company right now.

"Hey, Elle, how are my favorite author and her mini doing today?" Sparrow asked when Elle answered.

Usually she would shoot back that Sparrow didn't read much so she absolutely wasn't her favorite author, but today different words blurted out of her mouth without any conscious thought or decision on her part. "I'm pregnant."

Silence came down the line.

It lasted so long that Elle actually checked to make sure the call hadn't been disconnected.

It hadn't.

"Okay," Sparrow said, drawing the word out. "Not what I expected you to say. At all. Safe to say I'm not usually shocked into silence but you managed to do it. Should I say congratulations?"

That Sparrow asked that question made Elle really think about the answer.

For the last hour, she'd just been bemoaning her bad luck in life, with men in general, and how badly timed this was. Her fears that Rafe might actually come back to her because of the pregnancy and she would never know if he wanted her or just their child had also dominated her mind.

Now she shoved that all away and shut off her mind, allowing her heart to take over.

Was she happy about having another baby?

Everything else aside the answer was ... yes.

A small smile curled her lips up. "Yeah, you should say congratulations."

"Then big congrats, sister. I'm super thrilled for you," Sparrow enthused. "I almost hate to ask because I can actually hear the smile in your voice, but have you still been hearing from Panther?"

Texts had continued to come in from Rafe, growing in frequency over the last few days. While she sensed his regret over what had happened, and his desperation to talk to her, she wasn't ready for that. The texts might have gone unanswered, but she had read them over and over again.

I miss you.

I'm sorry.

I don't want to lose you.

I thought I was doing the right thing.

What was she supposed to say to that?

Understanding his desire to do what he felt was best for his child was something that as a mother she could understand. But as a woman, it *hurt* to be kicked to the curb for an ex.

"Yeah, he texts all the time, but ... I can't make myself answer," Elle admitted.

"It's scary, isn't it? Feeling like you're competing with someone else, that you aren't enough," Sparrow said softly. While Sparrow was all confidence and capability, Elle knew a little about how she and her husband had gotten together. Friends first, it wasn't until a random helicopter crash caused by someone targeting Sparrow's family had thrown the two together. Not over his wife's death, Ethan had fought the attraction between him and Sparrow almost until it was too late and he'd already lost her.

"It's terrifying," she agreed. After what she'd just been through with Ruthie, Elle would have thought she could conquer any fear, because nothing was scarier than having your child taken. But she was so tired of fighting just to get through each day. All she wanted was peace.

"Can I tell you something I haven't told anyone else?"

"Of course."

"Sometimes I still feel like I'm not good enough for Ethan. I know he loves me, but Sierra was his great love, and if she hadn't died they'd still be together. It can be hard not to feel like second best," Sparrow whispered, her voice raw with pain.

"Oh, Sparrow, that might be true, but Ethan *loves* you. With everything he has to give. I've seen the way he looks at you, he was lucky to have two great loves of his life. He wouldn't be able to stand losing you, it would destroy him. You, Connor, and Charlotte are his entire world," Elle said, her heart aching for the woman who still battled her doubts even while knowing she was loved.

"I know that in my head. I never doubt Ethan's love for me, I just worry that he'll compare me to Sierra and find me lacking. It's stupid, I know that, again my head is totally down for the facts, but my heart ... sometimes the doubts get the best of me."

"In Rafe's texts, he keeps telling me he thought he was doing the right thing. I know his parents divorced when he was young and he always felt on the outside. I believe he thinks giving Andy both parents together will make his son happy, and give him what Rafe never had. But I know that DNA doesn't equal happiness. I had both parents together and I grew up miserable. It's about love, and ... I was falling in love with him."

"Things are different now," Sparrow reminded her. "Panther has another child to think about."

"That's the problem. I don't want him with me for the baby, I want him with me for me. I'll always wonder if he wishes he had given Marcia a second chance for Andy's sake. I don't want that for me, for Ruthie, for Andy, or for this baby. Even if he did want us all, I don't know if I can get past the hurt of being kicked out of his house, a place he knew was where my daughter felt safe, like we were nothing. I'm angry, I'm scared, I'm hurt, and now I have two children depending on me to make the right decisions only I have no idea what they are. I'm so tired, Sparrow, and the pressure is too much. For months I've been living on adrenalin alone and I'm tapped out. I just don't think I have the strength to figure this all out."

CHAPTER

Twenty

March 25th
10:14 A.M.

Dad was stupid.

It was the first time in his life, Andy had ever thought that about his dad, but it was true.

He had always thought his dad was like a superhero, he was strong, and brave, and he fought bad guys and won. His dad was also lots of fun. They always did stuff together when he wasn't working, and Dad read him stories and tucked him in. Andy always knew his dad was smart enough to answer any question.

Well, he had thought all of that.

Not anymore.

Not since Dad made Elle and Ruthie leave.

Not since Dad wouldn't listen to him. Wouldn't let him call Elle and Ruthie, or go and visit them. Not since Dad didn't even care that Ruthie didn't have her ring and she'd be scared, and there was nobody to hold Elle when she had nightmares.

Dad was wrong.

Making them leave wasn't the right thing to do.

His dad kept telling him he had done it for him, but Andy didn't believe that. Marcia might be the woman who carried her in his tummy before he was born, but that didn't make her his mom.

Elle was the closest thing to a mom he had ever had, and Dad had made her leave.

It wasn't fair.

Sometimes he hated being a kid. When you were a kid you didn't get to make choices about your life, someone was always doing it for you cause they thought they knew better.

But Dad didn't know better this time.

There was something about Marcia that made Andy feel ... yucky.

That wasn't the right word, not the grown-up word, but it was how he felt. When he was with Elle he felt safe and warm, he knew she would look after him, knew she would care for him, knew that even though he couldn't always make choices himself that the ones she made would be good.

He didn't feel that way with Marcia.

When Andy tried to explain that to his dad, Dad had just told him that it was because he didn't know Marcia, and if he just gave her a chance then he would get to know her and come to love her.

But Daddy was wrong.

Wrong.

And it made Andy mad that his dad wouldn't listen to him and was treating him like a baby who didn't know anything.

He might only be eight, but Andy wasn't a baby. He was a big boy now, in the third grade, even though he did school at home and not at a school like most other kids his age. He could read, and his writing was real good. He always tried extra hard to make his letters look really clear just like they were in his books. He was good at math, loved numbers, could do his timetables, and division, and addition and subtraction were easy, he even knew fractions and percentages.

If he knew all those things then he could know what he was feeling, too.

"Okay, bud, Marcia's pulling up, I'm going to head out for a while," Dad said.

Andy ignored him and kept on watching cartoons. Only it wasn't so much fun watching them anymore without Ruthie with him. It was his job to protect her, make sure she didn't get sad or scared, and his dad didn't understand that. He hated knowing Ruthie might cry and he wouldn't be there to make her laugh instead, or play lots of games with her so she didn't have time to think about the bad man who had taken her.

"Hey, my favorite son." Dad crouched down beside the couch where Andy was sprawled out. "I love you, you know that right? You understand I'm not trying to hurt you, or Elle and Ruthie. I'm just trying to do what I think is best for you as your father."

"I know what's best for me, but you won't listen. You are hurting me, Dad. And you're hurting Elle and Ruthie, too, and I'm mad at you for that."

Dad sighed and he looked tired. More tired than sometimes when he came home from saving someone. Not even Dad looked happy with his choice to make Elle and Ruthie leave. So if none of them were happy, why couldn't Marcia go away and Elle and Ruthie come home? If Elle and Ruthie were there, Andy would spend time with Marcia if it made his dad happy, but she'd never really be his mom because he already knew he wanted Elle to be his mommy.

Elle would be the best mom in the whole world, she already loved Ruthie so much and Andy wanted a mom to love him that much.

"I know," Dad whispered, standing and kissing the top of Andy's head.

Ignoring Marcia when Dad let her in the door, he kept his attention fixed on the TV. Andy didn't know why Dad kept insisting on Marcia coming around every day to spend time with him. Didn't he know that as soon as he walked out the door she barely spoke to him? She didn't love him, Andy knew that every time he looked at Marcia, it was why he knew she would never really be his mom.

Dad always told him that it was important to know what you wanted in life and to go after it. You had to be brave, had to do what was right, had to make sure you protected those who needed it. You had to be a superhero even if you didn't have real superpowers like The Hulk.

So that's what Andy was going to do.

He was going to do what was right, he was going to protect Ruthie because that was his job, he just had to be brave to do it.

Leaving the TV on, he climbed off the couch and creeped over to the kitchen door to check that Marcia was inside. She was sitting at the table on her phone just like always so he went upstairs to grab his backpack. This morning when he got dressed, he had put all the things he needed in it, and now he put it on his back and put the superhero ring on his finger.

Ruthie needed this, she needed him and he wasn't going to stay away from her any longer.

If Dad wouldn't take him there then he'd go himself.

Back downstairs, he checked the kitchen again, but Marcia hadn't moved, hadn't bothered to check on him or ask him if he wanted to play with her. Yesterday, she didn't even make him lunch. Daddy was mad when Andy had told him that, but not mad enough to tell Marcia not to come back today or enough to call Elle and ask her and Ruthie to come home.

After he checked out the front window to make sure nobody was out there, Andy opened the front door and stepped out onto the porch.

Success.

Marcia hadn't stopped him, and his dad wasn't anywhere he could see, so there was no one to stop him as he ran for the trees. This was where he'd lived for almost his whole life, he knew every corner of the woods, he spent all summer and most of the spring and fall playing out there.

So he also knew a tiny little corner where sometimes the cameras didn't catch and there was a hole he could climb through in the fence.

Didn't matter if the cameras did see him because he knew his dad would find out as soon as he got home that Andy was gone. All he cared about was that he got to Elle's house before his dad could stop him.

If he could just make Dad and Elle spend some time together, he was sure his dad would remember how much fun the four of them had together, how happy they had been, and then ask Elle and Ruthie to come back home.

It had to work because he didn't want to feel bad that he wasn't protecting Ruthie like he'd promised her he would, or sad because Elle wasn't there, or angry that his dad wasn't listening to him. He never missed having a mom before Elle came to stay with them. How could he miss something he never had before? But now that he knew how cool it was to have a mom, he wanted Elle back, he loved her, and he knew she loved him, too. He could feel it when she smiled at him, and cooked his favorite dinner, and tucked him into bed at night with a kiss on his forehead.

Andy ran real fast. As fast as he could until he found the spot in the fence he'd noticed last fall. He'd been going to tell his dad about it, but then he'd forgotten all about it and only remembered again when he decided he had to go find Elle.

As he climbed through it, he was glad he'd forgotten because now nothing was going to stop him from going to Elle's house and begging her to come back home. He needed her, and he knew his daddy did, too.

CHAPTER
Twenty-One

March 25th
1:46 P.M.

Something had to change.

Panther knew that none of them could go on like this. He was miserable, Andy was miserable, Elle and Ruthie were miserable. It was pretty obvious that no matter how many times he texted, Elle was never going to text back. If he wanted to talk to her, attempt to fix the mess he'd made, then he was going to have to do it in person.

It hadn't even been a week yet, and he was already losing his mind without her presence in his life. Ruthie's, too, damn he missed that sweet little girl. The child gave the best hugs, there was just something about them that melted your heart when she wrapped her thin, little arms around your neck and held on like she needed you to know how much you meant to her.

That was his future.

Elle, Ruthie, and Andy.

Not Marcia.

Finally, reality had sunk in. It wasn't DNA that made a family, it was love. In the couple of years they had been together, Marcia had never shown him the same level of love Elle had in just over a month.

Just like he considered his Bravo Team brothers more his family than both his biological and step-siblings, he could consider Elle and Ruthie more his family than Marcia. There was no way he could control Marcia, if she was being honest and wanted back in on Andy's life then he wouldn't stop her, but he didn't have to give up his and his son's happiness for it.

Yes, he'd felt left out and unwanted as a child, but *that* was what had made him unhappy. Had his parents taken the time to make sure he felt secure in both his new homes, he could have found happiness even if he always had a lingering wish to have his parents together.

Together, he and Elle could build a family that would ensure both their kids knew how much they were loved and wanted. With Marcia he could never do that. Because he didn't love her, and sooner or later his son would pick up on that.

Andy didn't want his parents together, he just wanted a secure home life where he could grow and thrive.

As soon as he sent Marcia home, he and Andy were going to bake Ruthie's favorite cookies, then pick a few flowers that were starting to bloom in the mild early spring. And then they were going to stop by the grocery store to pick up ingredients for dinner.

After that, he was going to pray big time that Elle would let him in the door.

Sneaky move maybe, but he was pretty sure she wouldn't deny Andy, so he was absolutely going to use that to his advantage. Allowing his own childhood issues to mess with his head with what should have been an easy decision to make had been a mistake, but one he was determined to rectify.

It was time to look to the future and stop obsessing over the past.

Opening the front door, Panther looked immediately to the couch where he thought he would find his son. Andy hadn't made any effort to get to know Marcia and now that he understood just how angry his son was he got why.

Panther was trying to force something that, in reality, was going to take time.

Andy didn't know Marcia, she was nothing to him, and his son had bonded with Elle and Ruthie both, he missed them and blamed both Panther and Marcia for them being gone. He was proud of how smart his son was. Understanding what had taken Panther days to get. Family was the people you loved, who loved you in return, it had absolutely nothing to do with blood.

The couch was empty, though, and he wondered whether Marcia and Andy were making progress in building a relationship. He was glad, whatever happened he wanted his son to have as many people as possible to love him and support him.

Strolling through to the kitchen, he expected to find Andy and Marcia hanging out. Instead, all he saw was Marcia at the kitchen table with her phone in her hand. No Andy.

"Where's my son?" he growled, causing Marcia to jump, dropping her phone onto the table, and red tinting her pale cheeks.

"Oh ... umm ... he's watching TV."

"No. He's not. I just came through the living room and he's not there."

"Well then he's probably playing in the playroom," Marcia suggested.

"Why don't you *know* where he is?" he demanded. "You're not here to be playing on your phone, Marcia, you're in charge of an eight-year-old little boy. You should know where he is at all times unless you're playing hide and seek." Arching a brow, he mocked, "Are you playing hide and seek?"

"Of course not," Marcia grumbled, sounding irritated like she couldn't be bothered with the whole thing. Only this was their child they were talking about. "He's in the playroom. Or maybe upstairs playing in his room."

"Why don't you *know* where he is, Marcia?" Panther fumed as he stormed out of the kitchen to the playroom.

"He didn't want to play with me," she said like it was no big deal.

"So you just sat in there on your phone?" If he sounded incredulous it was because he absolutely was. He had thrown away the best thing to have ever happened to him after his son—and might not be able to get it back—because he'd always wanted Andy to have the childhood he hadn't. To know he'd done it all for someone who still didn't seem to care one iota about Andy made him furious.

"I can't force him to play with me," Marcia said defensively.

Defensive, not upset. She was angry with him for bringing it up but not sad that the son she said she wanted to help raise wanted nothing to do with her.

Andy was right. This woman didn't love him.

After finding the playroom empty, panic began to bubble inside him. Something was wrong. His son should be here. Andy rarely played in his room, he was usually either in the living room or the playroom, only both were empty and he had a bad feeling about it.

"Andy?" he yelled as he shoved past Marcia who looked bored, not guilty or concerned, and ran up the stairs.

There was no answer and just as he expected, the bedroom was empty.

Already knowing the answer, Panther ran to the dresser where he knew Andy kept the superhero ring, but it wasn't sitting there.

The ring was gone.

Which meant his son was gone.

Sending out an SOS text to his team telling them that Andy was missing, he stalked back down the stairs to where Marcia was waiting for him, lounging against the wall like she didn't have a care in the world.

It wasn't until he started advancing on her, making no attempt to hide his fury, that she startled and the first tinges of fear colored her eyes.

"Uh, he wasn't up there?" she asked, straightening.

"Nope. He wasn't. Why weren't you watching him?"

"He won't talk to me. I just assumed he was going to watch TV or play with his toys. He's probably outside, what's the big deal?"

"What's the big deal?" he roared. "Andy is eight. Eight. Do you get that? That means that you should know where he is at all times." Standing before her, he grasped her chin—none too gently—and forced her to look at him. "Why did you come back? It wasn't for Andy." That was now abundantly clear to him and he wished he had seen it right away.

At least Marcia had the good grace to look ashamed.

And guilty.

It was the guilt that tightened his gut.

"What have you done, Marcia?" he demanded.

"I didn't have a choice," she said softly.

"We *always* have a choice." Panther just hoped his choices hadn't cost him everything he held dear. "What. Did. You. Do?"

"I ... got into some trouble ... financially. Things spiraled and I racked up a lot of debt. Debt I couldn't pay off."

"What does that have to do with me and Andy?" They were divorced, whatever financial problems she'd got herself wrapped up in were not his responsibility.

"I thought maybe you would help, but I knew I would have to get in good with the boy first."

The boy. Not Andy. She couldn't even use their son's name.

"I knew how badly you wanted Andy to have the kind of childhood you didn't, so I thought if I came back and said I wanted a second chance, you would give it to me no matter what. Even if you were with someone else," Marcia continued.

Damn.

The woman had known him better than he knew himself.

"I thought all I would have to do was play happy families with you for a little while and then when I told you about the debt you would pay it off for me."

As angry as he was with his ex, Panther had to admit that the person he should be most angry with was himself. He had made the choice to throw away the good thing he was building with Elle and her daughter. He had chosen to allow his childhood to continue to control him and ignore everyone from his team, to his son, to his own instincts.

Releasing his grip on Marcia, he stepped away, no longer able to stomach having her anywhere near him. "There is nothing between us, I'd already made the decision before I came in here that I was going to try to fix things with Elle and only allow you to keep building something with Andy. My son deserves so much better than you for a mother, and Elle is everything I want for him. I don't think I ever loved you, Marcia. I don't think I knew what love meant back then. But I love my son, and I'm falling in love with Elle and that sweet little girl of hers. My son ran away because of you, because of your lies and manipulations. If anything happens to him, you can be sure I am going to make sure you're punished to the fullest extent of the law. Don't you ever come near me or my son again."

~

March 25th
   2:02 P.M.

Elle could feel her eyelids drooping as she sat on the couch beside Ruthie and watched another Disney movie.

Just like in her first pregnancy, she hadn't suffered from any morning sickness so far, and she hoped that, like last time, that continued, but she was exhausted. Last time around pregnancy had left her a wreck, barely enough energy to get out of bed to take care of the laundry, the cleaning, the cooking, and writing to pay their bills. This time around things didn't seem to be going any differently.

Only this time around things *were* different in so many ways.

Last time she had been eight years younger, and innocently hopeful that the baby would bring her the closeness with her husband that she could feel was lacking. She'd thought that having a child together would change everything. That her husband would see that he needed to step up more and help out around the house, and stick to one job and help contribute financially. That he needed to give her the emotional support she needed.

Instead, the baby was the final nail in their coffin, and her husband had filed for divorce six weeks after Ruthie was born. Looking back, it was easy to see that she had been so desperate for love and affection that she would take the scraps her ex gave her and blow them up to make them seem more than they were. She had been the same way with her parents. So desperate that anything they offered she would greedily accept.

It wasn't until she had Ruthie and finally experienced unconditional love that she realized that was what she deserved from all the people in her life.

Now she was almost thirty, she already had a child, so when the baby came along she was going to have to balance her time and attention between two children. Something Ruthie was going to have to get used to since she had always been the absolute focus of Elle's entire life.

Even though she had ended up being a single parent, she hadn't known that during her pregnancy, she'd thought she would be raising her child as part of a partnership. This time, at least, she knew she was going to have to do it all alone.

Already she was exhausted at the thought.

The buzz of the doorbell had her wearily shoving to her feet. Ruthie barely blinked, engrossed in every second of her movie marathon even though these were all movies she had seen before, most of them several times.

"Want more popcorn?" she asked her daughter as she stretched her back.

"Mmm?" Ruthie mumbled, making Elle smile.

"Do you want more popcorn after I answer the door?"

"Sure," Ruthie replied, never moving her gaze from the screen.

Still smiling as she headed for the door, expecting to collect more of the packages she'd ordered—although she really was going to have to toughen up and ask someone to pack up her and Ruthie's things that were still at Rafe's—her mouth dropped when she opened the door.

It wasn't the delivery driver standing on her front porch.

It was a four-foot-three, fifty-five pound, brown-haired, hazel-eyed eight-year-old looking up at her.

"Andy?" She dropped to her knees and dragged the boy into her arms, both overjoyed to see him again, but terrified what his presence meant. Had something happened to Rafe? Just because she was upset with him didn't mean she wanted him to be hurt. But if something had happened to Rafe, why was Andy here to tell her? This made zero sense.

"Elle! I missed you so bad," Andy said, hugging her tight.

Scanning the front yard, which was as empty as was the street, her confusion grew. How on earth had the boy gotten here? The little boy was wearing a backpack, and she got the sickening feeling that he might have run away from home.

She was way too intimately acquainted with the knowledge of what it felt like to learn your child had disappeared, and it wasn't something she would wish on anyone, not even her greatest enemy, and Rafe wasn't her enemy, things just hadn't worked out between them.

"Andy, what's going on? Who brought you here? Why are you here? Does your dad know?" she rattled off questions as she straightened, placing her hands on the boy's shoulders.

"I hitchhiked here and I'm not sorry," Andy said stubbornly. There was an angry gleam to his beautiful hazel eyes that she hadn't seen once while she'd been staying with the child and his father, and it made her heart ache. The last thing she wanted was for her and Ruthie leaving to have hurt Rafe and Andy's relationship, even if there hadn't been anything she had been able to do about it.

"Hitchhiked!" she squeaked, horrified at the idea of a little boy getting into a car alone with strangers. What kind of person picked up a child and didn't take them straight to a police station, or call the cops?

"It was easy. I just told them I got lost and that my dad was a cop and gave them your address, and they brought me right here." Andy said like it was all no big deal, while all Elle could think about were a million things that could have gone wrong with the boy's plan.

"Andy, you shouldn't have done that, it was too dangerous."

"I don't care. I wanted to see you. I missed you, Elle. I don't want that woman to be my mom, I want *you* to be my mom. I don't care what my dad says, he misses you, too. He doesn't really want to be with *her*, he wants to be with you. You're the closest thing to a mom I've ever had and I want you to come home. I want you and my dad to get back together. I miss Ruthie, I want her to be my sister, and I don't want you to ever leave again," Andy said, tears shimmering in his eyes by the time he finished his little speech.

"Oh, baby," she murmured as she reached down and picked him up even though he was really too big to carry. Elle wished that could happen, too, but the problem was she couldn't make Rafe want to be with her and Ruthie. Couldn't make him want to give up on whatever fears were guiding him. Couldn't even guarantee that if he did come to her and ask for a second chance, she would give it to him. Three children would be affected by whatever decisions she made, and she didn't take that lightly.

As nice as it would be to pretend the last week hadn't happened, it had, and there were no promises she could or would make to this child.

"I don't know what's going to happen with me and your dad, bud, but I do know that hitchhiking wasn't the answer." Just because she loved this little boy didn't mean she could allow him to get away with doing something so dangerous. *Especially* because she loved this boy it meant she couldn't let him get away with doing something so dangerous.

"I wanted to see you." He huffed.

"And I wanted to see you, too, but you know better than to talk to strangers, let alone get into a car with one," she rebuked. Regardless of what happened with Rafe, this little boy would always be part of her life because his little brother or sister was growing inside her. A permanent bond between her and Rafe, and between Ruthie, Andy, and this child.

"I don't care because it worked," Andy said, smiling widely.

"What worked?"

"You and Dad will have to see each other now. You'll have to talk, and that means you can get back together." His smile grew until he was beaming at her, so completely confident that his childish plan had worked and now the two of them would get back together.

Only life didn't work that simply when you were a grown-up.

There were no guarantees any of them were going to get the happy ending she'd write if this was one of her books.

Still, Andy was right about one thing. She was going to have to call his dad to tell him that Andy was safe and sound with her. Being upset with Rafe didn't mean she would allow him to suffer, afraid and wondering where his son was.

Whether she wanted to or not, she was about to come face to face with the man who hadn't just hurt her but her child as well. Hurting her, Elle could probably forgive, but hurting her daughter was a hard no. Although it was something she was going to have to work through because she was having a baby, and Rafe was the father, and he was going to want to be part of this child's life, which also meant being a part of hers and Ruthie's lives.

Right now, trying to figure out how it was going to work was too much for her exhausted and strung-out brain.

Setting Andy on his feet, she nudged him inside. "Go tell Ruthie you're here, she's missed you like crazy. Then the two of you get into the car because we have to take you back home to your dad."

Seeing Rafe again scared her. Just because she was hurt didn't mean her feelings had just vanished, and she so badly wanted to seek comfort in his strong arms. Elle prayed for strength to do the right thing for all of them.

CHAPTER
Twenty~Two

March 25th
2:18 P.M.

Thirty minutes had passed since Panther had learned his son had disappeared.

Since all evidence pointed toward Andy having run away, he was consoling himself with the fact that the boy was probably somewhere in the woods surrounding the compound.

His son was smart, Andy knew his way down to the road, all he had to do then was walk into town. It would take a long time for an eight-year-old, though, and at the most the boy had been gone for less than four hours, and that was if he'd left almost as soon as Marcia had arrived, so he might not have even made it to the road.

Honestly, what scared Panther the most was if Andy had gotten lost and was wandering around out there in the big forest. That would make him that much harder to find.

Because there wasn't a doubt in his mind that he knew where Andy was headed.

Elle.

Andy had made his feelings clear. He loved Elle and Ruthie, wanted them to be part of his life, and was angry that they'd been taken away from him. The boy wasn't just running away to run away, he was running with a purpose, he was running to somewhere.

Although he had debated calling Elle to let her know there was a slim chance that Andy would show up on her doorstep, he'd held off. To get to Elle's, Andy would have to walk the streets of the city and surely someone would stop a small boy walking alone to check he was okay. Calls had already been placed with the local police departments to alert him immediately if a young boy was found because anyone who saw him would definitely call the cops. Telling Elle about Andy would only worry her and she had been through enough.

Since he couldn't be absolutely sure Andy knew the way to the road and might have gotten lost, his entire team were out in the forest searching for the boy along with him. While Marcia had been completely unconcerned about their eight-year-old's wellbeing, his team cared and would do whatever it took to find him and bring him home.

Family wasn't blood.

If ever he'd needed another reminder of that, this was it.

No one on his team was biologically related to Andy, yet they all adored him and wouldn't stop searching for him until he was safe.

When his cell began ringing, Panther yanked it from his pocket, answering without even checking to see who was calling, assuming it would be one of his teammates, and he hoped they had good news.

"Lose something?"

The sweet, feminine voice was the last one in the world he expected to hear. "Elle?"

"Something of yours just turned up on my doorstep," she replied.

Relief almost knocked him to his knees. "Andy is with you?"

"Apparently he decided to run away from home and hitchhiked to get here."

Hitchhiked?

Now he felt nauseous.

If the wrong person had picked up his son, he might never have gotten him back. Andy could have been abused and murdered, or sold, or any number of horrific things.

Why would someone pick up a child and not call the police?

What was wrong with people?

Andy didn't look much older than his age, certainly not even old enough to be a pre-teen. If someone had spotted him trying to hitch a ride they should have called 911 or taken him straight to a police station.

"He hitchhiked?" Panther asked in a strangled voice. He was absolutely torn between grabbing his son the second he got to him and holding him tight, never letting him go, and giving out the mother of all punishments so Andy never tried anything like this again.

"Afraid so," Elle said, sympathy in her voice.

What must she be thinking of him?

There she was, a mother of a child who had been abducted, she had fought tooth and nail for her daughter, prepared to sacrifice anything to keep Ruthie alive, and there he was such an awful father that his son had run away from home.

Sighing, he sank back to rest against the nearest tree trunk. "I'll be there to pick him up as soon as I can. Sorry Andy caused all this trouble."

"It's okay, Rafe," she said gently. "Andy and Ruthie are in the car and we're already on our way to your place. I'll have your son home as soon as possible."

She was coming here?

And she didn't sound angry.

There was no way it could be this easy to get his second chance.

Could it?

There was no way he would let Elle leave until he'd apologized and done his best to explain why he'd made his choices. She was a mother, too, so she might understand. On the other hand, she was a mother of a child he had hurt so maybe she wouldn't be all that inclined to understand.

"Thank you," he said, wishing she could understand just how grateful he was to have her in his life, and how hard he would fight to convince her that he wouldn't repeat his mistakes. If she would let him, he would be there for her and Ruthie until the day he died.

"It's no problem, really. After all, I have to pack up my stuff at some point, can't put it off forever."

Elle sounded so tired. What he wouldn't give to be able to wrap his arms around her and just hold her, show her with actions that he was right there, she wasn't alone, all she had to do was lean on him.

This wasn't a conversation he wanted to have on the phone. He wanted her to see his face and body language so she would know he wasn't lying to her. But he also wasn't going to allow her to think that it was over that easily between them.

It was absolutely his fault that they were in this mess, but he was willing and prepared to do anything to fix it.

Anything.

"What are the kids doing?" he asked.

"Oh, um," she sounded surprised and paused, he assumed to look in the rear view mirror so she could see the kids in the backseat. "They're laughing and talking and watching something on Ruthie's iPad. They're holding hands, haven't stopped since they saw each other, it's the cutest thing."

"They missed each other." Drawing in a deep breath, knowing this was a battle he might not win no matter how hard he fought, he spoke from his heart. "Elle, he's not the only one who—"

His words broke off at the sound of screeching brakes, children's screams, and a muttered curse from Elle.

"Elle?" he called into the phone, straightening, his free hand curling into a fist.

"Rafe! There's a man, he has a—" She broke off and he heard the unmistakeable sound of gunshots before the line went dead.

Panic coursed through his system, the three people he cared about most in the world needed him and he wasn't there.

"Someone shot at Elle. She has Andy and Ruthie with her, in a car, on the way here," he shot off to whoever was within range to hear him, then took off at a run toward his cabin where he'd told Marcia to wait so he could finish telling her off once he knew Andy was safe and sound.

Now she held the answers he needed to getting his son, Elle, and Ruthie back alive.

Footsteps pounded the ground behind him so he knew at least one of his friends was following him, probably to make sure he didn't kill the woman who had come back to exploit his insecurities and used their son to do it.

As soon as he burst into his cabin, he yanked Marcia off the couch where she was sitting, and shoved her up against the wall. "What have you done?" he growled low, menacingly.

"Wh—?"

"Don't even start with me, Marcia," he warned. "Andy ran to Elle's house, she was bringing him home and someone shot at them. This is on you, isn't it? Who did you borrow money from?"

Marcia's eyes were wild with fear. "A l-loan shark," she stammered.

"Did they threaten you?"

"Th-they said that i-if I didn't g-get the m-money, that I w-would have to w-work it off at th-their club. Its why I c-came here. I thought y-you would help. I d-don't want to be a p-prostitute. If you didn't I ..."

"You what?" he growled. Given the danger his son was currently in he had little sympathy for the woman who had brought this on herself.

"I ... I thought ... the boy ... he's young and ... he'd be worth ..."

"You were going to sell my son?" he roared. What kind of mother was Marcia? What kind of human being? You could anyone even think of selling a child—their own child—to get themselves out of debt?

How could he have ever thought it was worth even considering working things out with Marcia to give Andy the childhood he'd never had?

Elle and Ruthie were the family Andy needed, they would love and support him, give him everything he needed.

Now if he couldn't get to them quickly enough he would lose all three of them.

~

March 25th
2:30 P.M.

Fear made it hard to concentrate, hard to think, heck, hard to breathe.

Her daughter's life was in danger again, and Andy's, too.

What did she do?

How did she get the kids out of this mess alive?

As Elle watched a man dressed in camouflage gear walk toward the car, carrying the biggest gun she'd ever seen, she pressed a hand to her stomach where her tiny little baby was nestled. How did she get this baby out of this mess alive?

"Mommy!" Ruthie cried from the backseat, and she met the children's terrified gazes in the rear view mirror.

"I need you two to promise me that you will do whatever I tell you, no hesitation, no questions asked. Can you both do that for me?" Elle asked. Getting these two out alive had to be her priority. She would do everything she could to keep herself and her unborn baby alive, too, but Ruthie and Andy had to be her number one.

"P-promise," Andy said with way too much understanding in his eyes for such a little boy. Given his dad's job, he knew more about their situation than Ruthie did.

"Good boy. Ruthie?"

"Promise, Mommy," her daughter said, tears streaming down her little face.

"That's my girl. I love you both, okay? Remember that. No matter what happens, know that I love both of you very much. My favorite daughter, and my favorite Andy." Giving the children what she hoped was a somewhat reassuring smile, she had no time to say or do anything else because the man reached the car and yanked open her door.

There was no doubt that he was absolutely prepared to use his gun to shoot them all. Him shooting up the car had convinced her of that.

Who was he?

What did he want?

It couldn't be a carjacking because his shots had rendered the car virtually unusable if the smoking engine was anything to go by. Was he a killer? Rapist? Why was he out here on the secluded road? They were close to where she'd pulled over to cry that first night she had driven out to Rafe's place. The chances of someone stumbling upon them were slim to none. All she could do was hope that Rafe got here before any of them died.

At least he knew something was wrong. Elle had intended to call him immediately so he knew Andy was safe, but then the kids had seen each other, they'd been so excited, and she'd bundled them both into the car. The whole drive she'd tried to make herself call, knowing she had to alleviate Rafe's fears for his son while battling her fear of talking to him after everything that had happened.

In the end her selfishness had delayed the call and that might just save their lives.

If Rafe got to them in time.

"Get out of the car," the man yelled at her as soon as he yanked her door open.

Shaking hands fumbled at the seatbelt, and it took her a couple of tries to get it undone so she could scramble out. By that time, the man had pulled open the back door and was reaching for the kids.

Something came over her as she saw that gun so close to her daughter and the little boy she would have loved to one day call her son.

No.

This man didn't get to traumatize these children any more than he already had.

"Stay away from them," she snarled as she sprung forward, shoving herself between him and the kids.

For a moment, the man appeared startled by her sudden intrusion. Then his eyes narrowed at her, and when he spoke it was with exaggerated patience like one would speak to a recalcitrant toddler. "Look, lady. Nobody has to get hurt here. I just need the boy. Once I have him you and the girl can sit here and wait for somebody to find you."

He was here for Andy?

Specifically?

So that meant this wasn't random. Someone wanted to hurt Rafe by taking his son. Or maybe this had something to do with Marcia. The woman had randomly turned up in Rafe and Andy's lives just days ago after no indication for seven years that she cared about them at all. What were the odds that this abduction attempt of her son didn't have something to do with her?

Odds didn't really matter right now. It seemed she had two choices. She could allow this man to take Andy and pray that Rafe arrived quickly enough to follow them, or she could do everything she could to protect the boy who might not be her blood, but who she already loved.

Yeah, there was no choice.

This man wasn't laying a hand on Andy if she could help it.

Behind her, the kids had already undone their seatbelts, she'd seen that as she launched herself forward, making herself a human shield offering some, even if not much, protection to the children. If she could keep the man talking maybe she could get him to lower his weapon a little. If she could do that, then maybe she could lunge at him, knock him down, buy enough time for the kids to run off into the woods.

Perhaps not the best of plans, but Rafe was coming, she just had to hold on until he got there.

"What do you think you're doing, lady?" the man grumbled, sounding less angry and more exasperated. Maybe he didn't think she was a threat or anything to be taken seriously.

Okay, so that was mostly true.

She had never touched a gun before, the only time she'd ever been in a dangerous situation was when she fought Jimmy Hillier. She hadn't taken self-defense, and all she knew about danger was what she wrote in her books. Researching danger was not the same thing as being in the midst of it herself.

But that didn't mean she wouldn't fight with everything she had to give to save the lives of those two kids who were depending on her.

"You can't have him," she said simply, doing her best to still the trembling of her body so she at least looked like a teeny bit of a threat.

"Look, lady. I don't know who you are and I don't care who you are. My girlfriend owes a guy a whole lot of money. Money she can't pay back. We came here to get the kid as payment so I'm going to take him. Like I said, you don't have to get hurt. You and the girl, who I can see is your daughter, can go on your merry way."

No way was she allowing this man to take Andy.

She couldn't allow this sweet little boy to be taken and sold by his heartless mother.

Trying her best to be brave, Elle straightened her back, drawing her small five-foot-two frame up to its full height. "I said you can't have him. If Marcia owes money that's her problem, it has nothing to do with her son."

"This would have been so much easier if the kid just bonded with his mom and agreed to go with her," the man muttered, seemingly to himself. Then he dragged in a breath like he was summoning patience he didn't have. "Lady, I'm not leaving without the kid. You're being stupid here."

"Maybe," she conceded. "But I can't let you just take Andy. I love him."

"Okay, I'm guessing you're the step mom, didn't know one was in the picture, but it doesn't matter. I didn't want to kill anyone, but I'm losing my patience. I can respect you trying to protect a kid you love, but simple fact is, I'm taking the boy. Doesn't really faze me leaving you and the girl behind dead, but I don't really want to make this messy. So I'm going to say this one more time before I kill you and the girl and take the boy by force. Move out of my way and give me the kid."

Elle knew she'd pushed him as far as she could. What she was going to do next was either going to get them all killed or give the children a chance at escaping.

Sorry, little one.

After sending up the silent apology to her unborn baby that she probably wasn't going to be able to save it, too, she screamed at the top of her lungs, "Kids, now! Run and don't stop."

As she said the words she launched herself at Andy's would-be kidnapper.

The sound of the gun seemed much too loud.

Fiery pain in her arm told her that she'd been hit.

But the force of her body hitting his, catching him off-guard, was enough to send both herself and the man to the ground in a tangle of limbs.

CHAPTER

Twenty-Three

March 25th
  2:40 P.M.

Panther was breaking every speed limit that existed to get to his family as fast as possible. There was no way he was giving up on Elle and Ruthie, he would fight for them, prove to them that they and his son were the future he wanted. The family he wanted.

As soon as he got the information he needed from Marcia, he was in his car and flying down the driveway. His team were with him. His family.

He had no idea how he could have thought—even for a second—that there would be any sort of happy family with Marcia.

Simply put, he didn't love her.

Which meant he could never have created the safe, warm family home he had wanted to give his son.

Never again would he be stupid enough to think that blood family was more important.

Now as he drove as fast as his car would go down the quiet road that led away from the compound, he prayed he wasn't going to lose everything that was important to him.

Since Elle's phone had cut off mid-call, he had no idea if they were close to her house or his. Depending on whether they were in the city or the quiet country road, it would affect how he and his team approached things. In the city someone would call the cops, who could arrive in seconds if they had been nearby, but he suspected they were in the woods somewhere. It was a much better idea to ambush someone where you weren't surrounded by many unknowns. In the city those unknowns would be exponentially more than in the forest.

"Did you get a location?" he demanded as he took a curve in the road way too fast. He'd already set up a program to hack Elle's phone and pinpoint her location, he was just waiting for it to tell him where his family was so he could go get them.

"About two miles ahead of us," Rock replied.

"We should pull over about a half mile out, approach on foot," Axe said, already taking over the op even though this was Panther's very life they were talking about. Without Andy what would he have? Without Elle and Ruthie his life would be bleak. He needed to get the three of them back alive and in one piece.

It was a good idea, would allow them to assess the situation before they jumped in which increased the likelihood of getting everyone out alive, but anxious energy was buzzing in his system, and all he wanted to do was get there as quickly as possible. In fact, he'd love nothing more than to drive his vehicle right up to wherever his family had been attacked and slam it into whoever dared to hurt what was his.

So even though every fiber in his body was screaming at him to get to Elle and the kids as fast as possible, he pulled the vehicle over to the side of the road a minute later. His team wasted no time, they all piled out of the car, weapons in their hands, prepared to run the final half mile and scope out how bad things were before coming up with a plan to get his family out alive.

They hadn't done much more than get out of the vehicle and start toward where Elle's phone was pinging when they all froze.

Footsteps.

Not the quiet controlled steps of someone who was out here hunting, but the chaotic kind of someone running for their life would make.

Muffled cries accompanied the footsteps, and Panther all but sagged with relief.

He would know that sound anywhere.

Since they didn't know who had ambushed Elle and the children, although he suspected it was someone associated with Marcia's debts, he had no idea how many people were there or how well trained they were. So instead of calling out to his son to tell him that daddy was here, he waited, and pounced the second his son ran past.

"It's okay, my favorite son, it's Dad," he said immediately, keeping his voice low so it wouldn't carry.

"Daddy?" Andy asked in a wavering voice that made his heart ache.

"Right here, buddy." Panther hugged his son tight against him and looked over to see that Scorpion had been the one to grab Ruthie. Although the girl wasn't struggling in his hold, she was pale, crying, and holding herself completely stiff as though afraid that even breathing wrong might get her into trouble.

The ache in his heart grew. The little girl had already been through so much and now she was hurting all over again.

Wondering if she would reject him given how he'd kicked her and her mother out of the only place they felt safe, he reached for her anyway. "Give her here," he said to Scorpion who immediately passed the child into his arms.

Instead of yelling at him, or telling to let her go, the little girl did the opposite. Her small arms wrapped around his neck and she began to cry as she clung to him. Andy was crying, too, and for several minutes Panther just stood there and held onto the kids, so very grateful they were there and they were okay.

Preoccupied as he was it took him a moment to realize that the kids were alone.

No Elle.

Glancing up to find his team had formed a protective circle around him and the kids, he realized that all this time he'd spent bemoaning never having had a real family as a kid, he had been surrounded by the best family anyone could hope for.

"You guys were so brave, but I need you to be brave a little longer," he said to the kids. "Where's Elle?"

"Mommy said we had to do whatever she said with no arguing," Ruthie said.

"Dad, Elle told us to run because the man wanted to take me. I heard a gunshot as Ruthie and me were running." Never in his life had Panther seen the serious and mature expression that was on Andy's face. He might be only a year older than Ruthie, but he understood exactly what Elle had done for him and the price she might have paid for it.

The sacrifice Elle might have made for him had fear stabbing like a million ice picks into his skin. A *decillion* ice picks he thought with an ache inside him that would never leave if he didn't get her back.

"You two are going to stay here with Scorpion and Trick while I go look for Elle," he told the kids, handing them off to the two men he knew would make Ruthie feel most at ease. Men he knew would protect his son and the little girl he one day soon wanted to officially make his daughter with their lives.

After kissing both kids, he left them behind and went to find the woman he loved.

As soon as he got her back, he was going to tell her how much he loved her. Who cared if they had only known each other a bit over a month? Actually that was longer than Tank, and Trick had known the women they were now with before they had declared their love.

Even before they reached the spot where Elle was they could hear a commotion. A man's angry voice yelling.

"You think I can't find two stupid kids in the woods? You didn't save them, all you did was make sure that instead of leaving the girl behind, I'm going to take her with me. She's pretty and I'm sure she'd sell for a bundle. And you, you're a beautiful woman, I think you'd fit in real nice at the boss' club."

The man continued to taunt Elle as Panther crept closer. He could see her car stopped pretty much in the middle of the road, there was some smoke coming from the engine and he could see the front windscreen had been shattered.

As he got closer still he could see that Elle was on the ground, propped up against the side of the car, a man was on top of her.

"Maybe I better give you a work over now, show you what happens when you don't follow orders," the man continued. Elle's top was already ripped open exposing a pale pink lacy bra. As awful as it was to have the woman he loved being pawed at by a man who was threatening to rape her, it was the blood smearing her left arm that almost stopped his heart.

She'd been shot.

Protecting his son.

Put herself in the path of a bullet just to give Andy a chance at escaping.

If he didn't already love this woman, that right there would have convinced him. How could he not love a woman that loved his son that deeply?

"I think I'll enjoy teaching you a lesson." The man shifted, covering more of Elle's body with his own, and for the second time in weeks he watched someone try to take something from Elle she wasn't willing to give.

People had better stop molesting his woman.

Angry, and every bit as lethal as the animal he was named for, Panther leaped at the man touching Elle.

~

March 25th
   2:50 P.M.

For the second time in less than two months, Elle had been prepared to allow herself to be raped in order to protect her daughter—and this time Andy as well—and buy time for Rafe to get there.

For the second time in less than two months, mere moments before she was violated, the pressure on top of her was suddenly ... gone.

Only this time, instead of a body dropping onto her, blood pouring down upon her, her would-be assailant was thrown sideways as another body connected with his.

Elle had to wonder for a moment if she'd hit her head when she'd fallen, or lost too much blood from what she was positive was a superficial gunshot wound, because she could have sworn it was an animal that leaped from out of nowhere.

A panther.

Dressed all in black, golden eyes glowing with rage, her panther attacked the man who had been moments away from raping her.

Dazed and relieved, she sank back against the car's hard side, closing her eyes and doing her best to ignore the sounds of the fight. The kids were safe. If Rafe was there that meant Ruthie and Andy were okay because she knew he would have secured them first before coming after her.

As he should.

The kids always had to come first.

It wasn't until a hand gently cupped her cheek that she blinked open eyes that suddenly felt much too heavy. Rafe was there, looking at her with what certainly appeared to her to be love shining from his gorgeous eyes.

But he didn't love her.

Couldn't.

Because if he did, he couldn't have just throw her and her daughter out of his home when he knew it was where they felt safe.

Didn't seem to matter how many times she told herself that, she couldn't be angry with him for doing what he thought was best for his child because she *was* angry with him.

Angry because her child had been hurt.

Angry because she had been hurt.

Angry because it wasn't the house that made her feel safe but the man inside it, and he'd taken away that security as though he didn't know what he was doing.

But he did know.

And he'd done it anyway.

Which was why she couldn't seem to let go of her anger.

Anger which was now bubbling up under the surface, ready to explode at any second. Elle didn't explode on people, she kept her feelings and emotions to herself, tried to be the good girl, to do what others expected her to do, and always do the right thing.

Only for the life of her, she didn't seem to be able to stop what was coming.

"You made us leave," the words burst out of her with a strength that completely belied what she was feeling, which was exhausted and strung-out.

Rafe winced, but his hand didn't move from where it cupped her cheek. "I know. I'm sorry."

"You knew Ruthie and I needed you," she continued completely ignoring his apology. Later she would listen to it, accept it, and do her best to move forward. But not right now. Not right now when she was scared, and tired, and shaking so badly her muscles were aching.

"I told you that my parents split up when I was young, created new families, and neither of them were interested in me. When Marcia found out she was pregnant with Andy I wasn't thrilled at first," he said honestly, seemingly unconcerned his team were standing around listening. "If I had kids I wanted to give them the perfect home. Everything I didn't have when I was a kid. It was why I married Marcia even though I know now I never loved her. It was why it hurt so much when she left. That perfect life I wanted for my son was gone."

Elle could sympathize with that. She, too, had wanted to give her child the life she'd never had. Two parents who adored her, lots of family time, making happy memories, playing and spending time together, she never wanted her daughter to feel unwanted like her only goal in life was to follow in her mother's footsteps.

Still, even though she could understand, had even felt the same way, the anger raging inside her didn't dim.

"I adjusted, gave Andy everything I could, but at the back of my mind, I guess I always felt bad about it. When Marcia showed up I didn't want her there, I didn't want to see her, I didn't want to ask you to leave, but I felt obligated to try to give Andy everything I didn't have."

She knew all of that, or at least had suspected it given the texts he'd sent.

The problem was, she could understand on some level where Rafe had been coming from, but if their situation had been reversed she would never have just kicked him and Andy out and taken her ex back.

She would have sat down with Rafe and talked things through, at the very least explained where her head was at.

But he hadn't done that.

He'd just acted.

Thrown her and Ruthie out knowing they would have to go to a hotel or back to the house that scared them both.

"I didn't want you to go. I don't love Marcia and I didn't want her back. I was miserable without you and felt like part of me was missing. I just ... felt stuck. Trapped."

For once his presence wasn't a calming influence on her. If anything, it felt like gasoline on the fire of her anger. "Then why didn't you talk to me?" she yelled in a voice that was very not Elle Cavey. It was too loud, too shrill, too angry. If both her parents and her ex could see her now, they would tell her she was overreacting, being a drama queen.

Fear of judgment always had her keeping her emotions bottled, but now she felt free. Maybe it was because she knew Rafe would never judge her, that he wouldn't hold an outburst against her. That even though he'd done something that had hurt her, he still cared deeply for her. Maybe even loved her.

"No excuses, honey. I should have. Absolutely. It was a mistake not to. I wasn't being a good partner to you, wasn't treating you like you were on my team. I messed up. Big time. I allowed my own insecurities and issues to trick me into believing I was doing what was best for my son but I wasn't. I was being selfish. Giving him what I needed when I was his age not what he needed now. I can't take it back—even though I wish I could—and I know I have no right to ask, but I'm hoping my mistake hasn't cost me a chance at a future with you and Ruthie."

He sounded so sincere, and he was completely owning the fact that he had hurt her, and wasn't pretending otherwise. He had also articulated why he'd made the choices he had, and he had texted her every single day telling and showing her that he cared.

That he wanted her.

But it didn't fix everything.

Desperately she wished it did but it didn't.

A sob broke free even as she tried to take it back. "I'm still mad at you."

A half smile wiped away some of the anxiety from Rafe's face and he cautiously reached out to take her hand. "So is that a yes or a no on giving me another chance? I'm really hoping it's a yes because I really want Rock to take a look at your arm, you're bleeding all over the place."

Oh yeah.

Somehow she'd forgotten about the gunshot wound, in comparison to sorting out her life and her and her children's future, it seemed insignificant. Although, now that Rafe reminded her it did hurt. A lot.

"It's a I don't trust you now and its going to take a lot of time and work to get that trust back but I'm not completely ready to shove my feelings for you aside and walk away. I guess since I'm having your baby I should give you another chance," she agreed.

Rafe's eyes about bugged out of his head. "Having my ...?" His gaze darted from her stomach up to meet her eyes and back down to her stomach. "You're pregnant? What? How? When? I ... a baby? We're having a baby?"

Closing the distance between his hand still hovering in the air between them, Elle laced their fingers together. "Birth control must have failed, maybe because of the antibiotics, I only found out this morning. I wasn't going to keep it from you, I swear, once I brought Andy home I would have talked with you. Are you ... okay with it? Having another baby, I mean. With me. It means whatever you want with Marcia won't happen." Suddenly her anger fled leaving her shaky and uncertain.

Instead of answering, Rafe grabbed her and hauled her onto his lap, banding his arms around her. "I don't want Marcia. Even before I knew that she put Andy in danger. Before I knew Andy ran away, I was going to come and see you, I couldn't stay away any longer. You're my future, Elle. The past is staying where it belongs. No more obsessing over my childhood. I have Andy, and now I have you and Ruthie, and a new baby." One of his hands covered her stomach, his fingers lightly caressing her bare skin. "Whatever it takes, however long it takes, I will earn back your trust, and Ruthie's."

Maybe it was time for her to leave her past behind as well.

Her parents might not have planned a child, then decided to attempt to mold the one they got anyway into someone who would follow in their footsteps, and her ex might have just wanted a slave, but

Rafe wanted all of her. She couldn't hold the mistakes of others against him, he was his own person with his own insecurities. He would make more mistakes, she'd make plenty, too, but as long as they acknowledged them, talked things through, listened to one another, and were open with each other, they would never have to feel alone or unwanted again. The time and work it would take to rebuild trust and build a solid foundation for a future would be worth it.

"Mom!"

Elle looked up at the sound of Ruthie's voice, and the next thing she knew both kids were clambering into the embrace she and Rafe were sharing. Her kids, all three of them, because she knew she would love Andy every bit as much as Ruthie and this baby.

Every bit as much as she loved Rafe.

"To the future," she said, putting her hand out.

Rafe's immediately covered it. "The future."

"To the future," Andy echoed, adding his hand to the pile.

"The future," Ruthie added, then giggled and put her hand on top of Andy's.

Sitting in the arms of the man she was falling in love with, with two kids on her lap, surrounded by five big, tough warriors, Elle finally felt like she had found where she belonged. Never again would she feel like she had no one at her back, that she was doing everything all on her own, now she had people who would support her, love her, and be there for her.

Her family.

CHAPTER
Twenty-Four

March 26th
5:55 A.M.

A peace he'd never experienced before had filled Panther the moment Elle had told him she was giving them a second chance.

It was still there more than twelve hours later.

He hoped it would last forever.

Although he was lying in bed, he hadn't slept a wink all night. Elle had been taken to the hospital at his insistence to get the wound on her arm cleaned and bandaged, and to get thoroughly checked out for both her sake and their baby's. At Elle's insistence, both children had also been checked out at the hospital and were thankfully uninjured.

Uninjured *only* because of the woman lying at his side.

Elle had literally saved Andy and Ruthie's lives, and even if he spent the rest of his life showing her how grateful he was it would never be enough.

She'd been scared terrified but she'd done what she needed to do. As soon as she was healed he was getting her and the kids some self-defense lessons so at least they wouldn't be as vulnerable in the future.

Bringing Elle and Ruthie back to his home had taken a little convincing. Elle wanted them to move slowly this time, not jump all into being a readymade family like they had before. While he wanted them here with him he knew she was right. So they had agreed that she and Ruthie would spend the night here, but in the morning move into the main building on the compound. That would give her and Ruthie some space and independence while they worked on rebuilding trust but also gave them a safe place to stay where they weren't haunted by bad memories.

Which was why he'd laid awake all night watching Elle sleep, stroking her hair, her cheek, her arm, and any part of her he could touch without waking her. More often than not, one of his hands was resting on her stomach, wondering at the miracle of their baby growing inside her. When he wasn't holding Elle or watching her, he was checking on the kids, and making sure they were both still asleep in Andy's room.

Every time he did he thought about the future. When Elle was ready to move in here the cabin would need to be extended. They needed another bedroom up here, at least one more, maybe two. Andy and Ruthie might be happy to share for now, so Mrs. Pfeffer's room could become the nursery, but as they got older the kids would want their own space. Downstairs, he was thinking of extending the playroom to make it suitable for three kids as well as enlarging his office so he could fit more in there and work at home more when he and Bravo Team weren't out on an op.

"Mmm," Elle moaned and rolled over, blinking open sleepy eyes. "You been watching me while I slept?" she asked when she saw him propped up on one elbow.

"Yep," he agreed. "Don't want to waste time sleeping when I can look at you, touch you, hold you, know that you're mine."

Her face softened and she gave him the sweetest smile. "I can't believe I slept so well."

"You were exhausted."

Elle nodded. "Pregnancy makes me tired, and ..."

"And you haven't been able to sleep at your house," he finished for her, knowing she didn't want to say it and make him feel bad. Which he did. Hurting Elle and Ruthie hadn't been his intention, but he couldn't deny he knew they would struggle alone. As much as he wanted to go back, he couldn't. All he could do going forward was show them that he would never let them down again.

"I was afraid of nightmares, of waking up alone, of scaring Ruthie, but knowing you were here beside me and that my daughter would feel safe in Andy's room, I guess I felt free to let go and rest."

"You are safe here, Elle. You and Ruthie both. I won't hurt either of you again. I swear. All I want to do is prove to you that you can trust me to be there for you when you need me." If there was a way to flip a switch and convince her he'd be all over it. But there wasn't. It was going to have to be a one step at a time kind of thing.

"Yeah?" Elle lifted a hand and trailed a fingertip over one pec, then traced the lines of his abs. "Here for me when I need you, huh? That sounds perfect because I need you now."

"Babe," he groaned, that wasn't what he'd had in mind. "You were shot, and you're pregnant."

"Not our first rodeo, we both know that sex isn't going to hurt the baby. And you heard the doctor, I was lucky, the bullet didn't hit anything important. I'm not going to lie and say it doesn't hurt because it does, but I don't see that it will stop us from having sex."

Was he really going to argue about it when all he wanted was to sink inside her, join their bodies together, and prove to himself that she was there and she was his?

"You let me do all the work," he told her as he rolled them so she was spread out beneath him.

"I think we've had this conversation before," Elle said with a chuckle that turned into a moan when he pushed her panties aside and slid a finger through her slick heat.

"Wet for me already, sweetheart?"

"For you, always," she said, moaning again as he thrust a finger inside her, stroking deep, adding pressure in the place he knew would make her squirm for him. Which she did.

Elle like this, in his bed, free from any inhibitions, opening herself up to him, was a gift he treasured. This Elle wasn't worried about pleasing others, wasn't worried about anything at all, she was just being, just feeling, and he loved that he could make her feel safe enough to be free with him, let her guard down, and be her true self not the woman she thought others required her to be.

Adding a second finger, he stretched her, and increased the pace as he pumped them in and out. His thumb found her bud and worked it as he brought his lips to hers, making love to her with his mouth. Their tongues dueled, his fingers continued to brush across that special spot inside her with each thrust, and he pressed harder on her bundle of nerves.

When she came apart for him, Panther swallowed her cries of ecstasy so the kids didn't hear them, and without giving her any time to recover, with her orgasm still rolling over her in waves, he moved down her body, pulling her panties down with him. As tremors still rocked her body, he swiped his tongue along her center making her moan. Then he began to suck, and lick, eating her with the hunger of a starving man.

Panther suspected he would always be starving for this woman.

This woman who filled a hole left inside him by past neglect, who stepped so seamlessly into the role of mother to his son that it was like she was born to do so.

Her fingers tangled in his hair as he ate at her, working her quickly toward a second orgasm. This time when she came he watched her teeth sink into her bottom lip as she tried to keep her screams of pleasure from waking the two children sleeping down the hall.

Two orgasms wasn't enough.

With her taste on his lips, he shoved off his pajama pants, and sank inside her in one smooth thrust. Her internal muscles were still quivering with pleasure, and she moaned as he filled her.

Knowing he could easily get a third orgasm from her, Panther crushed his mouth to hers, kissing her with every bit of emotion he had to offer. One hand balanced his weight so he didn't crush her, the other stroked her sensitive bud, and as soon as he felt her come he allowed himself his own release.

It felt so big.

So strong.

Nothing like he'd ever experienced before.

It felt like love.

As the last remnants of pleasure shuddered through his body, he carefully pressed closer to Elle. "I love you, my favorite Elle," he whispered in her ear.

Her body startled in surprise at him saying the words, but when he looked down at her she was smiling and tears shimmered in her eyes. "I love you, too, my favorite Rafe."

Smiling, he pulled out of her and quickly pulled his pants back on in case they had visitors before stretching back out beside Elle and pulling her into his arms. "Good, because I'm hoping I've earned your trust back enough to marry you before this little one makes his or her appearance."

"I hope that too," Elle whispered, snuggling close.

"Dad."

"Mom."

Two little voices called out moments before the door to the bedroom was flung open and Panther was glad he'd put on his pants right away. While Elle discreetly reached for her discarded panties, stuffing them under the bed, he distracted the kids.

"Morning, my favorite son, and my favorite one day daughter," he greeted.

"One day daughter?" Ruthie asked as both kids clambered up onto the bed. "What does that mean?"

Elle narrowed her eyes at him, but she didn't look all that annoyed. "It means that one day Rafe and I would like to get married, and that would make me Andy's stepmom, and Rafe your stepdad."

Ruthie's eyes lit up. "I'd have a dad?"

"You would," he told her, settling the little girl between him and Elle while his son bounced about.

"And I'd have a mom!" Andy said excitedly.

When he looked at Elle, asking a silent question, she nodded her approval. "You two will also be getting a baby brother or sister. Elle is pregnant."

Both kids let out excited squeals, and began asking a million questions which Elle tried to field while also attempting not to get squashed by Andy's bouncing, and Ruthie's wriggling. There was no way Panther could wipe the grin off his face even if he wanted to.

The family bed had just become his favorite place in the world because it was filled with his favorite people. The woman he was going to marry and the baby she carried inside her, his son and the little girl who would soon be his daughter. His family. The place he belonged.

Never again would he feel unwanted.

Not when he was surrounded by this much love.

CHAPTER
Twenty-Five

March 27th
   11:02 P.M.

Axle "Axe" Lindon stared at the warehouse just a couple of hours away from the compound.

Was this where Beth had been kept when she'd been taken from him?

So close to home?

Of course, he had known that the likelihood of her being held somewhere close to the compound was likely given that she had escaped on foot and returned home. But this was not quite three hours from home. Those eight long months his wife had been missing she had been within driving distance.

Hell, she'd been within walking distance.

Fury raged inside him. A constant companion in the twenty months since she disappeared. The eight months she'd been gone had been hell on earth, but Axe had kept reminding himself that everything would be okay when Beth came home.

Little did he know that when she did come home, she would have no memory of him, no memory of herself, no memory of the love they had shared.

His wife was a stranger to him. She slept in the spare bedroom in the cabin he'd built for the two of them because she couldn't stand his touch, and could barely stand to be around him at all.

What killed him the most was noticing how little by little she was opening up to the others, the guys on his team and the women they had fallen in love with.

Seemed he was the one Beth wanted to keep her distance from the most.

Axe knew why.

It was because he had failed her.

When his Delta Force team had first rescued her, he had promised her that no one would ever hurt her again. And he had failed. She'd been hurt. Horrifically. So badly her mind had to wipe itself completely blank just to function.

As badly as he hated the distance between them, he knew he deserved it. He had broken Beth's trust in the worst of ways, of course she couldn't stand to be near him.

The only chance he stood of getting his wife back was to destroy every single person who had hurt her.

Starting here.

Starting tonight.

"Move in," he ordered into his comms.

Moving like the well-oiled machine they were, Bravo Team advanced on the building. They had no idea if this place was linked to Beth's abduction but it was a lead, and he didn't care how slim a lead might be, he was checking out every single one.

Not that they'd had many. A key found on the bottom of the ocean, a survivor of the yacht blast, had led them here and he prayed that there was a reason for it. That answers lay within these four walls.

Circling the warehouse, his team approached from all directions. If anyone was in there they weren't slipping away into the night. Axe couldn't afford to let this op turn into a bust. He needed answers, Beth needed answers, and he had no intention of failing her again.

All was quiet, no gunshots pierced the night, no bright lights flipped on inside or outside the building, no voice shouted. There was nothing.

Nothing until Axe eased open a door and took a step inside.

Then the world around him exploded.

Picking him up and slamming him back down again.

Blackness descended and he slipped away.

When Beth's memories finally return will it bring her and Axe closer or push them further apart? Find out in the sixth and final book in the action packed and emotionally charged Prey Security: Bravo Team series!

Wicked Scars (Prey Security: Bravo Team #6)

Also by Jane Blythe

Detective Parker Bell Series

A SECRET TO THE GRAVE

WINTER WONDERLAND

DEAD OR ALIVE

LITTLE GIRL LOST

FORGOTTEN

Count to Ten Series

ONE

TWO

THREE

FOUR

FIVE

SIX

BURNING SECRETS

SEVEN

EIGHT

NINE

TEN

Broken Gems Series

CRACKED SAPPHIRE

CRUSHED RUBY

FRACTURED DIAMOND

SHATTERED AMETHYST

SPLINTERED EMERALD

SALVAGING MARIGOLD

River's End Rescues Series

COCKY SAVIOR

SOME REGRETS ARE FOREVER

SOME FEARS CAN CONTROL YOU

SOME LIES WILL HAUNT YOU

SOME QUESTIONS HAVE NO ANSWERS

SOME TRUTH CAN BE DISTORTED

SOME TRUST CAN BE REBUILT

SOME MISTAKES ARE UNFORGIVABLE

Candella Sisters' Heroes Series

LITTLE DOLLS

LITTLE HEARTS

LITTLE BALLERINA

Storybook Murders Series

NURSERY RHYME KILLER

FAIRYTALE KILLER

FABLE KILLER

Saving SEALs Series

Prey Security Series

Prey Security: Alpha Team Series

Prey Security: Artemis Team Series

IVORY'S FIGHT

PEARL'S FIGHT

LACEY'S FIGHT

OPAL'S FIGHT

Prey Security: Bravo Team Series

VICIOUS SCARS

RUTHLESS SCARS

BRUTAL SCARS

CRUEL SCARS

BURIED SCARS

WICKED SCARS

Prey Security: Athena Team Series

FIGHTING FOR SCARLETT

FIGHTING FOR LUCY

Christmas Romantic Suspense Series

CHRISTMAS HOSTAGE

CHRISTMAS CAPTIVE

CHRISTMAS VICTIM

YULETIDE PROTECTOR

YULETIDE GUARD

YULETIDE HERO

HOLIDAY GRIEF